CLASSIC CALLS THE SHOTS

CLASSIC CALLS THE SHOTS

A Case for Jack Colby, the Car Detective

Amy Myers

This first world edition published 2012
in Great Britain and in the USA by
SEVERN HOUSE PUBLISHERS LTD of
9–15 High Street, Sutton, Surrey, England, SM1 1DF.

British Library Cataloguing in Publication Data

Myers, Amy, 1938-
  Classic calls the shots.
  1. Detective and mystery stories.
  I. Title
  823.9'14-dc23

ISBN-13: 978-0-7278-8150-2 (cased)

All Severn House titles are printed on acid-free paper.

Severn House Publishers support the Forest Stewardship Council [FSC], the
leading international forest certification organisation. All our titles that are printed
on Greenpeace-approved FSC-certified paper carry the FSC logo.

Typeset by Palimpsest Book Production Ltd.,
Falkirk, Stirlingshire, Scotland.
Printed and bound in Great Britain by
MPG Books Ltd., Bodmin, Cornwall.

AUTHOR'S NOTE

Jack Colby has his own website and blog (www.jackcolby.co.uk) although my husband, James Myers, runs it for him. Jim plays a large part in writing his novels too, because without him the novel's engine wouldn't be going anywhere. With his extensive knowledge of classic cars, he has collaborated with me throughout on the creation of Jack Colby and Frogs Hill Classic Car Restorations and the cases in which they are involved, and I'm greatly indebted to him.

That Jack Colby sees himself in print is due to my agent, Dorothy Lumley of the Dorian Literary Agency, who kept her hand on the steering wheel, and to my publishers Severn House, who drove the novels past their finishing post. Along the way Jack was spurred on by Amanda Stewart, Gaynor Banyard, Tom and Marie O'Day, to whom many thanks. For specialist information I am grateful to Ian Stanfield, works manager of the National Motor Museum at Beaulieu, and to Roy Dowding of the Gordon-Keeble Owners Club and editor of its magazine *Keebling*. Among other sources, a Classic Cars for Sale web article on the Auburn; The Auburn, Cord and Duesenberg Museum in the US; and, for the story of Ramble, *Secret Service* by Christopher Andrew and *Blackwood's Magazine* were particularly helpful.

The plot and characters of *Classic Calls the Shots* are fictional, as are many of the specific locations in the novel, including Piper's Green, Stour Studios, Syndale Manor, the Gladden and Helsted estates and car parks, and also Shotsworth Security, Oxley Productions and Jack Colby's Frogs Hill Classic Car Restorations. Lenham, Charing, Pluckley and the Syndale Valley, however, are real Kentish villages, as timeless as the North Downs themselves.

ONE

'**N**icked from a film set? You're joking, Dave.'

He had to be. No crook in their right senses would steal a 1935 Auburn, even to order – especially from such a high-profile location. This Auburn is so rare and so beautiful that car lovers all over the world would faint in ecstasy if they were lucky enough to see one. As for stealing it: no way, for the same reason no one would pinch a Leonardo da Vinci. A slight exaggeration perhaps, as this car can still be bought, provided you've just had a lottery win in the six-figure range. But stealing such an eye-catching stunner is a breathtakingly risky job.

'No joke,' Dave's voice said gloomily at the end of the line. 'It's Bill Wade's – or was.'

Detective Superintendent Dave Jennings heads the Kent Police Car Crime Unit, and calls on the services of Jack Colby of Frogs Hill Classic Car Restorations, namely myself, whenever he sniffs something out of the ordinary about a classic car theft. As now. An Auburn 851 SC Boattail Speedster? I was hooked.

'Tell me about it, Dave.' I'd pay *him* to get this job. I knew about US film director Bill Wade. Who didn't? He lived in Kent for part of the year, no doubt living off the fat of the profits of his blockbusting *Running Tides*, which burst upon the world ten years ago. There'd been films in between, of course, but the one currently in production, *Dark Harvest*, was tipped to be its successor.

'Pinched from Stour Studios, near Lenham. Know the place?'

I did, because *Running Tides* had been shot there. I was still working overseas in the oil industry then, but Dad had been as excited as a boy with his first Dinky car because he'd taken a shine to the film's star, Margot Croft. He had caught a glimpse of her while the filming was in progress, but then his heart was broken because she committed suicide not long after it finished.

'I take it you've checked the usual channels?' I asked Dave. That Auburn must have broken all speed records on its way to its new owner if Dave was calling me in. His own team was excellent.

Dave likes talking in sound bites when there's something major afoot. 'Yup. Waste of time. Not a pro job.'

'Joyriders?' I asked. This was looking weirder by the minute.

'Went last Thursday night. Now Monday, so would have shown.'

A sigh of relief from me. That meant there was indeed a case and it was mine. 'When do I start?'

'Now. You're booked in with the bereaved. At his request.'

'Bill Wade himself?' This was turning into a *very* good day.

'Get your old jalopy on the road, and Jack . . .'

There had to be a snag. 'Tell me the worst.'

'If I knew what it was, I wouldn't need you. But I don't like the sniff of this case. There's something wrong somewhere.'

I've hired my beloved 1965 Gordon-Keeble out to film production crews on several occasions, so I've visited film sets before. Not so often that I wasn't looking forward to visiting this one, however, despite Dave's dire predictions. Usually there's a combined mass of cast and crew milling around together with a forest of technology in the form of cables, sound equipment, lights, cameras, dollies, boom arms, Steadicams etc. Amidst this, they are chatting, rehearsing, shooting, preparing, sipping coffee, studying scripts, call sheets and storyboards or adjusting make-up, hair or costumes – you name it. Humdrum workaday stuff, or so it seems, but at the magic words 'Going for a take' they spring into action like a Ferrari from the starting grid, and humdrum turns into magic.

I was looking forward to visiting Stour Studios, which are on the outskirts of Lenham village in the Headcorn direction. I once went to a recording of a TV show in the famous Maidstone Studios at Grove Green, but when I arrived at Stour Studios in my daily driver Alfa, they proved to be a different kettle of fish. They were not nearly as big as Grove Green, they were privately owned by Oxley Productions, and it was clear that at least currently it was entirely devoted to

Dark Harvest – and therefore to Bill Wade. I checked in at the security gate, returned a friendly grin from the guard, swept into the car park on the right and wended my way to reception with high expectations.

I knew that the studios had been converted from a farmhouse and its outbuildings, because I had visited the farm as a child with my father and been entranced by the baby piglets running about. It looked rather different now. The former granary, barns and outbuildings now made a compact complex round a central court; some had been converted, some torn down and rebuilt from scratch. Even so they'd made a good job of making the studios easy on the eye and the huge canteen I passed looked welcoming.

A large sign pointed to reception in the Georgian red-brick building that used to be the farmhouse, but now had a more businesslike air. The ground floor had been converted to provide a large modern entrance area – one that needed the word 'cold' before reception, however. At the desk to my left a grey-haired man in perhaps his late fifties and a severe-looking woman probably a few years younger were deep in what I would term 'animated discussion' of which the only words I caught were 'cow' and 'serve her right' apart from the accompanying F-words. On a better day she might have been attractive, and the man rather jolly, but today was clearly not a good one.

'Yes?' the woman snapped.

'Police,' I said curtly, in as good an imitation of Rebus as I could manage.

She stared at me as though this confirmed some long-felt suspicion.

'Here to see Bill Wade,' I added.

'Sign in.'

I signed.

'Upstairs – turn right, first door,' the man told me. 'Sooner you than me,' he added gloomily.

The directions were redundant, because as I went up the stairs the noise emanating from Bill Wade's office indicated where the action was. A woman's shrill voice produced the only distinguishable words through the closed door.

'I don't want him around.' A pause, then an emphatic 'Him or me, Roger!'

I was flummoxed. I'd never heard anyone produce that particular cliché before. Maybe that wasn't Bill Wade's office and this was a rehearsal, a script read-through – or had Hollywood really reached rural Kent?

Then I heard a low distressed murmur of men's voices. Two, I thought. 'Honey' was the only word I caught. This was getting better by the minute. Surely it was a script-reading.

'It's no good, Bill. You're ganging up against me. I won't have my professional judgement disregarded,' Mrs (or so I deduced from the 'honey') X continued in a higher pitch.

'Angie . . .' Both male voices provided this chorus.

'Is he staying or going?' Angie demanded.

'Goddammit, Angie, give me a break. I've got a car to find.' One of the males seemed to have reached breaking point.

This was a man after my own heart. Settle the car question first. It's usually easier. If that was Bill Wade, he deserved both his Auburn and my best efforts to find it.

The door was pulled vigorously open and a woman swept out. She was a shining processed blonde of about forty, and would have been a stunner if it hadn't been for the compressed lips and angry red flush. She was immaculately clad in stylish jacket and trousers, but there was no camera tracking her. This lady's anger was for real. She honoured me with a sideways look as she stalked past me, which implied that if this had been a better day there might have been a second look. She need not have bothered with the first because she wasn't my type.

Already I felt there was a touch of film noir about the situation, and I pressed ahead into the office, even more curious as to what I might be walking into. There were indeed two men there, and wearing my Philip Marlowe hat I quickly appraised the scene. Marlowe would have recognized it. Man sitting behind impressive and uncluttered antique desk, a man I recognized as Bill Wade from press photos. The other man was pacing up and down by the window and from the 'Roger' I'd just heard, it wasn't rocket science to deduce that this was Roger Ford, co-owner and producer of *Dark Harvest*. I had done some speedy Internet homework before I left home.

Bill Wade was quite something. Give him a field cap and he could have passed for Field Marshal Montgomery, wiry, pent-up energy, fifties, lined face, and ready to shoot on sight, and not just film. Whoever Angie was, I'd back Bill in a fight. Probably. His chair partly swivelled round as Roger Ford, currently staring grimly out of the window, as in all the best office scenes, said:

'He'll have to go, Bill.'

Time to introduce myself. 'Jack Colby. Here about your Auburn, Mr Wade.'

Instant attention from both men, and Bill Wade's gimlet eyes focused entirely on me.

'You've found it?' he barked at me.

'Sorry, not yet. You asked to see me.'

'We did.' It was Roger who answered. 'We need that Auburn back and quick.'

Roger Ford's co-owner of Oxley Productions and Stour Studios was his wife, Maisie, who came from some multi-billion-pound manufacturing company in the States. Ford was a big man in all senses. He was about my height, six feet, but a lot bigger where the hamburgers lodge. He too must have been in his fifties, grey-haired and with that assured companionable look that comes with success. A look that in my experience can quickly change to steel when matters go awry. As now, it seemed. I addressed Montgomery, however. 'I understood it was your personal car, Mr Wade?'

I knew it was. I'd seen articles about it. The car he'd owned for twenty years or so. A left-hand drive, one of the dozen or so hand-built 1935 Auburn Speedsters out of a total of just under a hundred styled by Gordon Buehrig. With its flamboyant body design and advanced technical specifications, this Auburn was truly a car for kings and film stars, among them Clark Gable. And his choice was Bill Wade's too. There were iconic photos of him driving around in it during the making of *Running Tides* ten or eleven years ago, in which he was often with the star with whom his name was 'linked', as they say: Margot Croft, my Dad's pin-up.

'Right,' Bill replied, eyes briskly gorging out my innermost secrets, 'but it's appearing in the movie. Which is why it was here and not locked up at my place.' If Oxley Productions had been found wanting, there was no suggestion of that in his voice.

Dave had emailed me a briefing, so I now knew Bill Wade lived in Mayden Manor, which was buried in the countryside near Sissinghurst. The Auburn however had disappeared from the studios complex three days earlier during the night of the third to fourth of June. As Bill's eyes bored into me, I could see just why Dave had called me in. I braced myself.

'What's your security like?' I asked.

'Good,' Roger Ford leapt in quickly. 'Magnetic pass needed to get in after ten. Anyone trying to get out of the gate without a pass brings the guards here in minutes. CCTV, which shows no sign of the car, security lights, no permanent guard between eleven p.m. and five forty-five a.m., but the grounds are patrolled every two hours. Nothing suspicious reported.'

Bill was pacing round the room like a leopard on the prowl, but he wasn't saying anything. I found that odd. If I'd had an Auburn pinched, and there was the slightest flaw in security, I'd have been screaming blue murder, but he wasn't. Even Roger Ford was relatively low key.

Dave had briefed me on the theft and security, but there's nothing like speaking to the horse's mouth for picking up any bad breath that might be around. 'Garage then: forced locks? Any stolen passes reported?'

'Neither,' Roger told me.

'So our car chum had both a pass and access to the keys.'

Bill Wade stopped pacing and fixed me with a look that made me glad I wasn't on one of his sets. 'A lot of people work here late, Jack.'

'Do they sign in or out, regardless of whether there's a guard on duty?'

'They're supposed to,' Roger growled, 'but don't always bother.'

'How many passes?'

'Around a hundred and fifty,' Roger shot at me in defensive mode. 'That's the permanent crew and staff. The cast and background – extras – sign for temporary ones. It's high at present. So double that.'

Great. 'And the car keys?'

'Master keys in the security booth. Locked,' Bill added drily, then came in for the quiet kill. 'You're not some Poirot, Colby. Forget how and who. Just get that Auburn back by next Monday.'

Seven days? Just like that? I goggled at him, struggling for sanity. 'You must know what you're asking.'

Roger Ford weighed in. 'We do. We need it. It's too expensive to reshoot scenes we've already shot in London. What are the chances? Dave Jennings said you had contacts.'

'I do, but not to produce stolen Auburns out of a hat. What about one of the new replicas?'

'At Oxley we only use the real McCoy,' Bill snapped.

I bit back the words 'let McCoy find one then' and asked, 'Why's it so important? Cars are usually kept in the background in films.' Not if I had anything to do with it, of course, but then usually I'm not consulted.

'Not for *Dark Harvest*. Believe me, if I could do without that car, I would. There's no way,' Roger said. 'Agree with that, Bill?'

Bill studied me for a moment or two and must have decided I was worthy of his full attention, because he stopped playing Montgomery and became reasonably human.

'One hundred per cent, I agree.' He sounded almost buddy to buddy. 'I do stories, Jack. Film's the only medium that can show them the way I want: the *whole* story. That's why I've been in love with movies since I was a kid. In my films you don't just see *what* happens; you see *why* and *how* without even being consciously aware of it. But it's there all right and it comes over if I strike the right mood. We use sound and lighting to get that mood and I layer one story over another story. The Auburn's in the second story. Background if you like, but vital. *That's* why I need it back. It's part of the movie. See?'

I didn't, not completely anyway. What I could see was why Bill was a great director. He knew where he was going.

'*Dark Harvest* is all about revenge, Jack. It lurks in the shadows,' Bill continued. 'The movie's set in 1935, around the time of your George V's Silver Jubilee, a time when everything looked reasonably hunky dory for Britain. Right?'

'Yes.' I knew the Jubilee had been a rave success – rather unexpectedly so, even for the King himself.

'It wasn't hunky dory. Waiting in the wings were Hitler, Mussolini, Franco and Oswald Mosley, all gearing up for fascism and in Adolf's case revenge for Germany's humiliation over the 1918 Armistice and the Treaty of Versailles. Add to that mix, by May 1935 the Prince of Wales' affair with Wallace Simpson was well under way and he was beginning to cosy up to Germany. Ahead lay deep trouble. He became King, then abdicated, all within a year of his succession. So all seems jolly rejoicing in May 1935 but in fact the past is catching up and is ready to explode into the future. That's the second layer. Understand?'

Not hard. I could manage so far.

'The cars are chosen for the second layer. Every time the audience sees one of them they're reminded of that. That's why we have a car adviser.'

Car adviser? Not Jack Colby, I noticed. Why didn't I ever get cushy jobs like that? 'What part does the Auburn play?'

'It's a bright new sleek American car, and it's seen with the formidable German Horch, Cabriolet Type 670, an Italian Fiat Tipo 508S, and the good old English Bentley, a 1933 Silent Sports Car. All reflecting the political situation.'

If Bill had set his mind to this weird theme, it was going to work. I was sure of that.

'That's why we need that Auburn,' Bill continued. 'Plus, as Roger says, we've shot several scenes with it. We already have a line on a replica but that doesn't interest me. Not one bit, Jack. We start filming on location next Monday with *my* Auburn.'

Director and producer aimed the full force of their considerable will at me, as if expecting me to produce it out of a hat. I only hoped I could. 'Not much time, eh?' Roger said grudgingly.

'No,' I agreed, poleaxed at this understatement.

'You'll do it, Jack. Want to see the scene of the crime? I'll get Tom to give you the tour.' Bill's lined face cracked into a grin, but it wasn't meant for me. Nor was it meant to be jovial. 'Keep him busy, eh, Roger?' He picked up his phone.

Whatever Dave had meant by his 'something wrong somewhere', I agreed with it. For all Bill Wade's undoubted leadership skills, so far this didn't strike me as a happy company. There could be trouble in store. The term 'film noir' might acquire a whole new meaning.

Tom proved to be the man I'd seen at reception. He seemed friendly enough, but abstracted, which was hardly surprising if, as seemed likely, his job was under threat. He introduced himself as Tom Hopkins, deputy assistant director. 'And before you ask me what that means,' he added gloomily, 'I'll tell you. Nothing. Assistant director is a big deal. Deputy doesn't exist in the deal stakes.'

'Power without responsibility?' I quipped as we set off. I was still brooding about this car adviser, and wondering whom they had chosen.

'Power?' He considered this. 'You could say that,' he said at last, as we walked over to the garages where the Auburn had been stored. 'You know what I was before I got this nothing job? Storyboarder. Now that's responsibility. Each one drawn by me after consultation with Bill.'

I knew about storyboards, the translation of a script into a series of artist's drawings to capture the proposed mood, continuity and action of the film and spot potential problems ahead. They are or were the great standby of the director and production designer. 'Aren't they digitalized now?'

'Can be, but not for Bill, they're not. We've worked together too long. He still uses film and hand-drawn storyboards. Trouble with computers is that they tell you something, but stop right there. No mood. My sketches fire Bill's imagination, and that's what he wants.'

'So what went wrong with that job?'

'Angie did. His blooming wife. You probably heard her in full force when you came in. So-called script supervisor, script editor and historical adviser. She's all for computers, got some kid wet behind the ears to rework *my* drawings.'

'You're very frank.' Extraordinarily so, I thought. I hadn't exactly sought this confidence, even though it was another useful indication that all was far from well at Stour Studios.

Bill might well only want me to get the Auburn back and no questions asked, but my success with that might well depend on what was going on right here.

'Nothing to lose,' Tom replied. 'Everyone feels the same about our Angie. She got me sacked as storyboarder, while we were shooting in London, on the grounds that she was script supervisor and Madam objected to the way I conveyed the mood. Too much emphasis on Louise Shaw's role, she said, which according to her threw the other relationships in the story out of kilter. I wouldn't change it, and she got me sacked.'

'It sounds like something that should have been sorted out.'

'Not when Madam falls out with Louise Shaw – the whole plot centres on her role. Besides, Bill was busy fighting with Madam over the time he was spending with Miss Shaw.'

Now that made sense. I like situations boiling down to straight human failings. I'd heard of Louise Shaw – who hadn't? – and she was a terrific actor. Is that why Angie disliked her? I wondered. Did she hanker after playing lead herself?

'So what are you still doing here?' I asked.

'Roger, Bill and I go back a long way, so they gave me a non-job to compensate. You'll see what it's like here. Shooting only began in Kent last week, after two weeks in London, but down here it seems different. We're cooped up together too much. We're at each other's throats, all of us, not just me and her. The chap playing Lord Charing, Brian Tegg, is fighting for his job too. Only one of his scenes has been shot as yet, and Madam didn't like it.'

'Isn't it always like that on film sets?'

'No,' he said simply. 'There's a lot of real nastiness here, but we don't know where it's coming from. Now this garage you wanted to see.' He stopped at one of the red-brick buildings that had been converted into a garage. 'Used to be the milking parlour, this lot,' he told me. 'Now we milk the Fords.'

I dutifully managed a laugh and he chuckled. All good-natured fun, perhaps, but perhaps not. Perhaps he too was embroiled in the 'real nastiness'.

The garage Tom led me to was the second last in a row of six, adjoining the canteen I'd already seen. They were obviously converted from stables, and at first glance they looked solid enough. Certainly the Auburn one was very firmly locked now with a large secure-looking padlock and security lights.

'Bill said there were four classics. Are the other three cars here?' I asked.

'Not yet. They arrive Monday.'

'It seems a given that someone got access to the key left at the security booth,' I said as Tom struggled with the padlock.

'Maybe. Maybe not. Could have gone out the other door. Here you are.' He flung the door open to reveal a now-empty garage.

Other door? I thought I must have misheard, but sure enough at the far end there was another double-doored entrance. I walked over to it, and found it merely bolted.

'Very useful,' I commented, and Tom grinned. 'I take it that was found bolted *after* the Auburn's theft?' That could be the only reason that Dave or Roger hadn't mentioned it.

'Yes. Easy enough to unbolt it during the day. The car was out for a while.'

'And then bolt it again during the kerfuffle after the theft was discovered.'

'If you say so. Police weren't interested.'

'Why on earth not?'

'Go outside and have a look.'

I pushed open the doors and he followed me on to the gravelled area outside. I saw the reason the police must have dismissed this exit. Staring me in the face were the waste bins and a rubbish dump on concrete hardstanding. There was just about room to get a car out here from the barn, but it would have had to turn sharply towards the rough grass bordering the boundary fence. With less than adequate headlights by today's standards, the Auburn wouldn't like that, but it could be done. What could not be done was to drive it straight through a fence with no gate in it. Like this one.

Aware that Tom was watching me, I walked over to it. It was of solid wood, about four foot high, running along about thirty yards before its job was taken over by a six-foot-high hedge. With his eyes on me, I checked every support post and cross-strut, without success. I could see no signs of anything being disturbed. On the other side of the fence was a farm track but for a car there was no way of reaching it.

I couldn't work out Tom's attitude. He wasn't eager for me to find any explanation of how the Auburn had disappeared, but on the other hand he seemed so devoted to Bill that he surely could have had no hand in its disappearance himself. 'Nothing there,' I said. 'Where does the track lead though?'

'Nowhere much. Joins up with another track and eventually winds up on the Lenham Heath road. The other way, it stops when it reaches the wood. No way through to a road there.'

He made no other comment. I can be pig-headed at times (Zoe and Len who work for me claim this is all too often) and I hate giving up so I took another look at that hedge: tall, prickly, green. No place for an Auburn. Then I noticed that some of the bushes didn't look in tip-top condition, so I took a walk alongside the hedge where the grass was long, but the ground not that bumpy, and there were no ditches. The closer I got, the unhappier the bushes looked. I got down on my knees and found that it wasn't my imagination. The ground had been disturbed here for a distance of about twelve feet or so, and on the other side of the hedge ran the farm track. It wasn't beyond the bounds of possibility that someone had carefully dug up these bushes, left them roughly in place, and removed them to take the Auburn through last Thursday night.

I decided not to share my discovery with Tom and he didn't pursue the matter. What I was doing must have been fairly obvious, however, and so I tackled it another way. 'How well known was it that this door was only bolted, not locked?'

'Anyone in the cast or crew – and staff, of course.'

'All three hundred of them?'

'You got it, Jack.'

In fact I might have got him. 'If Bill Wade is as popular as you imply, why should any of them want to pinch his car?'

'Bill's popular, but his wife isn't. I told you that. The Auburn is Bill's but Angie fancies herself in it and drives it around all the time. No one else is allowed to touch it without her say-so – even Miss Richey who drives it in the film.'

'So the thief is more probably someone who has it in for Angie.' Like Tom, I thought. 'Or could someone want to ruin the film?'

'No one wants that, Jack. Don't get that idea. It's going to be a winner – if Madam doesn't muck it up first. Want to see the rest of the place?'

The subject was being turned, and he took me over to the main leg of Stour Studios, opposite the garages. These were much taller, much grander buildings, and although one was the converted granary and another a barn conversion, the other two were purpose-built, as was the canteen opposite it.

Behind them in a field adjoining the complex stood what looked like the bottom half of the Eiffel Tower and in another corner the Brandenburg Gate with part of the Unter der Linden. 'That's where we shoot the exteriors,' Tom told me.

I dismissed this area as an exit route, as there was no way the Auburn could have reached it.

'Are these the studios or the production offices?' I asked Tom as we walked towards the nearest of the four buildings.

'Studios. Numbers One and Two for intimate scenes, Number Three for the big productions. Dressing rooms, Costume and Make-Up are here too. Next to this building is construction, set-dressing, storage, props, gaffer's and best boy's stuff and audio equipment. The next is the production offices, and the one after post-production. You've seen the canteen; above that is the green room and hospitality.'

There's jargon for you. Luckily I knew the gaffer and best boy were in charge of lighting, and the green room was where the cast could retire and meet guests. Every speciality has its own jargon, the combined shorthand and code of the trade. Even the car world has some. Jargon helps sort the insiders from outsiders, and here at Stour Studios I was definitely among the latter. That was good – I needed to be. Nevertheless I had to find the missing Auburn quickly, and I wasn't going to do it by hanging around admiring the place from the outside. I needed to get the measure of this cast and set, and the studio buildings were where they would be working.

I followed Tom eagerly as he went in through the door of Studio One. They'd just finished shooting there, but it was still full of crew and cast as well, judging by the thirties' costumes. I was so busy looking around me at the set (a rather splendid bedroom) and the overhead lighting, cameras and cranes that I forgot to look down as well. Which is why I wandered on to the carpeted set and tripped headlong over a cable stretched thoughtfully an inch or two above the floor level between a daybed and the set's wooden wall.

I partly saved myself from crashing headlong by grabbing at the bed, but still collapsed ungracefully on to the floor, sprawled out and staring straight at a pair of elegant feet shod in thirties' high-heeled ankle-strapped sandals.

TWO

'd seen photos of Louise Shaw before, even seen her in a film or two, but nothing prepared me for the real thing.

Louise Shaw would not win any run-of-the-mill beauty contests, but that did not matter one whit. Dark curls escaping from a red beret, warm concerned eyes – concerned for me – and a face as calm and perfect as Mona Lisa's. She was, I guessed, about thirty but in her case age was immaterial. 'Age cannot wither her . . .' I must have spoken out loud because she looked startled.

'Just worshipping at your feet,' I said cheerily, sitting up and checking my ankle which had twisted in the fall.

'You'd find that more comfortable if you stood on your own.' Concern had changed to amusement. 'Are they intact?'

I experimented by getting upright again. 'They are.' The black curls clustering at the nape of her neck and peeping out from the beret entranced me, but I tried not to stare. She was wearing a peach-coloured silk pyjama-type cocktail outfit, and it suited her.

'That's good.' She hesitated, clearly wanting to talk to Tom privately.

'He's OK, Miss Shaw,' Tom obliged. 'He's with the police.'

'Jack Colby,' I introduced myself, as Louise still looked uncertain. 'I'm working with the Car Crime Unit on the missing Auburn. Tom's showing me round the studios.'

'Losing that car was the last straw,' she murmured, then she couldn't hold back. 'What *is* going on round here? Tom, be careful. Angie's on the warpath. I've had another spat with her over my scene with Cora. She wants to have a go at you now.'

'She's already had it,' Tom said. 'It looks like the dole queue for me this time for sure.' He grimaced.

She looked horrified. 'She can't do that. Not again. I'll speak to Bill and Roger.'

'No use. She's got them both where it hurts. You don't need enemies like her.'

'Too late, I have. Anyway, it's right to speak out,' Louise said firmly, and won my heart for ever.

Then who should appear but Roger Ford himself. His assured look was in place, but it must be a necessary mask in his position. 'Sorry, Louise, sorry, Jack, but I need a word with you, Tom.'

Louise didn't move. 'Tom seems to think he'll lose his job again, but he's surely mistaken?'

Roger had conveniently already turned away, indicating that Tom should follow him off the set. Left alone (apart from a studio full of crew), Louise, clearly furious, looked ruefully at me. 'How about I finish the tour with you, Jack? I'm not needed by Costume for another hour and a half; it will help me cool off. Give me five minutes to change.'

It was an offer I couldn't refuse, much as I suspected she needed down time between calls. I waited outside in the sunshine, watching all the comings and goings. This inner courtyard was mostly paved and a decorative fountain now adorned the spot where I seemed to remember there had once been a well. There were many people around, but I didn't get the impression of general bonhomie. Far from it. Heads were down, any conversation seemed muted.

Louise returned right on cue, however, now clad in jeans and T-shirt which were somewhat at odds with the film make-up.

She must have read my thoughts. 'Working girl,' she quipped.

By the time she had given me the tour round both the production and post-production, not to mention the construction buildings, I wondered how films ever managed to get made. There were so many departments, so many different trades at work, and so many offices each with its own grand name that it was a miracle any one person could manage to be in charge. It also brought home to me just how many people might have been in a position to steal that Auburn – and in consequence that I needed to put aside all lustful thoughts about Louise and concentrate on my job. I made a supreme effort.

'Can you tell me what's going on here apart from the film,

Miss Shaw?' I asked, as the tour seemed to be nearing its
conclusion. 'Something seems wrong.'

'Call me Louise,' she said absently. Then: 'I don't mind
telling you. But first, do you think you'll get the Auburn back?'

'Truth is that I don't know. If it was a straightforward theft
I'd stand a better chance, but from what I've seen here, that
might not be the case. Any chance it was a home-grown job?'

'Every chance, I'd say. It could be disastrous for the film
if it's not found quickly. This is a relatively low-budget
film like *Running Tides*. That was one of those outsiders that
come out of nowhere and take practically every award going.
Roger's hoping *Dark Harvest* will do the same, but every
penny counts. If schedules get disrupted—'

'And Auburns lost.'

Louie smiled. 'Quite. You can see for yourself how much
planning goes into just one scene, and once Bill gets an idea
in his head, such as the Auburn, he won't be budged. But I
can't see why anyone would want to scupper the film. Quite
the opposite. We all have mouths to feed, people to look after.'

A husband? I wondered. I could hardly ask straight out.
Too early.

She broke the pause that followed. 'Do you know anything
about *Dark Harvest*?'

'Not the plot or your role, but Bill explained the revenge
theme and how the cars fit in.'

'Good. We actors don't usually notice the overall effect, the
mood, as we shoot scene by scene, partly because they're usually
out of order. On this film, though, if we look at the storyboards
before we shoot, or watch the dailies, the rough cuts, afterwards,
we can sense something unnerving, almost menacing.'

'Clouds in the bright blue sky?' I contributed, not very
brilliantly.

'At least one can see clouds. Here that's not always the
case. But this time it's not only the film itself, but the studios,
this set, this production. It seems dogged by bad luck at the
very least.'

'And at worst?'

'Someone intent on ensuring it doesn't succeed.'

'You talked of the Auburn as the last straw.'

'If the theft was only a practical joke,' she said, 'the car might reappear next Monday.'

'Why a joke? Have there been others?'

'A whole spate of them. That cable you tripped over. It shouldn't have been there. Dead against the gaffer's rules. It was probably meant for me. When we blocked the scene yesterday, I was to dash from the daybed to try to escape Cora's fury. I'd have fallen right over that cable, but Bill switched the move at the last moment.'

In anyone else I would have thought this a case of paranoia but this was Louise and I believed her.

'We've had a series of odd happenings, first in London and now here,' she continued, 'and several of them have involved me. Individually they mean nothing, but added together it's not only scary but ominous. I lost my mother's charm bracelet, my car wouldn't start but it proved to be something quite simple. There have been one or two threatening letters and other minor irritations. Angie's historical notes file was found in charred pieces. The worst hit was the caretaker.'

'What happened?'

'He's permanent staff and does all the maintenance work. His dog Henry made a good guard dog, but Henry was a great scrounger round the canteen waste bins. Sometimes his own plateful was put out for him, but last Thursday morning he was found poisoned.'

The day the Auburn was taken. Coincidence that the guard dog was eliminated? 'That sounds more than creepy, Louise. It sounds vicious. What about Angie Wade? Anything else happen to her apart from the burnt file?'

'She's public enemy number one, and she had a particularly vitriolic poison pen letter. She accused me of sending it, and being Angie she did it publicly. So the car, as I said, is the last straw.'

'Although it's technically Bill's?'

'Sure, but identified with Angie. The word goes round that "here comes Auburn Angie", not "Auburn Eleanor Richey" who drives the car in the film.'

'What part does she play?'

'Cora Langton.' Seeing this meant nothing to me, she continued, 'I'd better explain the plot. It centres on Tranton

Towers, as it's called in the film, which is owned by Lord Charing, big in government. I play Julia Danby, his discarded mistress, married to Charles but bent on revenge on his lordship. I plan it for the Jubilee Ball weekend at Tranton Towers. His son Robert is about to get engaged to rich American heiress Cora Langton, which would greatly help the depleted fortunes of the stately pile. However, enter the great seductress, me, planning to bust up the cosy engagement. The way I do it, you won't be amazed to hear, is by seducing Robert over the weekend. Robert falls for me in a big way, and the affair – once we've got rid of Cora temporarily – proceeds to the point where Lord Charing is so desperate that he tells his son about his own relationship with me. Shock, horror. His lordship then kills himself and, full of remorse, Robert goes back to Cora. Got it?'

I thought it sounded disappointingly standard stuff but I could hardly say so. She laughed, as she saw my expression.

'There's a twist. I then make the unhappy discovery that I'm actually in love with Robert. Too late, too late.'

'Sounds a negative sort of outcome,' I ventured.

'It could be, but not in Bill's hands. He's a genius. You wait till you see how it works out.'

'The mood?'

'Yes. Cora's the bright American lass with whom the good solid Englishman gets hitched, whereas Julia and husband are captivated by the fascists. Hence the cars. Miss America drives the Auburn, and the ultra English Robert drives the Bentley. Von Ribbentrop drives the German Horch, and I share the Italian Fiat with my fascist husband. Justin Parr's playing Robert. You've seen him on TV, I expect. He's a poppet.'

I disliked him already. 'The theft could have been intended to spite either Angie or Eleanor then?'

'Angie's the more likely. Ellie's harmless. She's new on the block, whereas a lot of us know Angie of old.'

'You couldn't have been in *Running Tides*? You'd have been in your cradle.'

'I didn't put you down as a line-shooter.'

'Fair hit,' I conceded.

'I wasn't in it. I was still struggling doing bit parts on TV and since then I've run across Angie from time to time.'

'Why does she have so much influence? She seems to act more like a prima donna than an adviser. Director's wife or not, she shouldn't be in a position to get Tom sacked once, let alone try for a second go. Why doesn't Bill or Roger rein her in?'

'Roger has a soft spot for Angie, chiefly because she's best chums with his wife, who holds most of the purse strings. Not an easy situation. Bill could overrule Angie, but he won't. Everything takes second place to the film while it's shooting. This film is going to be tricky, especially when we go on location next week, so endless squabbles with Angie won't help either Bill or Roger.'

'How much more shooting is there to do?'

'About another three or four weeks. It can't be more. We've all got other commitments after that, so we have to stick to schedule. It's one hell of a problem, and you, Jack, are the angel who's going to solve it for us.'

'Thanks for your faith,' I said wryly. Another three weeks and she might walk out of my life. I pulled myself together. She wasn't even in it yet. 'What about the car adviser?' I asked apparently carelessly. 'Doesn't he have emergency solutions?'

She looked at me rather oddly. 'He's not into detective work.'

'I'm glad. I wouldn't be here if he was.'

She laughed. 'How's the ankle? Can it make it to a brief look at the other two studios and then the canteen for a quick coffee?'

Louise's company was so enjoyable that it would be easy to persuade myself that hunting down the missing Auburn could only be done at the studios – and who was to say that wasn't right? 'Something is rotten in the state of Denmark', as some character in *Hamlet* observed. For me, substitute Stour Studios. Except for Louise. Nothing amiss there. Walking beside her, I felt as if I'd known her for ever and that it was going to continue that way.

The set dressers, she explained, were still finishing up in Studio One for the love scene between herself and Justin Parr being shot that afternoon. I tried not to imagine too vividly what it might consist of, and instead took a curious look at a few of the people who theoretically might have stolen the Auburn. The set was of a small drawing room and lighting technicians were focusing stand-based and overhead lamps, while around them buzzed half a dozen set dressers adjusting cushions, furniture, and family photographs.

'Is Justin around?' I asked, as we stood inside the doorway.

'No. Far too early. We're called for two thirty, another two and a half hours, and he's well known for walking in on the dot. Me, I need a few minutes on set to complete the change from being Louise to Julia Danby.'

'Is that difficult?

'No. It's a routine. I just shut my eyes and seductress Julia slowly takes over.'

I definitely didn't want to know what kind of love scene would follow. 'Show me how you change character.' I'd keep the seductress Louise for later – if and when.

She took me at my word. She shut her eyes and the face became expressionless and immobile. Then it began slowly to alter and when the eyes flew open again the woman before me was a stranger, full of contradictions, doubts, determination, malicious, vulnerable, and with the face of a Delilah. Then she relaxed and Louise was back with me.

'Did you see?' she asked doubtfully.

'I prefer Louise to Julia.'

'Thank you, Jack.' Then she kissed my cheek.

It had been meant lightly, but something had happened between us. From her look of sudden bewilderment she too realized that and wasn't sure she liked it. My move. I took her hand, and she smiled.

'Is there a Mrs Colby?' she asked.

'An ex of twenty years standing. Is there a Mr Shaw?'

'Yes.'

I knew life couldn't be this kind to me.

'Two in fact,' she continued. 'My father and my brother.'

'They're *wonderful* people,' I said fervently.

'You'll like them.'

This studio wasn't Number One, it was Cloud Nine.

'The tour,' she added pointedly, and I promptly leapt off my cloud and returned to business mode. Studio Three was vast. It was here that the Jubilee Ball was to be shot, and if someone had told me that there were a thousand people working on this set I'd have believed them. The crew was here in force, with generators, lamps, candles, cameras, moving platforms, Steadicams, and audio equipment, plus a construction team setting up the ballroom. There was accompanying noise, with shouts, cries and general hum so loud that it assaulted the ears. It was like being faced with the merry old land of Oz, watching people busily rigging lights, adjusting camera angles and polishing the floor. And Bill Wade was the wizard in charge of the lot.

'Crew time,' Louise told me, 'uncontaminated by cast or extras. We're not shooting here until tomorrow.'

'Are there many extras?'

'You bet, though they're often called background now. Roger's rubber-stamped a hundred and fifty for two days' work. Costume's been stretched to produce enough dress jackets and evening gowns for that number. Let alone the tiaras.'

'Would there be lists of both cast and background for the days when the incidents occurred?'

'Sure to be. Ask Casting.'

'Er . . .?' I tried to place this but failed.

'Their room's in the production building, first floor somewhere.'

'Great.' I could see that trying to approach the case by eliminating them one by one was likely to be a non-starter. I had to plough on, however, if the answer to the Auburn theft lay within the studios. It seemed Kafkaesque; I would be plunging through a never-ending fog towards some indication of where that beautiful object now was. In a scrapyard? No one could be so crass as to destroy it. A thing of beauty was a joy for ever, Keats said, and he would have drooled over the glories of the 1935 Auburn. Those amazingly elegant pontoon fenders, that breathtaking boattail, that gleaming cream paint . . .

'Let's have that coffee,' Louise suggested. 'I'll grab a sandwich too, and then I'll have to disappear. And you can get your cast lists. Did someone give you a security pass?'

'Someone did.' Reception had unbent sufficiently to hand me one with her own fair hand.

The canteen was plush and huge, so plush that I wondered how the hospitality suite could better it. I suppose the canteen needed to be on a grand scale with that number of cast and

crew to be fed and watered all day long. It was nearly lunchtime, and it was reasonably full. There were plenty of crew
here, plus some costumed cast, judging by the odd dress suit
and plus fours. One or two of the women were in slinky
cocktail dresses.

'I always feel half in character here,' Louise said. 'A sort
of betwixt and between place. Don't worry though. I won't
seduce you here.'

'Pity,' I said lightly. I was conscious that we both seemed to
be skirting round the edges of the next step – if there was one.

Muted conversations seemed the order of the day here too.
I could see Tom sitting at a table with several other men and a
pleasant-looking woman of about forty, all talking earnestly.
Louise and I found a table nearby and I went to get some coffee.
'This car adviser . . .' I began, as I returned bearing the cups.

'You'll meet him on Monday.'

'Who—?'

At that moment I saw Angie striding in, clad in designer jeans
and expensive jewellery, with – of course – large sunglasses on
top of her head and an expression that conveyed that she was
important. She looked both a joke and formidable, as she swanned
over to Tom. I couldn't hear what was being said, but the meaning
was clear, because Tom pushed back his chair, got to his feet
and walked out, white-faced. As he passed us, he managed a
wink. 'It's the push again. Collect the cash and go.'

One of his companions, a man who looked in his mid thirties,
with a gentle face and dark hair plastered back, no doubt for
thirties' style, stood up to confront Angie. 'You can't do this,'
he yelled at her, visibly trembling, as she stalked off to the
counter. 'Not again.' The room was suddenly hushed.

Angie stopped in her tracks and spun round. 'I have done
it, Chris,' she said coolly. 'Or rather Roger has.'

'We all know it's you who wants Tom out.'

'Sit down, Chris,' one of his neighbours said quietly. 'You
won't do Tom any good.' He was older, perhaps fifty or so,
and certainly wiser. Chris reluctantly obeyed, looking near to
tears either with frustration or fear.

'Good is what I want,' Angie said coolly. 'The good of the
film. Whatever it takes.' She was infuriatingly calm, seeming

almost bored. She must have strong cards in her hands, I thought, to risk being so unpopular.

'That's hard to see,' the older man remarked.

'No doubt it is – for you, Brian,' Angie said.

At this, Brian seemed about to leap up to defend himself, but the third man at the table ('Graham,' Louise hissed) stopped him. The woman ('Joan Burton') said sharply, 'Don't, Brian.'

Angie smirked – no other word for it – clearly aware that she was the object of fascinated attention. 'We require high standards here. From both cast *and* extras. Do remember that, Chris. I hope your work lives up to it. Yours too, Brian. And Graham, isn't it?' She then added as an afterthought, 'And even you, Joan.'

The meaning was crystal clear to everyone. Shut up or get out. No 'background' for her. They were mere extras.

With that, Angie decided to leave the canteen, perhaps thinking that coffee wasn't such a bright idea after all.

'Sure this isn't a scene shoot?' I asked Louise in wonder.

'I wish it was. She's for real, unfortunately. You think that's bad. You should hear what she spits out in a one to one confrontation.'

'As bad as that?'

'Oh yes. That's why I didn't intervene just now. It would have made things worse. Luckily she can't give me a lethal wound but others aren't in such a good position. Chris Frant and Graham East are basically non-speaking, although they're playing von Ribbentrop and the Prince of Wales respectively. Brian Tegg, the older man, might seem less vulnerable because he's a supporting actor playing Lord Charing, but she has him in her sights in a big way. If she gets nasty he could be recast even at this late stage because his big scenes are still to come. Joan's playing the housekeeper, another supporting role, but I think she's safe; she's everyone's favourite. Everyone's but Angie's, that is.'

'But Angie can't touch you?'

'Afraid she can. My script gets mysteriously changed every now and then. Nothing you can put your finger on, but the result isn't quite as strong as the original – which incidentally wasn't written by her. She merely tinkers with it.'

'What has she against you?

'I suppose it just comes back to power. I'm not part of the old gang, but Bill and I have to spend a lot of time together.'

'By old gang you mean from *Running Tides*?'

'Yes. Everyone at Tom's table stems from those days and there are others around.'

I took another look – Chris still looked white-faced, Brian Tegg seemed to be doing his best to cheer him up and Graham East, who was about Chris's age and seemed the serious, quiet type, was talking to Joan.

'Does Margot Croft fit into that story?' I asked.

'I suppose she must. I think Joan was a personal chum of hers, and Margot was Bill's property, as you must know, before Angie came along. Angie, like Joan, was an extra, and so were Chris, Brian and Graham. Tom was the storyboarder. Margot must have been quite a lady – Joan told me that Chris and Graham fancied her like mad, but they didn't stand a chance, although like Tom they worshipped the ground she trod on. So unfortunately did her husband, I'm told. Her suicide must have hit them all hard.'

'So Angie might see you as another Margot Croft?'

She flushed. 'Bill and I get on well – there has to be rapport between director and lead actors. Angie might have misconstrued it. Don't make that mistake, Jack.'

I took her hand in mine. 'I'm a magic bullet – I go straight to the truth.'

'Good. So find the Auburn.'

I laughed, and she added, 'Take care, Jack. The current situation is that Angie mustn't be crossed in any way, and for the sake of the film Bill and Roger have to rise above everything that's going on. I suppose as this is a film about revenge, Angie could be attacking the camaraderie that still lingers from Margot Croft's days.'

'Aren't there limits?'

'There are. And very soon Angie is going to reach them.'

I drove home through the lanes to Piper's Green like a kid after a visit to Santa Claus. I persuaded myself that despite the tantrums, there was a terrific film being shot, a terrific cast and director, and so everything was possible. No matter if there appeared to be a serpent slithering around in this paradise; it could easily be eliminated. Perhaps the nasty incidents were coincidental; perhaps the theft of the Auburn was due to some eccentric billionaire who had 'ordered' one. The prize for agreeing to find it was meeting Louise, and inside my pocket was a card with her mobile number on it.

All I had to do now was find the Auburn.

Frogs Hill Classic Car Restorations operates not far from the village of Piper's Green which is between Pluckley and Egerton on Kent's Greensand Ridge. I live in the farmhouse and a converted barn houses the Pits, which is the workshop where my team of two do what they love best – making the insides and outsides of classic cars whole again. They know everything about that process from bumper to bumper and whether it be an old Morris Minor or a Lanchester or a de Dion Bouton it usually responds to their caring hands. Len Vickers used to be a racing mechanic, which is why the Frogs Hill workshop gained its name of the Pits. He's wiry, sixty-something years old, a man of few words and unhurried action. His assistant Zoe Grant is just as caring, and just as slow because she loves her jobs so much she can't bear to finish them. She's about twenty-five, well behind Len in the age stakes, and together they make an unbeatable team. In short, the only flaw in the Frogs Hill business is the mortgage on the whole property, caused by my late father's addiction to purchasing every piece of interesting automobilia that he came across. Hence my involvement in police work to smooth the cash flow.

The lane to Frogs Hill is so little used that it does not rate highly on the Council's list of needed improvements and upkeep, and the drive to the Pits is of the same standard. Any car arriving is therefore well heralded. Len and Zoe know the sound of my Alfa though, so they usually don't even bother to look up as I come in. This time they did. I'd already told them about the missing Auburn and they had been as struck as I had been over the audacity of the thief. They had therefore promised to tap into the local automobile grapevine.

'Any luck?' I asked.

'Not a toot,' Zoe said. Len just grunted. 'How was it?' Zoe added, meaning of course Stour Studios.

'Just short of paradise,' I said smugly.

Zoe looked at me quizzically. She knows me well. 'I meant the car.'

'We've got six days from tomorrow to find it.' I tried to sound casual as I quickly scanned the cast lists I'd been given. They did not inspire me with hope. I had forced myself to do some thinking on the way back in between meditating about Louise. If the Auburn had been stolen to order from overseas, it must have been out of the country so quickly that Dave's team checked too late. The theft had only been discovered at shortly after 5.45 a.m. on the Friday morning when the studios opened, and Bill went to check on the car.

Another possibility was that the Auburn was winging its way inside a lorry to a destination somewhere in Britain. This was unlikely since so few 1935 Auburn cars come on the market that each one would be scrutinized extremely thoroughly. Bill's was left-hand drive too, which would help identify it in a trice. The third possibility was that it was indeed a practical joke and would turn up again on Monday. I just couldn't see that happening, however. The fourth possibility, fast becoming a probability, was that it was linked to the other incidents and might *not* turn up again.

Zoe had been mulling the problem over. 'We need outside resources, Jack. Local ones. How about Harry Prince?'

'Are you crazy?' I gazed at her in astonishment. Local car dealer and businessman Harry Prince's dearest wish in life is to see Frogs Hill fail and to make me an offer for the farm-house, the Pits and business that I can't refuse. Or that he *thought* I couldn't.

'All right then.' She'd seen my reaction. 'We'll ask Rob.'

I groaned. I liked the 'we' but Rob was almost as bad as Harry. He's Zoe's pet aristocratic layabout who unfortunately has a knack of picking up useful bits of information, provided it takes no effort. I still don't know what he does for a living. I know how he lives though. Zoe cooks for him. What else she does, I don't ask.

'If you must,' I said. Any port in a storm, after all – and storms there would be if I did not find that Auburn.

THREE

The Glory Boot is where I do my best thinking – usually, that is. It's an extension to the farmhouse and was built by my father to house his famous automobilia collection. I only have to walk through my living room with its comfortable old sofas and bookshelves, go through a sort of boot room-cum-general dump – and then open the door to Wonderland. It's here that my dad has left his soul. The Pits has acquired its own heady mix of high-octane fumes from the petrolheads who work there, but in the Glory Boot there is a feeling of, well, love. I have only to look at the posters, the models, the Giovanni paintings, and the loving scraps of old shop manuals to hop instantly back into my wondering childhood before I was daft enough to leave Kent for overseas and the oil business.

So why wasn't my mind racing round in top gear on Tuesday morning? Answer: I'd brought Louise home with me – only mentally, alas. In addition, I was aware that I couldn't keep an open mind over this missing Auburn because it had fixed on the fourth option that at best it was no coincidence that a wave of ill-conceived pranks was hitting the studios, and at worst something far more sinister. 'OK, son,' my father was muttering from his photo at the wheel of his beloved MG, 'so why the stop light?'

What was stopping me was where my gut feeling took me. What, if I had been nutty enough to pinch an Auburn 1935 for spite, would I do with it in the short term? If I wasn't a car lover, I would wreck it and return it so that everyone could see my handiwork – especially its proud owners. If I was a car lover, or at best someone who realized what a treasure this car was, I'd hide it somewhere unconnected with me to be found sooner or later – if it wasn't by then destroyed by mindless vandals. I hoped that the thief was a real car lover, and would hide it away somewhere safely. Where would that be?

If I were working at the studios but commuting from home, I could stick it in my own garage – but what would the neighbours say? Furthermore, that would mean my own car would still be in the studios' car park sticking out like a Ferrari in a banger race.

So where *was* the Auburn?

Dad seemed to have stopped his advisory service, as nothing came to mind, save that if I was correct and it was pinched by someone working on the set, crew or cast, then it couldn't be far away. Cast and crew could hardly take time off to drive it to John O'Groats. Which merely gave me the whole of Kent and maybe a bit of East Sussex to search.

By Monday. Now six days away.

Time to move. Louise's mobile number was burning a hole in my pocket but pride wasn't going to let me use it until I had some idea of where I was going with this commission. I'd rung one of my contacts who with luck would cover the grapevine of London and the home counties, but Harry Prince was, I had to admit, the unavoidable step I'd have to take next. He runs a big flashy garage near Ashford and several others too, including his newish acquisition, the Piper's Green garage, though he doesn't manage it in person. That's in Jimmy's loyal hands. He was the former owner's henchman and has worked there ever since Herr Daimler first decided to build a car. Jimmy prides himself on achieving the impossible over combining reliability with speed of service. I sometimes hope this will rub off on Len, but not so far. He tends to be a bit sniffy where Jimmy is concerned.

'Cranked your starting handle a bit late this morning, didn't you, Jack?' Zoe greeted me disapprovingly. 'Where have you been? Rob's been waiting for you.' There was a touch of reproach in her voice. Sometimes I think Zoe might have got the wrong end of the stick as to who owns this place. Certainly, Rob showed all the signs of possession. He strolled out from behind the Princess Vanden Plas that Zoe and Len were currently working on, and eyed me in what passes for a friendly manner for him. He is the clumsiest person around cars I've ever met and I eyed the Vanden Plas with trepidation as he placed his pudgy hand on the bumper to help him squeeze past. He's

not fat, exactly, he just has that well-oiled look that comes
from the confidence of knowing where you stand in life,
especially if it's high up the pecking order and even if it's not
deserved. He's shorter than me, but somehow . . . oh well,
he's Rob, that's all, and Zoe – though not infatuated with him
– accepts his presence in her life without quibble.

So far, I thought. One day this otherwise sensible sparky
girl will see the light.

'Zoe says you've a spot of trouble with an old banger,' Rob
said carelessly.

I froze. Old banger? 'It's an Auburn 851, *1935*.'

'That's good, is it?'

Even Zoe looked horrified and Len appeared to express his
indignation in person, wiping his hands on the oily cloth he's
treasured from the 1960s by the look of it.

'A beauty. Only ninety-odd produced. The queen of the
speedsters, either supercharged or non-supercharged. Company
lost money on every one of them,' Len added admiringly.

Naturally he approves of this approach. I sometimes think
he does his best to see he follows it through with the beauty
of his repairs versus the bill it finally produces.

'How can I help?' Rob said unenthusiastically.

'I've reason to think –' it sometimes pays to be pompous
with Rob because he understands pomposity – 'it could be
still in the neighbourhood. It's too conspicuous to escape
notice for one thing, and for another I'm betting on the fact
that the thief is staying locally and wouldn't have the time
to take it far.'

'No Far Eastern potentates then?'

'Unlikely. It's a known car. It wasn't featured in *Running
Tides* itself, but it appeared in a lot of photos of the star Margot
Croft. She was having an affair with its owner, the director
Bill Wade.'

Rob looked interested. 'That one of her standing by a car
with her hair blowing over her face on a Scottish moor?'

'The North Downs near Folkestone in fact,' I said.

'Whatever,' he dismissed this. 'Why didn't you say so
earlier? Had that photo stuck on my wall as a kid. Killed
herself afterwards, didn't she?'

'She did.'

Rob shrugged. 'Helps the image. So that was the car, then?'

'Yes.' I spat the word out with difficulty at this typical Rob observation on life and death.

'I'll help.' He made it sound as if I should sob with gratitude, but I could see that one off.

'Thanks,' I said offhandedly.

He grinned. 'Don't think I can do it, do you?'

'It's a tough one,' I said ambiguously. 'Especially as I have to find the Auburn by Monday.'

He didn't turn a single one of his mousy brown hairs. 'Leave it with me.'

I would, but only so far. There were lines that Rob could follow and other ones that I needed to do myself. The local pubs for one thing. There were two in Lenham, one in Sandway, not far from the studios, and another in Grafty Green on the Headcorn Road. Asking the regulars about it was a no-brainer. Its theft must have been in the dead of night, but with such an engine any car lover would be drooling at the sound even in his sleep.

'By the way,' Rob added, as thankfully he took his leave, 'I hear the film's being shot at Syndale Manor.'

'Yes,' I said cautiously. 'How did you know?'

'Nigel Biddington's a pal of mine.'

He didn't need to explain who he was. I knew. He was the son of Sir John Biddington, the owner of Syndale Manor.

'He's pretty desperate about the Auburn,' Rob added.

'Why?' I asked.

Rob grinned. 'Firstly, he's the car adviser on the film, and secondly he's dating Louise Shaw.'

I was still reeling from this news as I drove over to Charden, where Harry Prince lives. I needed to be in fighting form to seek Harry's help, and luckily the news of Nigel Biddington had shot me out of my corner. I wanted to go out and bash the world for treating me this way. In brighter moments I told myself that there was no way I could have mistaken those signs in Louise – but then, I had to admit, I'd barely met her. How could I know?

Charden is the far side of Pluckley almost in the Ashford suburbs, and Harry's home is next door to one of his garages. This one was his original investment, and the house was like his choice of cars: big, monstrous, showy. The only difference is that the cars are classics and the house is modern. Once I'd fought my way through the technology that guards his house from those who would like to put Harry in his place, he greeted me quite affably. I like his wife, but there was no sign of her today.

Harry, as I said earlier, is first in line to write a cheque for Frogs Hill Farm and the Glory Boot in particular. He too is on the big showy side. He's also an old rascal, but when the chips are down he can be surprisingly straight. It's when the wheel's still spinning that one has to watch him.

'What can I do for you, Jack my lad?'

Jack his lad seethed, but I needed his help. 'Auburn 1935, left-hand drive. Pinched from Stour Studios last Thursday night.'

'Yeah, I heard about it. Shouldn't be hard to find, even for you.' He sniggered.

'What did you hear, Harry?'

'Only that it had gone,' he said hastily. 'Public knowledge.'

'Nothing more?' I was suspicious.

Harry looked shifty. 'Not our fault, Jack.'

I had been right to be wary. '*Our* fault?'

'Security,' he said carelessly. 'I've got an interest in the firm that runs it. Shotsworth Security. First class, they are.'

Harry has his fingers in so many pies it's surprising there's a crust left anywhere. 'Well now,' I said. 'Fancy that. I'll pop in and have a word with them. Nothing more you can tell me?'

Harry seemed oddly relieved. 'No, and ain't that odd, Jack? You'd think I would have heard *something*.'

'That's goodish news, Harry. If you haven't, it confirms what I think. It's a spite job. Someone at the Studios.'

He blenched. 'I wouldn't be sure of that, Jack. Hearing nothing isn't always good.'

He actually looked quite worried on my behalf and he was still staring after me with a somewhat puzzled look on his face as I drove away. I had no doubt that he could have told me more, but had no intention of doing so. And that was bad news.

Next port of call was the hotel where the crew and some of the cast were staying, although not the stars, who were tucked away on the Downs. Some of the crew commuted to the set daily on a need-to-attend basis, as did the extras and a few of the cast. That still left quite a number to be put up locally and Oxley Productions had taken over a big hotel on the edge of Harrietsham, the next village from Lenham on the A20 towards Maidstone. The pleasantly rural name, The Cricketers, refers to the village's excellent cricket facilities in the early nineteenth century, which had fostered the career of Alfred Mynn, otherwise known as the Mighty Mynn or the Lion of Kent. The name was all that was rural about the hotel, which was large and modern and didn't even try to look ancient, though it sported a few tubs of flowers around its forecourt.

My guess was that whoever took the Auburn was probably staying here. Car commuters or local residents would face more problems over planning a theft such as that. From the hotel, however, it would be possible to walk to or from the studios, provided one didn't mind crossing a couple of fields. That would solve the need to leave one's own transport in the parking lot at Stour Studios. There was also, I'd been told, a bus that picked up those who needed transport in the morning and returned them at ten p.m. at the end of the filming day. That wouldn't cover anyone who was working late, which on Thursday night, the DOP's lists had told me, had included crew, extras and a few of the cast.

I ordered a coffee from reception as the bar was unattended. When it arrived it was lukewarm, but it served its purpose by giving me an excuse to wander round the hotel and stroll out into the garden at the rear. That makes it sound enticingly large, which this garden was not, although it was well tailored. My interest, however, was in the car park that lay behind it. I hardly expected to find the Auburn waiting for me, but there were two lock-up garages which I eyed thoughtfully, even though the chances of the Auburn being inside were virtually nil.

I looked up at the North Downs rising gently behind the village. From here the Downs look green and pleasant and always remind me of the Psalmist's: 'I will lift up mine eyes unto the hills, from whence cometh my strength.' I know the Downs well. Narrow lanes that used to be smuggling and trading routes criss-cross them, and in between are hamlets and isolated farms aplenty. Any one of them could be hiding the Auburn. Beautiful though the Downs look, man has tampered with them; they have been fought over, dug up for quarries, and used to hide crime from prying eyes for thousands of years. They are timeless and they like you to know it, so it can be eerie up there as well as beautiful. Despite my addiction to cars, I love walking, but on the Downs, particularly in some areas, I often feel my steps quickening and it seems hard to realize that civilization – if one can call it that – is so near at hand. History and prehistory not only lie here, they shout at you.

I returned to reception and produced my police credentials. The receptionist was unimpressed – until I mentioned *Dark Harvest* and Stour Studios. It turned out she was a film fan, and it was seventh heaven for her to have the hotel full of crew and staff. Once, she told me with pride, Justin Parr himself had come in and was ever so nice to her. It took a while for me to get her back to solid ground.

'Do the crew mainly use the bus?' I asked.

'Sometimes,' she said helpfully. 'It comes back about ten fifteen. The bar closes at midnight, but some of them are still sitting around long after that. I work the night shift every so often.'

'Do many of them eat here?' From what I'd glimpsed of the menu I didn't think that the Roux brothers masterminded the Cricketers' kitchens, and it was far more likely that the film crew and cast ate at the Studios. The food on film sets is usually excellent.

'Not often,' she conceded.

'Were you working night shift last Thursday by any chance?'

'Yes.' Her face lit up as she realized she could help me.

'Anything special happen that night? Anyone come in during the small hours?'

She looked at me in wonder. 'Of course. There's a lot of clubs in Maidstone.'

I realized I was going to get nowhere unless I had specific names. One last hope. 'Do you have CCTV here?'

She brightened up again. 'Not here. In the car park.'

That was something at least. I'd alert Dave to that one. 'What's in the lock-up garages?'

'I don't know.' Her face fell. 'I could get Winston to show you.'

'I'd like that.' I smiled at her, and she cheered up. Winston proved to be a lad of not more than twenty and spic and span in a uniform I recognized including the yellow jacket. The same firm as the Studios employed. 'Shotsworth Security?' I asked as we set off through the garden. He nodded.

'Good firm to work for. Why do you want to see the garages?' he enquired.

'Part of a major crime investigation,' I assured him, as he unlocked the first padlock and threw the doors open. All that greeted me was an empty garage.

Winston thought this very funny. 'No crime there, sir.'

'Good heavens! The bird has flown,' I exclaimed solemnly.

'Perhaps he's nesting here.' He chuckled as he unlocked the other one.

That too was empty. 'Second bird flown too?' he asked.

'You never know in my line of work.' To make him feel he wasn't being cheated, I carefully noted the clues of the empty garages into my Blackberry, and we parted good friends.

I spent the rest of the day locally, trying local pubs to ask residents and staff if they'd seen the car. Without success. All that told me was that it had probably turned left into the Lenham Heath road, which had fewer houses along it and connected with the A20 running between Ashford and Maidstone. The next step was obvious: the next morning, Wednesday, I would check out the security at the studios with the guard himself. I didn't want to run into Louise without some sort of trophy progress, but short of broadcasting an appeal to the nation, nailing down how and when and whither this car vanished was the pathway to finding it. I was reasonably happy with the 'how' at least, and even the 'when'. Now came the hard part.

Having checked in at the barrier, I decided to park first and then walk back, but the best of plans can be held up by a beautiful blonde. As I parked, a rather smart Bentley just drew up and the blonde was emerging from it. She looked familiar and I realized that I had seen her on my TV screen.

'Would you be Eleanor Richey?' I asked.

She turned blue, blue eyes on me. 'Why yes, I would. And you are?' She was cooing with all signs saying welcome, and her accent told me she was no English rose, but a fully fledged American beauty. The coo in her voice was not, I thought, a response to my charm but because it was her natural manner.

'Jack Colby. I'm part of the police hunt for the Auburn.'

She looked impressed. 'I love that car. I felt a million dollars driving it.'

'Of course.' I smote my head in mock disgust at myself. 'You're playing Cora Langton, aren't you? I thought they weren't doing the car shots till next week?'

'Angie let me try it, the sweetie. She knew I was nervous about it, so we took it for a drive last Thursday and let me take the wheel. We went into Lenham Square and back. Caused quite a stir.'

I imagined it had. Lenham's a good centre for exotic cars, being near the A20 and the Chilston Park country hotel, plus its being a stopping point between London and the Channel. I doubt if it sees many Auburn 1935s, however. The village has a magnificent central square, surrounded by picturesque houses from medieval days onward. Cars can park there, and the Auburn would have had the whole population gaping at it.

I wondered whether it was significant that the car had been taken on the Thursday night. Did I really think that someone had spotted it in the square, tracked it to the studios and arranged to pinch it that speedily? Not possible. Stealing a classic takes a bit of thought and planning. Even so I noted that the car had been in use that day.

Eleanor and I walked to the studios together, and I left her at reception to return to the security barrier. But then I ran slap into Bill Wade.

He was not amused. 'What the sweet hell are you doing here?' he demanded. 'Expecting to find my car? Got any leads on it yet?'

One has to be positive with the Bill Wades of this world. 'I know how the car could have left the complex. Now I'm covering other ground.'

'What ground, where?' he snapped.

'First step the security guard and the DOP again – I need the list of who was on call last Friday.'

'The car went Thursday night.'

'I know.'

He held my glance, and nodded, professional to professional. 'Good. Let's go see Greg. Roger will want a word with you about insurance after that.'

I didn't ask who Greg was. It had been Rick I spoke to yesterday. But I'd lose all credibility if I queried it. Instead I followed in Bill's wake as crew and staff scattered to either side like the waves of the Red Sea as he led the way to Greg's domain on the first floor of the admin building.

It turned out Greg didn't have the list; it was on somebody called Jackie's computer. Bill simply stood there. Greg got the message and the list shot through in double-quick time. He handed it over to Bill who skimmed it, and passed it to me. 'Roger,' he reminded me. 'Now. Talk to Ken later.'

So off we went again. 'Tell me how my Auburn got out,' Bill commanded. I obeyed but he was not that impressed.

'Good work over that hedge, Jack. But the joker still had to get into the garage to get those doors open.'

Time to win a brownie point. 'Not if he went into the garage during the day and unbolted the rear door ready for that night.'

'Still had to get in through locked doors.'

'Not that day. Your wife was out with Eleanor Richey in the Auburn.'

'Ahead of me there.' He brooded as we crossed the courtyard. 'So it's someone here.'

'Looks that way, but not certain.'

A piercing look came my way. 'What are the chances of my getting it back?'

'Soon or sometime?'

'Both.'

'Soon – slim. Sometime – fifty-fifty.'

'As bad as that? Someone here has it in for the film, that what you think?' he shot at me. 'Angie loves that car. Always has. I owned it before I met her, I was driving it during *Running Tides*, but I guess she reckons it's hers now, not mine. You'd best have a word with Angie. She thinks there's something odd going on about the cars for this production.'

'If that's so, that does affect *Dark Harvest*. Any reason why it should be the target?'

'No, but I've had security tightened. There are other cars to bear in mind – the Bentley, the Horch, the Fiat. Any or all of them could be next to go.'

That was a looming disaster that I hadn't thought of, but I did a good job of treating it coolly.

'Could be,' I answered, 'but the joker has made his point with the Auburn, so the others might be safe.'

'I want that Auburn back,' Bill said drily. 'It's special.'

I agreed. And there was something else that was special too: Louise. I caught a glimpse of her as we came out of the building, but she didn't see me. It was all I could do to refrain from rushing after her to demand what Nigel Biddington was doing in her life, but I managed it. In any case, Bill was frogmarching me to Roger's office so I had no choice.

His office was beyond the reception desk I'd visited on my earlier visit. Bill strode right by the desk and thumped on Roger's door. There was no reply.

'Is he in, Jane?' he asked.

'I think so. He was earlier.'

Bill didn't deal in uncertainties. He gave her a scathing look and marched into the office with me close behind. The room was empty but the patio doors were wide open. 'Must be in the garden,' Bill said briefly, and out we went.

I remembered that farmhouse garden. It had been a delightful one, even for a boy of my age, perhaps eight or nine. It wasn't large, but instead of depending on open space for its effects it was an intricate puzzle of intertwining paths, little bridges over a running stream, tiny waterfalls and arches of roses. The farmer's wife had probably created it as her own private domain and the studios had not altered it, as far as I could see, although it must take a lot of upkeep. Perhaps Roger Ford liked to relax here. I remembered there were a couple of stone seats hidden away in concealed nooks.

Bill strode to the middle of the garden and looked around, but there was no sound or sight of Roger.

'Not here either,' Bill grunted.

'Maybe he's dozed off,' I said, putting my head round a trellis covered with sweet-smelling roses.

And then I saw it. I saw the blood first and gagged. Plenty of it was dry but some had trickled into a tiny pond and coloured it red. I forced myself to look further. And there lay the body it had come from. It looked very dead.

I must have let out some kind of noise, a retch maybe, for Bill hurried to my side. Just what I didn't want, but I was too late.

The body was turned away from us, but it was a woman's and I knew immediately whose it was. It was Angie's.

FOUR

Neither of us moved. I registered that there was some insect buzzing nearby and that incongruously a bird was singing and the sun burning on my arm. Then I found myself punching in 999 on my mobile even though my mind was still fighting to get back in gear and Bill was half walking, half staggering towards what was left of his wife. How could I say stop? There was no doubt it was Angie even though half her head had been blown away. The gun was lying at her side to prove it.

My eyes stayed on Bill even while I was talking on the phone. That done, I made another one – to Dave Jennings – to tell him he had been right. There *was* something wrong somewhere. Nightmarishly wrong.

Bill had squatted down by the body and his hand rested protectively on his wife's yellow silk trousers. The matching jacket was blood-soaked.

I forced myself to action, walked over to him and pulled him to his feet. 'Out,' I said gently.

He looked at me like a hurt animal, but for once in his life Bill Wade acquiesced. We must have been silent because when we went into the building – through its rear door this time, not the office patio doors – everything seemed strangely normal. Only Louise, who was chatting to Jane at the front desk, read my face correctly, looked from me to Bill and became very still.

'Angie's dead,' I said briefly. 'The police are on their way.'

She gave a half gasp, steadied herself and took charge of Bill. It was high time. The phrase goes 'beside himself with grief' but Bill had gone *inside* himself. He seemed to have shrivelled into grey old age, his power ceded without a murmur. 'I'll take care of him,' she said. I must have looked fairly shaky myself, because she added, 'Are you OK, Jack?'

I nodded. So I was, on the surface at any rate. I could

function. With Bill gone I dealt with the receptionist, thankfully not the gorgon of my first visit; Jane was a sensible girl in her mid twenties, even if understandably out of her depth at the moment.

'Police?' she queried, looking scared as well as shocked.

'Afraid so.' I decided not to specify why an ambulance would not suffice. 'I need your help now. Who's your closest reliable ally?'

A moment's thought. 'Tom Hopkins and Julie. I job-share with her but she's around. And Ken Merton – he's at the security barrier.'

Where I knew he would be needed. 'Page Julie and Tom then, to help us guard this building. No one gets in before the police. Not even Roger Ford.'

She took my point. 'Where . . .?'

'In the garden.'

She went a shade greener, if that were possible, but she had her wits about her. 'What about the gate?'

'What gate?'

'There's one into the garden on the far corner. It's not always locked.'

'Stay here, I'll check.'

I dashed back and forced myself back through that garden, steeling myself to pass Angie's body again. The gate took some finding since it was masked by two tall hedges with a narrow winding path between them. The gate was open and I wasn't going to touch it. I cursed the fact that I hadn't yet bought a mobile that took photos. Then it was back to reception where Julie, the older woman of my first visit, had now joined Jane and both of them were looking at me as though I had personally engineered this crisis. No Tom yet, so I despatched Jane to guard the open gate and left Julie in charge of the building to repel all attempts to enter it. She'd be good at that. Then I hurried down to the security barrier to put Ken Merton in the picture. His cheerful face grew highly suspicious; he needed convincing that I wasn't a maniac and that the police were really on their way. And then, only then, did I return to the farmhouse to wait.

*   *   *

Waiting is the worst part of bad times such as these. The police arrived rapidly – and without the usual procedure of PCs first checking and reporting on the scene. I suspected it was my name relayed through Dave Jennings that had brought DI Brandon out with the whole works so promptly. He nodded without enthusiasm as I explained how I was involved and what I had done and not done at the crime scene, including checking the gate. Crime scene? Brandon certainly seemed to be treating it as one, not surprisingly. I couldn't see Angie Wade committing suicide.

The cordons were up all round the farmhouse and the garden, including that useful gate. The cast and crew had been corralled into Studio Three, but Jane and I were escorted to the cast's green room above the canteen for easy access. This was the comfortable social area for them to meet between calls if they wished. Not much comfort here at present, however. Jane and I felt like two overlooked passengers on the *Marie Celeste*. I wondered what had happened to Bill and Louise but the question was answered when Louise herself joined us and collapsed on to a sofa.

'Hope you don't mind,' she said, 'but I didn't feel up to dealing with questions en masse in Studio Three. Bill and Roger are with the police now, so I'm off duty for a while.'

That shook me. 'Is Bill up to questioning?'

'Believe it or not, yes. He was pretty wobbly but when Roger arrived, it seemed to put him back on track, at least on one level. He was beginning to talk logically again by the time the police called him, and Roger too.' A pause. 'What happened, Jack?'

Those dark eyes held mine steadily. 'She was shot in the head,' I told her. 'The gun was at her side.'

'So it could have been suicide?' Jane asked.

'I don't know,' I said flatly.

Louise reached out and touched my hand. I'd like to have poured out the horror of it, but I couldn't, not with Jane present.

'But if it wasn't suicide, that means someone murdered her,' Jane said, horrified. 'All these awful things that have happened, the dog and the car and now *murder.*'

'We don't know they're connected,' Louise said promptly. 'Nor do we know she was murdered.' She looked so desperate that I decided to join in. In any case, talking about it was inevitable, and however callous it might sound, it could also be helpful.

'Murderers don't usually announce their intentions in advance,' I pointed out.

'It's one hell of a coincidence,' Jane muttered defiantly.

'Angie hasn't always been the target of what's been happening,' Louise argued.

We said no more, perhaps because we all saw where this might lead. Was anyone else going to fall victim?

Jane broke the silence as she burst out again, 'Mrs Wade loved that garden. It's so unfair. And I didn't hear *anything*. No shot, nothing.'

'There was probably a silencer on the gun. What time did you begin work this morning?' I asked.

I'd been so caught up with Bill and the sheer ghastliness of the scene that I hadn't thought about the time element.

'The same as usual,' she wailed. 'The cast and crew and some of the staff begin at six but the office doesn't open until eight thirty.'

'Were there a lot of people going in and out this morning? Did you see Angie go in?'

Jane shook her head. 'But she'd been in. I knew that. She'd taken her post. She and Mr Wade and Mr Ford all have their own keys, so they can get in at any time. And there's the gate of course.'

There was. There were also the open windows in Roger Ford's office. 'Is Mr Ford's office the only one on the ground floor?' I asked her.

'Yes. There's a waiting room of sorts across the entrance hall, but no one used it this morning. Mr Wade's and his wife's are on the first floor, both overlooking the garden.'

'Is that her regular office?' It seemed strange to me because she was a consultant on the film, and so technically an outsider and not part of Oxley Productions.

Jane pulled a face. 'She made a fuss and so she got it.' Then realizing these were ambiguous words, she burst into tears and Louise comforted her. 'I'm sorry,' Jane wailed. 'It's the shock. Did she . . . did she die while I was there or earlier?'

'I don't know,' I said again. I had found Angie at about
twenty to ten, and the blood, I recalled, was congealed. I
comforted Jane by reminding her that the side gate was open
when I found it, albeit that for all she knew I had pulled it
open myself before asking her to guard it.

'Were there a lot of visitors this morning?' Louise repeated
my question.

'You, Miss Shaw. Mr Ford came in and out, and so did Mr
Wade.'

'Did they stay in their offices long?'

'I don't know about Mr Ford, but Mr Wade never does. Not
on a shooting day.' Jane looked dismayed at yet another
ambiguity.

'Filming usually begins at six thirty,' Louise explained
hurriedly. 'It takes a bit of time for us to get costumed, and
the crew to sort themselves out so we tend to arrive here about
five forty-five when the gates officially open. From about six
fifteen or so, Bill is usually on set continuously.'

'Was he today?'

She looked at me stonily. 'I don't know. I wasn't on call until
eight. And if it's relevant I don't know about Roger Ford either.'

I had to persist. 'He must have been in his office at some
point, Jane, because the windows were already open when Bill
and I went through them at twenty to ten. Was the rear door
to the house locked? If it was, perhaps that's why Angie went
through the patio doors. Or perhaps she was with him when
you arrived at eight thirty?'

A step too far. Much too far. Jane closed down. 'I unlocked
that door like I do every day when I come in. Other than that,
I really couldn't say.'

Louise stepped in. 'I'm sure Jane would support me, Jack,
and indeed everyone at Stour Studios, when I tell you there's
no way Bill or Roger would have been involved in Angie's
death. Bill adored her. He was a lion to everyone else but a
pussy cat where she was concerned.'

'Even when she effectively threatened his film?'

'They would sort it out between them. Murder wouldn't
come into it. Angie was sharp. She knew there was a line she
couldn't cross and she rarely did.'

'She seems to have done over Tom Hopkins. He was sacked yesterday.'

Louise hesitated. 'That's true.'

'Tom,' Jane said, 'is *never* sacked. I saw him around this morning just as usual.'

Had she indeed, I thought. Then why hadn't we seen him since Angie's body had been discovered?

My second and more formal interview with Brandon was unexpectedly straightforward. He had established himself in one of the front ground-floor offices in the production building, and the whole of the farmhouse was cordoned off as a crime scene. Brandon and I had taken each other's measure on a previous case, and though I can't say the rapport between us was strong, he didn't seem to be automatically assuming I was in the frame for this murder. He is serious, with a one-track mind, the automaton type. Keeping one's nose to the trail you are on is a good attribute for a copper, but he can carry it too far, until you wonder what makes him tick when he's at home with his wife and kids. He listened with only one or two interruptions to my story.

'This car theft,' he said at last. 'You think that was part of this dirty tricks campaign?'

'From what I've been told, I do. Angie Wade was as fond of that car as Bill was, and she was identified with it by everyone here.'

'And she wasn't popular on the set.'

'An understatement.'

'Any line on that missing car yet?'

'No, but it's early days. I have a feeling that it's not that far away.'

'A pricey job, from what Dave tells me.'

'He's right,' I agreed. 'Too rare to be an easy mark.'

'So the theft could have been a warning to Angie Wade. But why bother to warn her? Seems odd.'

'I agree. She told her husband there was something weird going on over the cars.'

A pause while the automaton gobbled up this information. Then: 'You're going on looking for that car?'

'Unless called off by Dave or Bill Wade.'

'Good. Keep in touch over anything I need to know, will you?'

Good? Was this really Brandon letting me on the ground floor? I decided to put this to the test. 'What time was she killed?' I asked.

'She arrived with her husband in their BMW more or less on the dot of six. He seems to be a stickler for punctuality. Estimate is that she'd been dead between two to three hours when you found her. Some leeway necessary.'

That meant she'd been killed between six and eight, and so that open gate figured even higher in importance. Anyone could have used it.

I tried another question. 'Who opened the patio doors in Roger Ford's office? It could have been Angie herself. The rear door was locked until eight thirty.'

'Not yet known, but it could have been. Roger Ford denies opening them. Says he was only in there first thing this morning about six fifteen and they were shut then. After that, he was dividing his time between the studios and production building. Question is, why should Angie Wade have decided to spend a bit of time in the garden that early?'

I'd no answer to that. 'No chance it was suicide?' I asked.

'Would you like it to be?' Brandon asked surprisingly.

'Yes.' If it was murder, I could see a very messy road ahead.

Brandon turned into a human being. 'Don't get too involved, Jack. You're no use to us that way. Answer: we need the lab report, but suicide doesn't look likely.'

'Not from where I'm sitting either.' I rose to go.

'By the way, Jack,' he added, 'the gun's a Smith and Wesson thirty-eight pistol, with silencer. Bill Wade says he owns one.'

When I returned to the green room, it was empty, but Louise had left a note that she and Jane were going down to the canteen to 'join the others', so I made my way there. When I reached it, I could see that 'the others' meant everyone at the studios. It was, to my surprise, already lunchtime, and the canteen, despite the circumstances, was doing brisk business. I stood in the doorway for a moment or two, thinking about what Brandon had said: 'Don't get too involved.' Perhaps it was too late. I spotted Louise at a table with Joan Burton and – yes – Tom Hopkins. Sacked or not, here he was. At another table Eleanor Richey was deep in conversation with someone I recognized from TV as Justin Parr. I felt an outsider, even when Louise introduced me to Justin, who seemed amiable enough. But he was a heart-throb, and I usually distrust that kind of face in case it's a mask for something quite different going on beneath. I wondered whether it was in his case, then decided I was getting obsessively suspicious because of the shock of what had happened.

The sole subject of the subdued conversation was obvious, and I wasn't sorry when one of the runners came up to me with a message from Roger Ford. Could I join him and Bill in Studio Two? I whispered to Louise, 'I'll call you,' and she looked pleased.

I walked over to the studio and found Roger and Bill at a table with a plate of untouched sandwiches, glasses and a large carafe of water. Both still looked in shock, although Bill seemed slightly better than when I had last seen him, as if he were winning the fight he had set himself.

I murmured my sympathy to both of them, and was glad that it was not brushed aside, but gracefully accepted by both men.

'She was a good friend,' Roger said quietly, and it seemed to me he was sincere. Bill said nothing and his eyes were moist. I tried to push the thought from my mind that other people didn't have such favourable impressions of his late wife.

'Sit down, Jack,' Bill said, and as I obeyed he barked out at me: 'This Brandon, Jack. Good at his job, is he? You work for the police, so I reckon you know.'

'First class,' I said, meaning it. I didn't much like the bloke, but credit where it's due.

'And are you?' he shot again.

That took me aback. 'I'm good,' I replied. 'That doesn't mean I score one hundred per cent – no one does.'

'That's what Brandon says. So here's where we're at, Jack. Roger and I want you to hunt down that Auburn as arranged. Brandon's going to find out who killed my Angie, but you're

in a different field, and we need you too. This Dave Jennings
you work for – I've spoken to him, and he says you have a
nose for car trouble of all sorts. I told you Angie said there
was something mighty wrong about the cars. That was as we
drove here only this morning, and now she's dead.'

'It could be—' I began.

Brushed aside. 'Coincidence. I know that, but she said cars,
not car. That means more than the Auburn. She wouldn't have
been talking about the studios' general parking lot, she meant
the cars that Oxley's hired – the Bentley, the Fiat, the Horch
and my Auburn. We've also got a day's filming coming up for
which Oxley's hired a whole lot more. Someone's killed Angie,
Jack, and if the cars are the link, I need to know. Name your
own rates, I'll pay.'

I was stymied. 'I work for the police, but you have a car
adviser. Wouldn't he do the job better?' I could see problems
ahead if this job clashed with Dave's, or worse with Brandon's.

'Nigel? He's wet behind the ears compared with you.
Besides, you're new on the block, and that's valuable.'

'Did your wife say anything more about the cars?'

Bill's face twisted in pain. 'No. I'm not proud of myself,
Jack. I get absorbed in the movie and Angie knows that. She
said she'd tell me tonight or over the weekend. She knows
what I'm like.' The pain must have got worse as he must have
realized he was talking of Angie in the present tense, because
he glared at me. 'So whatever it costs, I'll pay you well.'

I tried to work my way through this, but couldn't. 'I can't
do it, Bill – I'm already working for the police. I have to be
independent.'

The keen eyes were on me. 'Neither Roger nor I killed
Angie if that's what worries you. Let's do it this way. You
work for the police. You tell them anything they need to know.
Anything.'

That sounded OK to me. 'In that case, I have to ask you
two questions. First, what would Angie have been doing in
the garden at that hour? It can't just have been chance.'

Bill struggled to keep emotion from overwhelming him.
'She's crazy about gardens. Keeps a strict eye on the gardeners
Oxley employs. That so, Roger?'

Roger nodded. 'We employ two ladies to look after that garden and where we shoot the exteriors. You'll find their number in the book – Garden Easy is the name. Janette Paul and Daphne Marsh. Been working here for years.'

I knew Daphne. She was a chum of Liz Potter who was the love of my life for a year or so when I returned from the oil business. We parted amicably and are still great friends.

'Second question,' I said. 'Have you reached a decision over what's happening to the film?'

'We have and it's not been easy,' Roger replied as Bill was beginning to look grey with the effort of trying to seem rational. 'These studios are closed until at least the weekend because of the crime scene. Monday, the shooting goes on as scheduled up at Syndale Manor. Angie was a trouper. She'd understand.'

Bill did his best to achieve something like a grin. 'Six a.m. Monday, Jack. *With* the Auburn.'

By the time I returned to Frogs Hill, the news was out. It travels fast. Albeit it was only that a woman had been found dead at Stour Studios, with no details, but my trusty team was eager to know what was going on. Zoe appeared, spanner in hand, as soon as she heard the sound of my Alfa drawing up in the forecourt. Len was close behind her.

'Who's the woman?' she demanded.

'Angela Wade.'

It takes a lot to stun Len. 'Bill Wade's *wife*?'

'Yes.'

'Owner of the Auburn?'

'That was Bill's, but she drove it a lot. It was a classy car.'

'*Was*?' Zoe raised an eyebrow. 'Given up, have you?'

She was right. I was thinking in terms of the Auburn being gone for ever. I supposed this was because Angie's death had capped it in horror. It put matters in perspective. If I was going to sort out what Angie meant by 'something mighty wrong with the cars' I needed to get the Auburn right back on the agenda.

'I meant *is*,' I told her.

'Good, because Rob has a lead.'

FIVE

All I had wanted was a quiet evening with a stiff drink after the shocks of the day. I did not want to have to think about Rob, who, so Zoe informed me, would be coming to pick me up at nine o'clock the next morning. This was unfair of me, especially if Rob actually had come up with something helpful. Was that likely? Knowing Rob, it could possibly be on the cards. On the other hand, he could be leading me way off target and wasting valuable time. Not that I had any real hopes of finding the car by Monday, but at least I didn't need to be driving along false avenues.

I retreated to the farmhouse, considered the question of eating and discarded it. I'd make myself a sandwich when my stomach had settled down. I'd even do without the stiff drink. Even Dad's haunting presence must have sunk into gloom because when I made my way to the Glory Boot, it didn't have its usual resonance – especially when Dave Jennings rang my mobile.

'What's all this about Angie Wade? I heard you'd found the body.'

'Whatever you were told, it's probably right.'

'What's your take on it? Connected with our job or not?'

'Could well be. Bill Wade told me his wife was talking about something being wrong with the cars – meaning, I assume, the other cars hired for the film. That might be some-thing to do with her death, or completely irrelevant.'

'Did you tell Brandon?'

'Yes. He's asked me to stick around. My stock seems to have risen.'

'Let's hope the Footsie keeps it that way,' Dave said drily.

I hoped so too. My stock all too easily goes down instead of up.

'I might have a lead over the car,' I told him. Overstatement, since it was only Rob.

'If you find it, your job with us ends, Jack. It will be over to Brandon and I doubt if he'll pay.'

'It isn't over,' I pointed out, 'until we find who nicked the Auburn.'

He grudgingly agreed, but the word 'budget' hung over us both.

Rob turned up about ten o'clock, not nine. He drives a Range Rover Vogue Edition, and invited me to share it with him. I still wasn't feeling too great so I made no protest, although I wouldn't choose to be driven by him on a Peking to Paris rally.

'Where are we off to?' I asked, as he revved along Frogs Lane to the annoyance of my stomach.

'To see Clarissa.'

'And she is? The latest gorgeous blonde in your life perhaps?'

'She's in her mid eighties, with Alzheimer's, so go gently.'

With her maybe. Rob wouldn't be so lucky if this was a wild goose chase.

'She lives in the Gladden Estate at Charing. Know it?'

I did. It was on the A20 on the Lenham side of the village and was one of those new doll's-house estates with attractive town houses and larger ones divided into several flats. It even had a few shops to make it a jolly community. The door to Clarissa's flat was indeed opened by a gorgeous blonde. I looked suspiciously at Rob but he was completely oblivious, because he was too busy chatting her up. She eyed him up and down and I fretted until he had run out of steam. We all had a merry laugh or two and then she led us into a cosy over-warm room where a silver-haired lady who could have auditioned for Miss Marple was sitting by the window in an upright armchair with a small table in front of her loaded with her needs, which included a newspaper, *Radio Times*, audio player and a radio.

Clarissa smiled at me benignly. 'You're the vicar, aren't you? I remember you.'

'No, Clarissa,' Rob told her firmly. 'This is Jack Colby – he's interested in the car you told my father you saw last week.'

'Car?' she repeated doubtfully. 'I think I sold it.'

My heart sank, as Rob tried his best. 'This was a very
special car. You said you heard it one night about a week ago.'
    She still looked puzzled, but then brightened up. 'You don't
mean the Auburn, do you? The 1935?' When we nodded, she
added, 'Why didn't you say so earlier, Rob? Of course I
remember it.'
    Could this be a set-up, I wondered, taken aback at the sudden
briskness of Clarissa's tone. No doubt she thought she remembered one, but had the idea been planted in her mind?
    'A cream-painted one—' I began.
    'The colour is immaterial, Mr Colby,' she interrupted reprov-
ingly. 'In fact the one I saw was indeed Cigarette Cream, the
colour that had featured in one of the charming advertisements
for Walker Cigarettes. I'm surprised that a vicar can afford
one, however.'
    'I'm actually a classic car restorer,' I murmured.
    'How do you find time to fit that in with your religious
duties?' Another reproving stare. 'Dear Rob is a classic car
restorer too, of course. Perhaps you work for him?'
    I turned a bemused eye on Rob, who did his best to look
innocent. I decided in the interests of the Auburn to ignore
the slur. 'Do you remember when and where you saw it?' I
asked her.
    'Of course I do. I sleep badly, Mr Colby, and sometimes
sit in here during the night not bothering to go to bed. It was
about two o'clock in the morning. I have a chiming clock – a
Thomas Tompion. Such a comforting sound at night. It had
just struck two. I was dozing, and the engine woke me up. It
is quite unmistakable. I looked down into the road and was
not surprised to see I was right about its being an Auburn. A
speedster. *Cream*,' she added meaningfully. 'A left-hand drive,
I believe, as I had no clear view of the driver. I remember my
father telling me about the car, when he worked in America
in the 1930s. He was full of praise, stating that it symbolized
the resurgence of America from the depression. Later he bought
an old one himself.'
    I found this hard to credit despite the specific information
she had. 'You're sure you weren't still dozing?'
    Wrong step. 'I may be old, Mr Colby, and I may be inexact

on some memories but on cars I am never mistaken. My father taught me well, and my late husband ran a garage.'

I felt duly abashed, and once she observed this she continued happily, 'It was a moonlit night on a well-lit road, you see. Thankfully our taxes still seem to cover street lighting. I saw the car passed twice. This road comes to a dead end, with only a turning circle, and thus the car had had to return. It frequently happens that drivers lose their way and take this road by mistake. I mentioned it to my godson Peter, that's dear Rob's father, who was most interested. I had heard that there was an Auburn somewhere in Kent and there could scarcely be two. Rob is so knowledgeable.'

Dear Rob, who could confuse a Mini with a Maserati without blenching, smiled demurely.

I ate my way through several biscuits and a mug of coffee supplied by the blonde and we talked cars. I also heard more about Dear Peter and Dear Rob. Memory is an odd thing. On cars Clarissa was crystal clear, on everyday living she faltered. As I left, she said brightly, 'Give my regards to your dear wife. Mary, isn't it?'

I agreed that it was.

'I thought so,' Clarissa said complacently. 'It was a woman driving the Auburn. Perhaps it was her?'

It was Thursday morning, and I had three and a half days left before the Auburn had to be at Syndale Manor, plus several nights if needed. I wondered if Bill Wade would notice if the Auburn wasn't there. His insistence on it might have been a knee-jerk reaction. There were formalities with any death, let alone one in these circumstances, and they might well take all the stamina that Bill possessed. Nevertheless Monday was a date I could not miss. Was I any further along having heard Clarissa's story? A woman at the wheel? I could hardly take that seriously when she herself said she had no clear view of the driver, especially as she had lost the plot by that point of the conversation. Where did it leave me though? Only that the thief of whichever sex had been making for Ashford, or the nearby turn-off to Canterbury, or even Dover, and had taken the wrong road.

Rob drove me back to Frogs Hill, and disappeared with my

thanks and a flourish of his pudgy hand. I retreated to make some routine follow-up phone calls. Unfortunately no news is not always good news. Harry Prince had nothing to offer, nor did my London contact. All he did tell me was that there was a lot of movement in what he tactfully termed 'the trade', especially in Kent thanks to its proximity to the Channel and eager buyers in Holland and Belgium. That fitted in with an offhand remark from Dave that his unit was increasingly bugged by insurance investigators. That shook me. Perhaps I was wrong, and the Auburn had been a victim of a straight theft after all.

Great. Back to the starting grid.

I went round to the barn-cum-garage where I keep my Lagonda and Gordon-Keeble, a sight that always cheers me up. The Gordon-Keeble has only recently recovered from an accident in the cause of British justice. That it recovered at all is thanks to Len's painstaking care in making good the damage. Specialists in fibreglass bodywork had to be called in for serious consultations over their patient. Under its post-operative care in the Pits, however, its metallic maroon finish now glows out to the world again. Every time I slither into the driving seat of this car it feels like coming home. Like the Glory Boot, it welcomes me with its own special smell.

It needed a run so I decided to take it over to the studios to see if Ken Merton was anywhere around. It was a gorgeous day and the Gordon-Keeble purred its majestic way through the back lanes with its usual spirited oomph. Once the Lenham Heath road, which the Auburn must have taken last Thursday night, was the main route to London, but it was hard to imagine that stage coaches, wagons and horses once filled it.

When I reached the studios, there was no sign of Ken. This was a crime scene indeed, and the outer cordon was in front of the security barriers. I cursed, but at least the Gordon-Keeble sounded pleased that we'd come out. Its V8 rumbling burble was music to my ears as I drove my stately way back to Frogs Hill. Where I hit pay dirt. There was a car outside that I recognized. If I was right, it meant that dreams sometimes come true. Louise was somewhere around.

I found her in the Pits, examining the inside of a gearbox

at Len's side. She had a smudge of black on her right hand
which suggested she had been given a practical role in the
proceedings, voluntarily or not. She looked up and grinned.

'Have you joined the payroll?' I joked. It was a feeble effort,
because it was the first time I'd seen her on home turf and for
a moment she seemed a stranger.

'Considering any offers – but I'd hate to sabotage your
business. I don't know a gearbox from an axle.'

Len was looking protective and didn't want to let her go
before he had explained every single cog and shaft to her, so
I suggested I made coffee all round in the farmhouse. Len, as
I predicted, couldn't bear to be parted from the smell of the
Pits, and said that, thanks, he'd take his in here. Louise thankfully got the right message, as did Zoe. Louise sat at my
kitchen table looking completely at home. In jeans, white
blouse and overshirt she looked a far cry from the famous film
star image beloved of the press.

'Am I holding up your search?' she asked. 'I had to get
away from the hotel – it was beginning to get to me and the
press have winkled out where we're staying.' This was at
the Buckhurst Hotel, which was hidden deep on the Downs
towards Faversham further east than the Manor.

'You're not holding up anything. The search is stalled, with
only one slight lead. How's Bill?'

'Not good. He's staying with Roger and Maisie – they live
at Headcorn, which is handier than his own home and he gets
company.'

'It doesn't seem very likely that the film will begin again
on Monday.'

'You underestimate Bill. The film will go on, even though
he adored Angie and even though the police are daft enough
to think of him as a suspect.'

'Men have killed adored wives before now,' I pointed out.
'There was an implication that the gun was his.'

'It wasn't. The police found it safe and sound at his home.
Anyway, Angie knew how well off she was. She wouldn't step
out of line one inch, because Bill gave her all she needed.
Devotion, money – and power. That sounds tough on her but
that's how it was. I can't spin you a yarn about how wonderful

she was, Jack. She was fine on a good day, but from my angle she was far from fine.'

I had to say it. 'Because of the issues between you.'

She looked me straight in the eye. 'Yes, but without reason. Bill and I got on well but no sex.'

I decided not to comment. 'Could Tom have been involved? He had plenty of reason to dislike Angie.'

'Don't go there, Jack. You've met him. You can tell he wouldn't harm a fly even though he seems to be suspect number one for the police. I suppose that's with reason, as she did get him sacked twice. Of course he's old-fashioned but nothing wrong with that if Bill wants it that way. We all understand his boards. Tom pours love into the sketches and there's mutual dependence between him and Bill. She didn't like that either.'

I remembered uneasily that Tom could not be found when Jane had paged him on Tuesday morning.

'Where did the so-called "old gang" as a whole stand over Angie?' Tom was part of it, after all.

'The *Running Tides* group? No love lost there either, even though Angie herself was an extra. I suppose she might have felt that the others were closer to Bill than she was. *And* closer to Margot Croft. But I don't believe any of this has any relevance, Jack. That's the past. The trouble is in the here and now.'

'OK. What about Eleanor Richey and the other stars? Did they hit it off with Angie?'

'Eleanor and Angie were on good terms. Eleanor drove the Auburn after all, and Justin seemed to get on with her. But then he gets on with everyone. The others weren't obviously antagonistic. I can't see why any of them would want to *kill* her though.'

'To stop her wrecking the film?'

She stared at me. 'Not sufficient. I know that means we're back to—'

'Tom,' I supplied for her.

'And me?' she asked quietly.

'I don't see you in that role.'

'Thanks.'

A silence fell between us for a moment.

'Jack, I should come clean,' she admitted. 'There *was* more trouble in the here and now. Angie was busy meddling with the scripts of more characters than mine and Brian's. There were others. I heard rumblings.'

'Do you think the film will settle down after all this?'

'Too soon to say how it will be affected. The shooting goes on. It's fair to say that any actor with a bit or small part gets used to having their parts chopped down or even out. It goes with the territory. It's an up and down life and that's why our home lives and private relationships can be so up and down. Joan's been through a sticky divorce, Chris Frant's wife left him a year ago and Graham – who's gay – is having partner trouble. Brian has a disabled wife. Perhaps that's why they stick together, but Angie might have seen it as a conspiracy against her. They stick together because they need support.'

'Do you, Louise?' I said quietly.

She looked up at me. 'Not me, Jack. Born under the original wandering star, that's me. That's inside me just as much as each of the parts I play. It drives me on. But some actors never get that chance, because fate intervenes or the parts aren't there, or they run up against other difficulties. I've been lucky though. I've been given the opportunity to wander from part to part and so I have to use it.'

'Not tempted to put roots down?'

'Of course.' She looked round my kitchen and out at what she could see of my garden through the windows. 'I'm no gardener,' she said regretfully.

I gave her space. 'Nor me. I attack it with a mower periodically but otherwise my garden and I have a live and let live arrangement. I let it live until the bushes start advancing through the doors. At the moment the roses are saving me from shame.'

She hesitated. 'I *am* sometimes tempted.'

I couldn't stop myself. 'By Nigel Biddington?'

'No. He's a friend.'

'How do you define that?'

'Someone I wouldn't go to bed with.' A smile. 'Inquisition over?'

I nodded, dizzy with relief.

'Then may I see the Glory Boot that Len told me about?' she asked.

'You can.' I led her past the comfy sofas and bookshelves in the living room, through the boot room and into the Glory Boot itself. She walked in, looked around and said spontaneously:

'Oh I like this.'

'Even though cars aren't your thing?' I asked doubtfully.

'Yes and no. I know nothing about car mechanics and technology but I like old cars in context. Is that too stupidly romantic for you?'

'Nothing about cars is stupid. Nor over romantic. But define that for me, please.'

'The way they fit into history. The cars, the picnic baskets, the celebs of the thirties and forties in their jalopies, the cars they chose, the way they reflect the way of life they trundled through as youngsters.'

'The owners or the cars?'

'Oh, the cars. *They* were young once too. That's why it's surely good to treasure them in their old age.'

Somehow I found her in my arms and I was kissing her. Hard. Unplanned, heading I knew not where. My arms were round her and I wanted her more than anyone or anything in the world. What's more, she wanted me, even though she at last pulled back.

'Where are we driving to, Jack?'

'You know.' A gentle kiss this time.

'Now?'

'Why not?'

'Here?'

We settled for the comfort of upstairs.

Two hours later I floated down to somewhere near earth again, but what we said to each other isn't part of the Auburn's story. Only of ours, and that would run and run.

Twenty-four hours to go. Less. The Auburn swam back into my consciousness early on the Sunday morning, as I watched my Louise drive out, back to the secure hotel on the Downs. We'd had two whole days and three nights together. In theory anyway. On the Friday, Louise had to drive back to the hotel where Bill had indefatigably insisted on blocking and discussing scenes for the forthcoming week at Syndale Manor. I had thrown myself into checking cast lists, who was and who was not present before and after the disappearance of the Auburn and when Angie died. All three relevant days had required full crew and cast plus a selection of extras. As a result of this spadework, therefore, I was little further forward.

I'd also popped into Liz Potter's garden centre in Piper's Green where the two ladies of Garden Easy would meet me. Yes, they said, they did work for Oxley, and no they had not been there on the Wednesday morning that Angie died. They had a regular slot with Mrs Wade to work in the garden but that was not one of their days. On Wednesdays they were employed at Hampton Court. That meant if Angie was summoned to the garden, it was not by either of them. If she went down there on the spur of the moment, her killer could not have foreseen that and it must have been an opportunist murder – not possible because of the gun. So she was summoned there – but by whom?

I couldn't be sure that Clarissa had not been dreaming with her story about seeing the Auburn, but on the other hand I still had no other line to consider. I needed to haul my brain back from where it was dreaming with Louise and refocus it on the car.

I focused. Lack of information from outside sources reconfirmed my conviction that whoever had pinched the Auburn was employed at the studios and would therefore need to show up for filming at six a.m. on the Friday morning. Where did that leave me? If he or she was working alone, then he or she had to get from wherever the Auburn was now residing back to the studios or to be picked up by the shuttle bus.

So far, so good. Or bad, depending on how one looked at it. Therefore the thief either walked back to the hotel after hiding the car or walked directly to the studios. Or, I realized glumly, he could have had his own car waiting for him near the hiding place. Or he took public transport. It would have been a tad memorable if he arrived at the studios by bike. Given the clocking-in time, buses were out and trains barely possible. Cars might draw attention if they were left unattended in a country lane while they awaited their owner. A handy empty barn? Unlikely for a non-local cast or crew member.

I sat down with the ordnance survey maps of the area and

drew a neat circle in the area that public transport was available – namely the Ashford to London route. Rural stations on that route included Lenham and Harrietsham from where the walk to the studios would easily be possible. Even Headcorn might be conceivable, though X would arrive at the studios somewhat sleepy from the long walk.

The Lenham and Harrietsham line also stopped at Charing, however. *Near to where Clarissa had seen the car.* I was trying not to rush to conclusions, but honour demanded that I found Bill his Auburn in less than twenty-four hours. And then there was Louise. There was a seventeenth-century Kentish poet with the romantic name of Lovelace who wrote: 'I could not love thee, dear, so much, Loved I not honour more.' That sentiment strikes a trifle strange to modern ears, but it galvanized me. Auburn or bust.

I rang Len at home, which was normally off bounds, but that was immaterial. Len sounded thrilled in fact; perhaps he thought I was summoning him over to the Pits. He certainly seemed to lose interest when I mentioned the Auburn, but for once I didn't care.

'Where would you a hide a car in a hurry, Len? Any car, not just an Auburn?'

A grunt came back. 'Cows.' Or that's what it sounded like.

'Sorry?'

Another grunt. 'With cars. Other *cars.*'

'Yes, but this is an Auburn, Len. It would stand out like a Bugatti in a boot sale.'

'Wraps,' he said.

'Which scene?' I got muddled with film jargon.

'Covers,' he yelled. 'Under covers.'

Even I got to the next step. 'Private car parks.'

'Worth a go,' he said, and put the phone down.

I rushed over to my maps again. Suppose Clarissa had been right on target. If the thief had mistaken the turning, it would suggest he was heading either for a house or road nearby, or for the main turning for Canterbury. From the latter he was less likely to get back to the studios in time without a taxi, which would be traceable. From Charing it would be only three miles or so to walk back to the studios. I could remember no suitable car park in Charing village, so I thought again about the estate where Clarissa lived. They were town houses, with no sign of their having their own garages. Residents needed somewhere to park, as would the shoppers. I began to feel sick again but with excitement this time. I remembered that breakfast with Louise had been a long time ago and forced myself to make a sandwich and eat it (ghastly though it tasted). Then I leapt into the Alfa and drove like a knight of old determined to win his spurs.

Coming from the Pluckley road, I had to turn right into the Gladden estate. Instead I turned before that into an inconspicuous entrance marked P which led – to my great pleasure – into a small underground car park. For a nervous thief coming from Lenham, turning into the estate would be a natural mistake to make.

A nice jolly-looking security guard wearing the by now familiar uniform of Shotsworth Security watched me take a time ticket from the machine. Then I got out and showed him my police pass and he became even more jolly, although I sensed a certain strain in the jolliness now. I parked the Alfa and as I got out I noticed that Mr Jolly had left his booth and advanced into the parking lot to check up on me. I waved to him, as I strolled around, but saw nothing of interest, so I went down to the next level in the bowels of the earth. There I found what I was looking for. Several cars tucked away – not together – and under a cover of some sort. I peered beneath one, and found a Jaguar XK150. Nice, but not the Auburn. Then I walked up to the next one, and tried that. Eureka!

I'd found it. The Auburn itself in all its glory.

I was conscious of a prickling feeling at the back of my neck and knew I was being watched. It was a sense I had valued ever since my oil business days, when it could mean the difference between life and sudden death. Maybe here too, but I was less worried when I saw it was only the jolly-looking chap from the security booth.

Only he wasn't jolly any longer.

Especially when I told him the police would be coming to take the Auburn away. It wasn't that he looked about to bash me – he was a lot shorter and flabbier than me anyway. But he did look extremely nervous.

SIX

For all my relief, recovering the Auburn seemed but a small victory in the context of Angie's death and I felt it would do little to dispel the shadows cast over *Dark Harvest*. I waited patiently by the car for Dave's team to arrive. Mr Jolly, whose real name I had forced out of him to be Nathan Wynn, had disclaimed all knowledge of Auburns or indeed of any other car in his domain. Guess what – he just worked here and the car must have come in on someone else's watch. Was the car park manned by night? With great relief, he agreed it was not. Was there CCTV? There was, but before I got too hopeful, he added, 'Doesn't cover every corner of course.'

'What about this one?' I asked, pointing to the Auburn's hiding place.

Guess again. 'Not a chance.' Happy grin.

To Dave's team it was only one more stolen car and it was Sunday afternoon, as Dave had pointed out on the phone. The wait for his team was a long one, even though I knew he had been winding me up. Fair enough, I supposed. For me it presented a different scenario. One step had been accomplished, but the next foot forward was wavering around in mid-air. The Auburn was possible evidence in a murder case and so on Brandon's plate as well as Dave's, but without anything tangible to link the two Dave was in the driving seat for the moment. I was glad, because it helped me keep them separate, rather than trying to spot links where none might exist, for all Angie's cryptic words to Bill.

'When will you be able to release the Auburn?' I'd asked Dave hopefully on the phone. 'It has to be at Syndale Manor by six a.m. tomorrow.'

Brief pause. 'Believe in miracles, do you? Think the entire Kent police force is going to turn out on a Sunday to check out the car overnight?'

'I hoped—'

'No way. Tuesday, Jack.'

'Eight am. Monday,' I bartered.

'Three in the afternoon.'

'Ten in the morning.'

'Eleven,' and Dave rang off.

It was his job to relay the news to Bill and for that I was duly grateful. Dave must have hidden powers of persuasion because no irate phone call from Bill followed. Nathan was still presumably in his booth, but I remained guarding the precious Auburn. I decided to leave the wraps as they were, save for the place where I had heaved them up earlier, though I longed to see the lady totally unclad with black tarpaulin.

The team arrived complete with a low loader an hour and a half later and watching them winch the Auburn aboard was nerve-racking. I felt personally responsible, and no doubt Bill saw it the same way. A 1935 Auburn Speedster was special.

The next morning an uncertain sun was doing its best to cheer me up as I drove the Auburn along the A20 towards Syndale Manor. Dave had told me I could have the honour of picking it up and returning it to the film set. On the whole, I'd have preferred them to do it on the low loader, but the word 'budget' floated around, and I would be facing Bill in person. I comforted myself that this way I could realize my dreams and actually drive the stunner. The darling just seemed to float along, although if I'd been eight inches shorter, I might have had trouble seeing out over the bonnet. For me, though, it was a glorious moment, even though the lanes to Syndale Manor, once one has left the A20, are not wide. In places meeting another car involves contact with scratchy hedges, ditches and mud, but I had little choice of route. There are two ways of approaching the Manor and both of them involve stretches of single-track lanes that set classic car owners' hearts a-quiver. I took the Doddington road through Wichling, which is so small that you are past it before you recognize it as an independent village. Nevertheless it has an active church, which dignifies it by the name of village rather than hamlet. It is high up on the Downs and that whole area can be creepy, very creepy in rain or mist or low cloud. The Pilgrims Way, the ancient road from Winchester to Canterbury, runs along the Downs between Wichling and the A20 and its atmosphere suggests that the humble cars on the main road are a mere nothing compared with the ghosts of pilgrims past. Except, of course, for the Auburn, which is hardly a mere nothing. I was still savouring every minute of this drive, although the wipers were hardly efficient when I tried to remove some bird dirt that had blessed the windscreen.

With the weather still meditating on what mischief it might produce and my anxiety to avoid responsibility for the slightest mark on the Auburn, I was glad when, having turned down the even narrower lane to Syndale Manor, which boasted grass growing through the tarmac in places, I saw the Manor's open gates on the right. It lies in the Syndale valley, the better known end of which emerges near Ospringe, on the A2 to Canterbury. Smugglers, pilgrims, Templars, prehistoric traders – they have all used this valley and add their own history to that of the travellers on the Pilgrims Way, which is a relatively recent name for a track going back to prehistory. Like Dad in the Glory Boot, their ghosts still hang around.

As I proceeded up the Manor drive, a sign pointed to the field where cars were to be parked, and I was about to go in when a horrified security guard (Shotsworth Security, naturally) leapt out of nowhere and frantically waved me onwards.

'You're *production*,' he yelled at me, goggling at the car. 'They're waiting for you up *there*.'

Is *there* Heaven? I wondered, as I drove onwards. It was one form of it, I discovered. The guard had obviously rung the great news of my arrival through, because as I turned a corner I was greeted by an amazing spectacle. In the background against an unexpectedly blue sky was Syndale Manor. I'd seen pictures of it, but the real thing was stupendous. Georgian, mellowed yellow stone, dignified, huge, and with beautifully proportioned windows, it was a gracious sight to behold.

To my right in the shade of a line of trees I glimpsed the usual cluster of day caravans and trailers, and to my left was a field full of what looked like the catering vans and loos, together with an array of tables. All these I briefly registered, but what transfixed my astounded eyes was what lay ahead of me. It seemed the entire crew, cast and staff were lining the driveway for my triumphant arrival, or more probably the Auburn's. They were waving madly, and there was even a modest cheer or two. Striding towards me in the middle of the drive like a sheriff in a Western was Bill Wade.

He and I both drew up with about six feet left between us. I got out of the Auburn and indicated he could take over the driving, but he didn't move.

'About time,' he grunted. 'Hurt, is she?'

'Not a scratch.'

'Inside damage?'

'None that I or the police could see.'

We looked at her together, admiring the cream paintwork, the four chromed external exhaust headers and all the other glories of this wonderful car.

'That's bad news,' was Bill's remarkable conclusion, and not unnaturally it threw me off track. 'It means someone had it in for Angie, not the car or film,' he went on to explain.

'But you both loved it.'

'Sure. It's part of my life.' He stared at it some more and then nodded – to himself, it seemed, not to me. Then he snapped into gear. 'We're shooting arrivals,' he told me.

I thought for a crazy instant that included me, but I realized this probably meant the arrivals at 'Tranton Towers' for the Jubilee ball weekend.

'The Auburn's called for two o'clock. Be there, Jack.' He turned to go, and then stopped. 'And thanks.'

'Won't you drive her in?' I asked.

I thought for a moment he would refuse again, but if so he changed his mind. I left him to it, and walked behind as the Auburn, with its owner at the wheel, slowly made its way to play its part in what would surely become movie history, just as *Running Tides* had done.

The crew and a few cast closed around him and it was business as usual. Bill was surrounded by so many people that he was almost invisible. Not inaudible though, as his orders came over loud and clear. The professionals were at work. I waited for a while, watching technicians adjusting lighting

angles on Syndale Manor's front entrance and the two four-
wheel drives with their rear-mounted cameras manoeuvring
their way through the mass of people.

I saw the other three classics driven up one by one, joining
the Auburn now parked to one side of the forecourt. The Fiat
508S Tipo, the Bentley Silent Sports and the Horch were so
distinctive that I expected the whole crew to stop in their tracks
to applaud. They didn't of course. Nor did the various members
of the cast I could see gathered in groups. I spotted Louise,
dolled up in a slinky 1930s silver-grey suit. She'd told me that
silver grey, highly fashionable in May 1935 because of the
Silver Jubilee, was part of Bill's colour strategy agreed with
his cinematographer. He'd been angling for some kind of effect
such as Jack Cardiff had used for the Other World in *A Matter
of Life and Death*, but it hadn't worked. Hence the use of the
silver-grey theme, which was a compromise – not something
that Bill was used to. Compromise or not, it suited Louise.

The Horch, bearing 'von Ribbentrop', was the first car to
be shot 'arriving' at the Manor, and I saw Chris Frant setting
off in it towards the gate, followed by the four-wheel drives
carrying Bill and camera crews. A bevy of other crew members
and a small group of extras rushed after them. Should I join
them? It was a wrench but I stayed where I was. The one
thing one can bank on with the film production is that there
will be a lot of waiting around. It was only eleven thirty, and
I had over two hours before the Auburn took the limelight. I
preferred to use the time, not waste it.

I spotted Louise talking to a pleasant looking fair-haired
man in modern jeans and leather blouson, who looked vaguely
familiar.

'Jack!' Louise had spotted me and was waving, not I thought
to her companion's pleasure. So naturally I joined them. 'You
wanted to meet Nigel Biddington,' she said. 'Nigel, this is
Jack Colby. He works for the police.'

'The chap who found the Auburn?' he asked.

Nigel was about thirty, and at first his expression was one
that I tend to associate with Rob and his ilk, which usually
translates for me as: 'Do I wish to know you?' Today it didn't.
His face lit up with pleasure.

'The star of the show himself,' he continued. 'You saved my bacon, I can tell you. I thought I was going to have to produce a miracle at short notice.'

He seemed sincere and inoffensive, and I could believe Louise's claim that he was a friend only. Still, first impressions aren't always right.

'I'll have to leave you two car buffs,' Louise said. 'I'm on call shortly. As soon as the Horch reaches the forecourt my far from beloved husband and I have to rush out to greet von Ribbentrop. This is Chris's big moment; he only has two words to speak in the film – *"Guten Tag"* – and this is the scene, so we have to make sure it goes well for his sake.' She excused herself with a quick touch of my hand, which reassured me that our nights together had been no dream.

Nigel and I then talked serious cars, as he showed off the Bentley and the Fiat. He knew his stuff, I grudgingly granted. He even knew all about the famous 'Bentley Boy' Woolf Barnato, one of Dad's childhood heroes. I realized that Nigel's face had struck a chord with me as one I'd seen around at various car shows and gatherings.

'Where did you hire the cars for the film?' I asked. 'From an agency?'

'That or from people I know through my day job. I'm a car insurance broker.'

I could see him being rather good at his job. 'I saw you at the Wheatsheaf, I think. Or Dering Arms at Pluckley.' Both have regular classic car meets.

'Probably. Good hunting ground for this job. Did you know we're having thirty more classics here this Saturday? The whole day's devoted to them.'

That sounded good to me. 'Terrific. I'll be here. Did you get the Horch from an agency?'

'Difficult. I tracked it down from someone I know.' He was so vague I wondered what the mystery was.

We were still deep into discussing the Car Day, as Nigel referred to it, when Roger Ford joined us and added his profuse thanks. 'Might save the premiums going up next time, eh, Nigel? The insurers have been having some big payouts recently, Jack, and couldn't believe their luck over the Auburn being recovered within the thirty days before they had to fork out.'

'Where are you keeping these classics?' I asked.

'We've special security garages set up here for two weeks. I don't think there'll be more trouble.'

'You think Bill's right?' I asked. 'That it's Angie that the thief was targeting, not the film?'

'I darn well hope so,' Roger said with feeling. 'Oxley Productions can't afford much more of this. He must have realized that this didn't sound good, because he added, 'Don't get me wrong, Jack. Angie was a good friend, and what's happened is a personal nightmare – both for Bill and me. But Bill's chosen to push forward with this movie, and the only way it will work is to keep distance between the movie and Angie's death. We don't know where we are with the studios, but what's going on *here* is safe ground. Understand?'

I did. 'The known, not the nightmare.'

He shot me a keen look. 'You've a foot in both camps, Jack. OK with that?'

'Both camps?' Nigel queried. 'The Auburn's back.'

Marshy ground. I didn't want Angie's comments to Bill spread around.

'There's still the paperwork to do,' I said easily, 'plus the need to find out who took the car in the first place, plus the possible threat to the other classics.'

'Of course,' Nigel murmured. 'Better safe than sorry.'

But were they safe? I wondered. Even in these glorious surroundings it was not only the shadow of Angie's death that hung over the company. I had a feeling that they were characters in a film of their own, caught up in a web in which they were totally unaware of the spider working amongst them.

It took over an hour – a remarkably brief time apparently – to get the Horch up the drive, and even then its final arrival displeased Bill. I could hear his voice ranting at the unfortunate Chris Frant – for pulling up the Horch too quickly. By that time lunch was in full flow and I had just provided myself with an interesting pasta and salad when Eleanor Richey, looking gorgeous in a powder-blue silk suit and matching hat, pounced on me.

'You're *so–oo–oo* clever,' she cooed at me.

'Luck,' I said modestly.

'Nonsense. You're good.' She tucked her arm in mine. 'The police should be asking you to find out who killed poor Angie. Can't you help them out? You're so *brilliant*.'

'Not my role,' I said. 'I'm still looking into the dirty tricks campaign. Did you suffer from it?'

'I guess we all did. ' She pulled a face. 'It was poor darling Louise who really suffered. Bill likes her so much.'

Ouch. That was delivered with such apparent sweetness that I mentally winced. I picked up the implication though. It wasn't hard. 'Is there any possibility that Angie could have been behind the dirty tricks?' I played with the idea that someone had found that out, and used it against her by stealing the Auburn for real.

Eleanor did her best to look aghast. 'Of course not. Although she did put people's backs up. She was so possessive over Bill that anyone who looked at him twice was in trouble. I guess I shouldn't say such nasty things about her, but it's just unbelievable that she's dead. And now the Auburn's here, waiting for me to drive it *alone*. I was trying to pluck up courage for a practice drive. I suppose you wouldn't come with me?'

'Not without Bill's permission,' I said hastily. Honey traps I did not need.

'Nigel's will do. He's in charge of the cars,' she said coolly.

I gave in, duly found Nigel, and checking that the way was clear after the Horch filming, we drove down the drive and back in stately fashion. Hardly to my surprise she was a confident driver, showing no signs of the nervousness she had claimed, as she chattered on. On the way back we passed Louise, about to go into the catering area. She stood to one side and saluted as we sailed past. Perhaps it was my imagination but an eyebrow was raised, rather like Zoe's trick. I gave Louise a wave and a friendly toot, and caught her in the mirror laughing.

By the time I managed to prise myself away to follow her, Louise was already established at a table with Justin Parr – they looked all too cosy together, but when Louise indicated that I should join them, he greeted me with genuine interest.

'So you're Bill's flavour of the month,' he said.

'You could have fooled me,' I said cheerfully. 'I thought I was in the doghouse for being over five hours late.'

'Not today.'

'How's he coping with the filming?'

'It's the only thing keeping him going, I reckon. If he keeps centred on the film, he doesn't have to think about Angie and police,' he said quietly.

'Are there any police here?' I asked. It was possible that Brandon would have posted someone here – just in case – but I hadn't identified anyone as yet.

'I thought *you* were the police,' Louise joked.

'Don't let DI Brandon hear you say that,' I said hastily. His goodwill to me would only stretch so far. 'Is Shotsworth Security in sole charge here?'

'I think so,' Justin answered. 'They seem pretty good.'

I didn't like to point out that one major car theft, a series of petty crimes and a murder wouldn't count in my book as 'pretty good' – but if Justin thought it so, best leave it that way. He and Louise must be used to being hemmed in by guards. I made a mental note, however, to keep my eye on Shotsworth Security as far as I could.

I'd spotted Tom and Joan at another table, and so mindful of my role here, I decided to make my excuses (with deep regret) to Louise and Justin.

'See you at close of play, Jack?' Louise asked.

'Done,' I said happily.

Justin looked interested. 'I thought I had your undivided love, Louise,' he joked.

'Job-share,' I quipped.

Louise blushed and I loved her even more. How could this woman play a scheming seductress on screen and set and be such an angel off it, when Eleanor Richey played a sweet American on-screen and came over as a prize bitch off it. The acting profession is an interesting one: does the role hide the truth or reveal it?

When I joined Tom and Joan, Joan was already in costume and told me she had to leave because she was due at Make-Up. 'Are you employed again?' I asked Tom cautiously, when we were alone.

Tom ostentatiously looked around for possible spies. 'I re-employed myself at Roger's suggestion.'

'Deputy assistant DOP again?'

'No. Roger thought Bill could do with more practical support. He suggested I brought my hand-drawn storyboards back. Usually they're a pre-production tool for the director and cinematographer but Bill likes them around all the time, so I've stuck them up in the ops caravan. We know it's a risk. With Angie's death so close, it could go either way, but Bill hasn't objected yet. Roger thinks they might help draw the company together by opening up discussion. We're gambling that Bill won't think it's an insult to Angie. Want a look?'

I did, and we walked over to the ops caravan which was out on its own, away from the day caravans allotted to the stars. I noticed a couple of security guards prominently patrolling the area – necessary, I supposed, as fans could easily evade gate checks by climbing over walls or fences. And so, it occurred to me, could anyone bent on mischief.

There were no guards around the ops caravan. It was open to all comers. I followed Tom up the steps and into the world of *Dark Harvest*.

On one side were neat small sketches, on a series of what looked like computer printed templates. 'These are the thumbnails for the rest of the week, including Car Day,' Tom told me. 'Bill uses them to either stick up in front of him or scribble notes on. But these,' he said with pride, pointing to the much larger hand-drawn charcoaled sketches, 'are the real thing. Today's and tomorrow's detailed storyboards.'

I had looked at the Car Day thumbnails with interest but it was clear that to Tom a car was a car, even if it was a precious classic. On the other hand, the hand-drawn dramatic sketches of the cast in a series of situations and emotions came across with power and with what I imagine Bill had meant by 'mood'. There was Julia Danby – not the Louise I knew, but a sultry, vengeful woman. There was the innocent American heiress, the beleaguered Lord Charing, his son Robert Steed, and a dark-haired Italianate man whom I imagined must be Charles Danby. All of these sketches brought across a brooding sense of what was to come. I wasn't sure if I liked the result, but it was certainly a winner.

'How's Bill with these?' I asked.

'Hasn't seen them yet,' Tom said awkwardly. 'Roger suggested I just put them up and hope that Bill would . . . Ah.'

His eyes slipped past me and I turned round to see Bill standing in the doorway. Tom and I stood there like naughty schoolboys, as he marched in and surveyed the storyboards. We held our breath waiting for Nemesis.

'Saw them earlier, Tom,' Bill said at last. 'Good work. We'll go with these. Got the rest?'

Tom nodded, stunned.

Then it was my turn. 'Jack, seven this evening after shooting if everything goes OK. You too, Tom. We're showing *Running Tides* in the Manor. There's a home cinema down in the basement. Everyone to be there. No exceptions.'

Bang went my quiet evening alone with Louise, and I wondered why Bill was so keen for everyone to see it, even me.

Syndale Manor was to be used chiefly for external shots, although according to the storyboards I'd seen the staircase and entrance hall were also being used this week. The Manor was not open to the public and when I went inside it seemed very much still a home, albeit one that had both benefited and suffered from conversions over the years. Large rooms had been divided into smaller ones, and there was no longer a ballroom. The cinema in the basement had apparently been the idea of Sir John's grandfather who had a passion for Gloria Swanson and for Charlie Chaplin, and set it up in the 1920s. It held about sixty people at a guess, not everyone as Bill had said, but tonight I could see that included the cast, a few lesser acting mortals, department chiefs – and me.

I could see no sign of Bill as I took my place in the back row. This wasn't modesty on my part, but because I wanted an overall squint at the audience. Nigel was in the front row and I thought I saw Louise next to him. I was wrong, because she appeared a few minutes later, scoured the audience and then made her way to me. I sat there with an idiot's grin on my face, especially when she kissed me on the cheek. Nothing like the back row of a cinema for sweethearts. Well, that used to be the case, although now any row will do. The back row held a special place in my heart, however, so Louise and I held hands. For the rest, I could wait. Just about.

Running Tides was set in the First World War around the Folkestone and Dover area and Lille in northern France. It was based loosely on a real story about a French agent, a girl code-named Ramble, a British RFC pilot flying fighters on the Ypres front with whom she fell in love, a Belgian spy and a British agent working out of Folkestone. After the war one of the heads of British Intelligence wrote a novel loosely based on Ramble's story, in which Ramble survived the war and became a nun. In real life her story was different. She was captured and died miserably in prison a month or two later. *Running Tides* was closer to the latter scenario. The theme sounds fairly run of the mill, and so it might have proved in its execution had it not been for two factors. The first was Margot Croft playing Ramble, and the second was its director, Bill Wade. I could see now why Bill wanted us to see it. Its mood said that it was not just a film about three or four people in wartime, but a film about all time. Country against country, betrayal, love, and danger, and more importantly a warning for the future, a theme that *Dark Harvest* would continue.

I'd seen some of Margot Croft's films before – she was only twenty-nine when she died, so there weren't that many featuring her mature work, but they were outstanding. In *Running Tides* she was mesmerizing. With her dark hair and eyes, and her steady expression, there was something about her that reminded me of Louise. I wondered if Louise reminded Bill too of Margot Croft? And whether Angie had noticed?

I could see Bill now. He was standing in the doorway of the cinema, eyes fixed on the screen during a close-up of his former lover. Even from here I could see the agony in his eyes.

SEVEN

Dinner with Louise on a summer's night under the stars. The only hitch in this paradise was that we were sharing it with fifty or so other people at plastic tables in a field with utilitarian-looking catering vans. The velvety sky, kindly provided by providence on what might be the year's only day of true summer in this volatile-weathered country was an inducement to drink and talk – except that I had to pass on the drinking. Nothing wrong with talking, I supposed. I had no choice, short of sweeping Louise off in my Alfa, and there was no way I could do that. There had been something about *Running Tides* that made it fitting for those who had been part of its success to be together, and even those who had not been so involved seemed to have their place here tonight. A community spirit? There was certainly that, although the talk was muted, as though everyone had been affected one way or another by seeing the film again. Perhaps, it occurred to me, that was why Bill had wanted us all to watch it.

Maybe he had personal reasons for that, as Angie had been an extra in the film. No, that didn't fit, because there was his relationship with Margot Croft. It was not until after the film and after Margot's suicide that Angie had entered his life. Moreover Bill struck me as someone who was guided by instinct in his creative work, but by logic outside it. An interesting combination.

The food was even better in the evening than it had been at lunchtime, and both evening and diners became mellow. Joan, Chris, Graham and Brian joined their table up with ours, so it was a companionable occasion. A middle-aged housekeeper in *Dark Harvest*, in the earlier film Joan had been a snappy young woman at Folkestone intelligence HQ. The intervening years had added a whole generation to her two small roles. In any case, she was the pleasantest period housekeeper I'd ever seen.

I hadn't spotted Chris in *Running Tides* and put my foot in it by saying so. He didn't look pleased. 'I was there all right,' he told me. 'Just wasn't playing the fighter pilot – tried for it, but too much competition. Even in those days a Wade film was something special and the world and his wife were lining up for it. I landed up as a pilot taking off on the same mission as the hero.'

'And now you're Chris von Ribbentrop,' Joan laughed. 'You get a taste of both sides in our profession. You too, Brian, first a German soldier, now Lord Charing.'

'A rich and varied career,' Brian agreed gravely. 'I remember playing a gorilla way back in my youth in some sci-fi film. Pretty hairy job that. At least I've risen to having a peerage and a stately home.'

'Not to mention having me as an ex-lover,' Louise joked.

'Pity about the ex,' Brian said.

At which Graham chimed in with a reference to his male partner, and the atmosphere grew temporarily cooler. I remembered that the partnership was going through a bad patch. Time, I thought, to bring matters back to the present.

'I didn't see Angie in the film either,' I said. 'What scene was she in?'

'A French peasant in the market. Easy to miss,' Chris said promptly, then made a face. 'Sorry.'

'She didn't go out of her way to make friends,' Louise said comfortingly.

'That's what I told the police. They'd heard about our spat with her in the canteen,' Chris said.

'She went much too far,' Joan said fairly. 'Did the police grill you over it?'

'To a cinder,' Chris admitted. 'But I told them that if I'd been planning to murder her I'd hardly have had a stand-up row with her in front of half the company.'

'What did they say to that?' Louise asked.

'What the police always do. Nothing. Then they turned to other matters, such as where I was on the night of Thursday the third when the Auburn disappeared. Most of us seem to have been through that line with them. I told them we were shooting late that day. Graham and I had something to eat, then left about ten thirty or so.'

'We drove back to the hotel in my car,' Graham took over, 'for which I am truly grateful because otherwise I might have a starring role at the top of the suspects' list. Luckily CCTV showed us signing out of the security barrier. Then they started asking about last Wednesday, and I told them we all got the bus to the studios like good little boys.'

'They had a go at me because I arrived early that morning,' Joan said. 'They pointed out I wasn't on call until nine o'clock so apparently I had plenty of time to nip over in my house-keeper's best black to murder Angie and exit unnoticed by the side gate. When I asked why I would want to murder Angie, they told me the same as you, Chris. Nothing.'

'Me too,' Brian said. 'My guess is that I'm right after Tom on the suspects' list. Angie was pretty vocal about my short-comings as Lord Charing and was eager to put the matter right in her own sweet way. The bus arrived at six, but I didn't think to get a witness to where I was every minute before I went on set.'

'Difficult situation,' I sympathized. 'But unless there's forensic evidence the police have a long haul on their hands.'

'Do they have any?' Louise asked uneasily.

'I don't know,' I said truthfully. 'I'm not in Brandon's confidence – but humour me. If there are a hundred or so background cast, surely the odd one is not missed even if supposed be on the set?'

All four stared at me as though I was a quaint old dinosaur who hadn't waddled over a film set in his life.

'The odd one is *always* missed,' Joan explained kindly. 'Especially on one of Bill's films. Even if the casting depart-ment misses one or two, he has a sixth or even seventh sense – he somehow knows if the grouping doesn't look or feel exactly as he remembers it from the last take or his plan for the scene.'

'How?' I asked curiously. I knew directors stood in for God, but this seemed remarkable.

'Overall feel for costume, height, expression . . .' Joan answered vaguely.

'Anyway, there's a discipline to it,' Chris added. 'Not only do we check in on arrival, but if we didn't do so for costuming and make-up that too would be noticed, so would incomplete call sheets.'

'Were the call sheets OK last Wednesday morning?'

Chris looked blank. 'I don't remember. Do you, Graham?'

'We did ten takes of the Berlin scene – that was an exterior. I don't remember any problems. There were long intervals between takes though. It would be on record if there were any absentees.'

I was sure that Brandon would have that covered. 'What about consultants and outsiders like me? Do they always get here at the crack of dawn?'

Louise was not fooled. She knew I didn't mean myself. 'If you're thinking of Tom and even,' she added lightly, 'Nigel, the answer's no. You don't have to check in with anyone except at the security barrier. Tom was around that morning, and so was Nigel. He'd come in to sort out a quibble on the insurance on Car Day.'

I offered to drive Louise back to the Buckhurst Hotel, and to my disappointment she accepted. I'd no real hope that she'd seize the opportunity to come to Frogs Hill with me – a four thirty or so dawn rise to be at the studio at six is not conducive to relaxed sex, so I was not surprised at her decision. Just these few moments alone with her were precious, however. The hotel was way off even what passed on the Downs for the beaten track. It was guarded by high walls, massive iron gates and no doubt a couple of pit bulls and Rottweilers.

I parked outside and as we were walking up to the hotel entrance the thought of guard dogs reminded me of the one tenuous link so far between the dirty tricks campaign and the theft of the Auburn. The guard dog had been poisoned that day. And if they were linked, then Angie's death must surely have been the end target for the campaign.

'I take it that wasn't the first time you'd seen *Running Tides*?' I asked Louise. It was still dusk, and the stars weren't yet out for their nightly display but it felt as though they were beaming their approval anyway.

'I watched it on DVD when I first knew I'd got this role last year. That doesn't have the same effect as watching it on a large screen like tonight. It came at us head-on, didn't it? Margot Croft was a great actor.'

'She was inspiring,' I said sincerely. 'Does Bill ever talk about her?'

'Never. And not, I think, just because Angie would have screamed blue murder. Oh damn,' she said softly, 'the things one says.'

'Inevitable. You're in Margot Croft's mould, Louise. You're heading for greatness. Oscars looming.'

I meant this seriously and she took it that way. 'Not like Margot, though. She was a natural. I've had to work at it – I might get there one day, but I'm not certain. This film . . .'

'Might get you there?' I finished, as she paused.

'I told you I was a wandering star, Jack. That's what the ancient Greeks called the planets that shoot across the sky. That's the excitement of this profession – you never know where it will take you. It could spin me up to the top or it could drop me down amongst the has-beens and never-made-its. All of us start out thinking we'll hit the heights. There's a moment – a tide in the affairs of men that taken at the flood leads on to fortune. Shakespeare was right, as usual. There are turning points in life and in careers.'

'Doesn't luck play a part too, if the right part comes at the right time?

'Yes, but I don't think it's the major part; something within oneself decrees whether one can see and then grasp what the wandering star offers. Commitment, luck, the sheer ability to recognize it. Mostly our chances at fame and fortune pass before we've grabbed them. Now I am in a film for Oxley Productions that follows a success like *Running Tides*. I feel that star's right above me, Jack.'

'Is fortune what you want? Or fame, or both?'

She considered this seriously. 'I'm not sure one can balance fame and fortune with the flame within.' She laughed self-consciously. 'Flame – that sounds precious, doesn't it? But that's what it boils down to. If it burns brightly enough to light the way ahead, you have to take it. Either one chooses regular work at any cost, or one has to go out on a limb and satisfy the need within.' She turned to smile at me. 'So on I go.'

'For ever?'

'Sarah Bernhardt was still playing new roles at nearly eighty and with only one leg. She had fame and fortune enough and on she went. Still driven.'

'But not wandering.'

'No,' she replied. 'But then I'm not nearly eighty.'

'For that,' I said fervently, 'I am most grateful.'

I woke up the next morning wondering about the quibble over the cars that Nigel had come in to discuss with Roger. Something about them had definitely upset Angie, and insurance could well be the issue at stake. It would be a good place to start, and there was no time to waste, as Car Day was only three days away, so I headed for the Manor.

Roger Ford had the privilege of a room in the house itself, not a caravan, courtesy of Sir John Biddington, who had allotted him a room at the side of the house overlooking the gardens.

'What can I do for you, Jack?' No mask today. Roger looked weary and was sitting by the window with the computer in front of him on a small table. The screen was blank.

'Cars,' I said.

He heaved a sigh. 'Talk to Nigel.'

'Not yet. I need your impartial input.'

'I'm not impartial. I've got a film to make without busting the budget.'

'I need to speak to the top man. You.'

'That bad? You got me, Jack.' A glimmer of a grin.

'You remember what Angie told Bill about the cars? That there was something wrong somewhere?'

I didn't feel comfortable talking to him about this, but couldn't put my finger on why. I'm supposed to have a nose for trouble, but sometimes it's hard to tell the difference between trouble and having an off day.

'Sure I do. Found out what she meant yet?'

'Still plugging away. How much was Angie involved with that side of admin?'

'Not at all, except over the Auburn. She was as mad as hell when it went missing. She took it personally.'

'As perhaps she was meant to, but I need your take *before* I start jumping to conclusions.'

'The buck stops here.' Roger made a wry face. 'Too right. But I've so many bucks pulling up here at present that cars don't seem that important. But shoot away.'

'You've got four very expensive motors out there. Is the insurance side of things in order?'

'That's done through Nigel Biddington. I've had enough to do over the Auburn in recent days so I know there's nothing wrong with his service. The insurance company is secure enough. The fact that the car was undamaged cheered them up, but not me. It suggests it was pinched out of spite, which might put the others at risk. The company is happy with the precautions so far.'

'Could the thief have it in for Oxley Productions?'

'Oxley?' That stirred him up. 'That's a crazy idea. Why?'

'It's worth taking seriously.'

He stared at me as though I was the last straw in person. 'I'll step up security even more. I'll have guards sleeping in those damned cars if need be.'

'What insurance do you have for Car Day?'

'Twenty-four hours only. Nigel's taken care of it.'

'Is Oxley itself insured?'

He took my point. 'Uninsurable for that degree of risk. Loss of the day's filming could be covered but not all the attendant problems. A nightmare in fact if we can't film. But it won't happen, Jack. Maybe Bill misheard what Angie said.'

I supposed that was just possible, but I had to go on. 'She died, Roger. If not over the cars, what else? Tom?'

'The police think so. They've hauled him into the station twice, but he's not been charged. Anyway I gave him a job, so it would have blown over. Motive gone.'

Time to tread delicate ground. 'I gather your wife was close to Angie. She must have been very upset.' This might be an implication too far, but I had to ask it.

He didn't seem to take offence. 'Yeah. They were both background performers on *Running Tides* – that's what brought them together. Maisie was brought up in the States and movie-mad, so she pleaded with her folks to let her see what the movie world was all about at first hand. She was real keen on Bill's films, so that's what she chose to go for. She met Angie and stayed friendly. Maisie's a peaceable woman and dropping old friends isn't something she'd do lightly.'

Peaceable or not, I thought, Maisie and Angie had managed to clutch the producer and director respectively, I reflected. Not bad going.

He was a smart man. He must have guessed what I was thinking. 'During *Tides* Bill was a single man, and I was mid-divorce. Bill had been divorced for some years. No problem. I married Maisie in due course and here we are ten years later, no intention of changing the situation. Bill wasn't so lucky. He never even noticed Angie on set – that came later – but he was obsessed with Margot, and that was a problem.'

'That led to her suicide?'

He hesitated, then said, 'She was what I guess you'd call fragile. She was married, had a bust-up with her husband over Bill, but wanted to continue in a threesome with both husband and Bill. Husband was reluctant but prepared to go along with it. Bill wasn't. He wasn't trying to blackmail her into choosing him – not his style – he just decided he should go. She couldn't take the shock of being rejected, as she saw it, and that was it. Bill took a long time to get over it. As for the Auburn, she and Bill very publicly went around in it all the time. Because she was the more public face, it became *her* car in a way.'

'And later Angie's,' I pointed out.

'Yeah. Angie's *and* Bill's. Don't take that too far, Jack.'

But I did. A token of victory for Angie. Margot Croft's car. Margot Croft's man.

As I drove back to Frogs Hill, I thought more about Angie's death and where I (and Brandon) should be looking. There was undoubtedly a fork in our road ahead. The cars were one angle, the one I was officially following up. There must have been a reason for Angie's words to Bill. Roger, however, had found nothing amiss with the insurance, so unless he was involved in some kind of fraud – which seemed extremely unlikely – there was no immediate way forward on that front. Saturday would be the day that might produce another lead.

As for the second angle, scratch the surface of the *Dark Harvest* company and there could be quite a few who wanted Angie Wade out of the way, although that was a long way from using murder as the solution. Louise had pointed out that the past was indeed past, and people killed for reasons stemming from the present. That brought me back to happy-go-lucky Tom again, who had been ousted from the job he loved and suspected that he might not be saved another time. I had little doubt that Brandon was hot on his case. Apart from Brian Tegg who was teetering on the brink of losing his role of Lord Charing, there were no other obvious candidates in this category. I needed to scratch deeper.

When I reached Frogs Hill again, I went straight to the Pits. It had not escaped my notice that there might not be enough in the kitty to pay the mortgage at the end of the month unless my work force was galvanized into meeting a few deadlines.

To my surprise neither Zoe nor Len was there. I could see that they *had* been there, but nothing otherwise. Abducted by aliens? This was surely the only thing that would drag them away from their precious grease pit. I went outside again, and this time noticed a familiar car tucked round at the side of the Pits barn. I was glad it was out of sight. To have that monstrous canary-coloured horror desecrating the forecourt of Frogs Hill would put off potential customers.

'Harry?' I roared.

No reply. Had Zoe and Len taken him into the farmhouse – not the Glory Boot, I hoped. Was he already ransacking it? Valuing it? I rushed straight to it, but thankfully it was undefiled by Harry. So where was everybody?

There was only one place left. Grimly I went into the garden and out of the side gate to the barn-cum-garages where we keep Charlie (our old low-loader), my treasured Gordon-Keeble, and the Lagonda. Sure enough, there were my staff and Harry, who was puffing away like a chimney before the clean air act.

'Nice old jalopies.' Harry grinned at me.

'Anything I can do for you?' I enquired.

'You could do a lot for this place. I've been telling Len

here and Zoe – good team you've got, Jack. I'd look after them like a shot.'

I gnashed my teeth in frustration. Len looked a bit sheepish, but Zoe looked as though Harry were a knight in shining armour.

'We could work up a nice little business here,' Harry kindly offered. 'You need capital, Jack. Don't forget that. Spend money to make money. Any time you want to talk it over—'

'The only thing I want to talk over with you, Harry,' I countered pleasantly, 'is Shotsworth Security.'

He went rather pale. 'What about it?'

'You have the contract for the Gladden estate car park, haven't you?'

'So?' he ventured cautiously. 'I don't run Shotsworth. I just co-own it. Heard you found your Auburn at Gladden though, so you owe me.'

'Permitting property on the stolen list into the car park? I don't think so. Especially if there are others.'

There was a strange silence. 'Stolen, Jack?' Harry said at last. 'I'm told it was a practical joke. Someone working there.'

'Told by whom?' I pressed. 'Nathan Wynn, one of the security guards at Gladden?'

Harry decided to put up a defence. 'So what? They've been doing their job OK. No fiddling books there.'

'Making anything on the side, though?'

'Watch it, Jack. I've got witnesses,' Harry pointed out virtuously.

Bless them, Zoe and Len were chattering furiously to each other, thus rendering themselves incapable of bearing witness. Their dialogue drowned my next words too, which was just as well. 'If you're mixed up with anything, Harry, it won't look good for you. Not with Dave Jennings after you. I've looked after you so far.'

Harry promptly got down to business. 'You know I'm straight, Jack.'

'Within wavy lines,' I agreed.

'Keep in touch. I'll look into it. If I find there's a glitch –' he gave me a sideways glance – 'you won't hear about it, but the problem will go away.'

At least *he* went away. That was a start. Indeed he almost ran, and I wondered where his next destination would be.

I knew where mine was – and hoped I didn't meet Harry there. I took a brief detour to the Pits whither Zoe and Len condescended to return to tell them I had a date with Gladden Car Park, but I'd be back to discuss work schedules. Rob was hanging around so the word 'schedules' ran like water off a duck's back where Zoe was concerned, and Len merely nodded and commented that the Porsche 356 just brought in needed attention.

Later, I promised myself. Right now, there was something that needed my urgent attention at Gladden. *Before* Harry was able to have a chat with Nathan Wynn.

Nathan wasn't on duty when I drove into the car park and I didn't recognize the new guard. He was big, and unlike Nathan didn't even pretend jollity.

'Police,' I told him, flashing my pass, but he seemed uninterested. I drove on down to the lower level and parked. I then had a look around to see how many cars were under wraps today. There was a Focus parked where the Auburn had been, shining and sparkly clean. No wraps on that. Three cars were covered, however, so I went to investigate them. The Jag I had seen earlier was either no longer here or had moved to another place before donning its veil of tarpaulin. Of the three under wraps, one proved to be an ancient Renault that hadn't moved since they stopped walking before cars with a red flag. It had on it a licence that was out of date by five years, and it had lost a wheel. Maybe the owner was never coming back or didn't need a car up in paradise. The next one was an Aston Martin DB4, and the third—

I never got a chance to find out. I was vaguely aware of two shapes whirling out of the shadows, then I was seized from behind with a hand round my throat and another one punching my stomach. Then I was on the hard concrete floor and saw a large boot heading straight for me.

EIGHT

A & E in a large hospital late in the evening invites no sympathy for its patients – to staff and other sufferers I was just a middle-aged lout who'd been in a punch-up. By the time I was unloaded from the ambulance, however, I was past caring about anyone save what was left of myself. In due course I was given various tests delivered with icy glances, kept in overnight for a further X-ray, and duly written off the next morning with severe bruising and a couple of busted ribs. My feelings weren't noted on the official record.

'What happened, Jack?' Zoe asked when she duly picked me up in her old banger – a twenty-five-year-old Ford Fiesta. She looked concerned so I knew I did not present a handsome picture. It takes a lot to stir Zoe's compassion – unless you're Rob of course.

'Someone objected to my strolling through the Gladden car park.'

'Why go back?' Zoe asked. 'You'd found the Auburn.'

'Wondered what else might be there.' It would have sounded weak to anyone but Zoe. She was on my wavelength.

'Did you find it?'

'Not sure.'

'Typical,' Zoe said kindly. 'Try harder.'

'You try harder with three busted ribs.' I had added one for luck. 'I sniffed round cars under wraps, but don't know what they told me.'

'Old age, she said even more kindly.

I tried to be more specific. 'The Jag I saw the other day had gone. And under the other wraps were an ancient Renault Tourer with only three wheels and an Aston Martin DB4. There was another one I didn't get to see. That's why I'm not sure. OK?'

'No common denominator. I told Rob you were going—'

'Rob?' I interrupted, horrified. My fate in Rob's hands?

'Zoe, he's a chum of Nigel Biddington,' I croaked. She isn't usually such a dope.

'So?' She looked startled, and I remembered that I'd had to keep Angie's doubts over the car scene to myself. As far as Zoe knew, Nigel was merely the insurance-broking son of the upright Sir John. Which of course he might be, I was forced to concede in fairness. Nevertheless, even if Nathan Wynn had been one of my assailants, there was another one to account for. Maybe Nathan kept a tame hit man for such events as my arrival, because someone had clearly known of my movements. I doubted whether Harry Prince could have got the message through in time, although I suppose it was theoretically possible.

'Not wise to spread my movements around,' I said as mildly as I could.

She looked at me scathingly, as we drew up outside Frogs Hill. 'You think Rob would stoop to bashing you up? Or Nigel? Have a look at the *Kentish Graphic*. It was published yesterday.' She fished around on the back seat and produced one of the local rags. The front page blared out that the full story of the tragic death of film director's wife Angela Wade could be found on page five. Page five, baulked of hard news on the said death, considered whether the theft and miraculous recovery of 'her' stolen and valuable car could be a clue to her killer. It was, the story cunningly continued, an interesting fact that the man who found Angela Wade's body also found the missing vehicle, said to be 'priceless'. It also provided 'the man's' name and address. Mine.

I groaned and slumped back in the car seat.

'You always wanted to be on the front page and now you've made it,' Zoe said encouraging. 'Anyone in Kent could have been following you around yesterday.' Then she glanced at my face and became more human. 'You toddle off to bed,' she offered, 'and I'll heat up some soup or make coffee or something.'

Bed did not appeal – for one thing it reminded me of Louise, which was a painful memory in the circumstances. James Bond might manage to continue his love life no matter what, but we mere mortals aren't so indefatigable. Hardly to my surprise, my mobile had disappeared, but luckily I don't keep details of my sensitive contacts in it for just this eventuality.

Once inside the farmhouse, I crawled to the sofa and investigated the landline. It had six messages on it. Two were from Louise, wanting to know where I was. The mere sound of her voice was frustrating, both emotionally and physically. The second said she'd heard what had happened and would be over as soon as she could. I couldn't ring back because she had explained that Bill banned mobiles within a dozen miles of his sets, on the grounds that he paid for his cast to stay in character. Taking time off for lunch was OK though, because it was shared with the rest of the cast and therefore *in* character. Mobile calls would take them *out* of it. I could leave a message but I'd rather wait until I could speak to her in person.

Dave had rung me too, and the rest of the calls were from Bill Wade. I decided to get up to date with Dave first. After all, Gladden was on his turf. He was all sympathy.

'Can't pay you compensation, Jack. Budget, all that stuff. Bad news you being duffed up. Insured, are you?'

I wasn't actually. I told him what I'd found in the car park, then thought to ask him: 'Have you got an Aston Martin DB4 on your stolen list?'

He checked. 'No.'

Bang went that theory. 'A Jag XK150?'

'Yes.'

'Too late. It's gone.'

'Number?'

Car numbers come easily to me, so I reeled that one off and for good measure the Aston Martin's too. Dave checked both. 'No Aston on the list whatever the number, but there was a Jag XK150. Not the same number, although that means nothing. Suspicious though.' A pause. 'I don't like the smell of this, Jack. Want to do some more scouting?'

'They know my form now.'

'No problem,' he told me cheerfully. 'This Shotsworth Security . . .'

'Owned by Harry Prince but not, I think, run by him,' I supplied.

'It isn't. Know Mark Shotsworth?'

'No.'

'You should do. He runs it. He doesn't move in the rarefied circles of classics though. More in the grab everything you can nick line.'

'Which side of it? Harry's normally our side.'

'The other. Did GBH a few years back.'

'And runs a security firm?'

'Reformed character.'

I felt my ribs protesting. 'Maybe.'

'Just a guess, Jack. Talking of classics, there's another local wee lamb out there bleating for its mother.'

'Name?'

'Bugatti Type 57. Year 1937.'

Something between a gasp and a whistle emerged from my lips. 'They'd be crazy to hide it down there.'

'Some people are crazy, Jack. Does no harm to keep an eye out.' With a few more kind words he rang off – which left only Bill to call.

Bill didn't waste time in sympathy in the messages he'd left. Each time he merely said: 'Ring me, Jack.' When I did so, he got to the nub of the matter immediately. 'Gladden car park. That where you found my Auburn?'

'That's right.'

'Why? Did you ask yourself that?'

'I did. There could be several reasons. I'll find the right one.'

'I already have. Angie was right. The cars, Jack. Something stinks.'

My body reminded me of that all too painfully.

For all Bill's eagerness for me to be on the hunt, I slept a lot of that day, missing a call from Louise, who had sneaked a mobile into her caravan.

I woke up at about six on Thursday evening with the setting sun streaming in the window and forced myself to read the offending article in the local paper again. Stour Studios were always a prime source of material for the local press one way or another, but seldom quite so dramatically or horrifically as in these last eight days. The national press and TV had been present in force at the studios and most of the reporters had found their way up to Syndale Manor. Which can't have pleased Sir John. Nor Bill. Fortunately security was heavy, with police and guards at the gate and patrolling the grounds. Not surprisingly, Brandon's press conferences had not satisfied press hunger, but intensified it. Murder on a film set is newsworthy enough, let alone when the victim is the director's wife and the director is Bill Wade. Years ago rumours that Marlon Brando had been spotted in east Kent had set off a kerfuffle of speculation and rumour that ran and ran for many a long year. It was a given therefore that the *Kentish Graphic* would make the most of local drama. Its territory is wide, covering the whole of east Kent and most of the west too.

I knew who was responsible for yesterday's article, without even looking for a byline. This was Pen Roxton's work. I've known Pen for years on and off. She is a redoubtable journalist; she's physically tiny, slender, hair in varying shades of yesterday's blonde, sharp-nosed, squeaky-voiced and eagle-eyed, and she has the ability to melt into the background at will. It's when she emerges out of the undergrowth in one tremendous rush that the ferret in her takes over. One word, and she is in for the kill. I know quite a few who have crossed swords with her, but never before had the pleasure of either seeing her at work or being the rabbit she was hunting.

I suspected that moment had come, as I read her current handiwork skilfully blending fact and fiction. Super-sleuth Jack Colby had apparently told 'our reporter' Pen Roxton that I was hot on the trail – not specifying whether of the murderer or car thief, but somehow also managing to imply that the finger of suspicion for both was firmly pointing at me. Fortunately Pen has more than one finger, and nor does she like events to prove her wrong, so she was also pointing at several other people. The tragic Bill Wade had his turn. Pen had done her homework on *Running Tides*. The tragic Bill had first lost his great love Margot Croft to suicide and now his beloved Angie *who* had been an extra on the same film. My italics, but I could hear Pen panting her eagerness to promote suspicion loud and clear.

Roger Ford came off lightly, portrayed as the embattled producer dogged by scandal and trauma. Nevertheless, he was

putting a brave face on it. 'I believe in *Dark Harvest*,' he had
apparently confided to Pen. 'I believe in Bill; I believe in his
ability to surmount this devastating tragedy.'

Devastating? I wasn't yet on Roger's wavelength, but one
thing I was sure of was that he wouldn't speak of 'devastating
tragedy' to Pen, even if like most people he took refuge in
the familiar when grappling with events that lay outside expectations of what life should offer.

Pen had a go at Joan Burton too, having cottoned on to
the fact that she too was in *Running Tides*. 'So I asked Joan
what the great star Margot Croft had been like to work with.
She has been compared with Greta Garbo, but off set what
was she like? "She was my friend," Joan told me quietly.
"How could I describe her? Her loss was a devastating
tragedy and for me still is. We all adored her, men and
women. That link still holds us together – Bill, Roger, Chris,
Graham, Tom, Brian – we seldom speak of her, but we *know*
we are all thinking of her."'

I could imagine how Bill had reacted to this story, if he had
even bothered to read it. My guess was that he would ignore
it by blitzing his way through to what was more important:
solving Angie's murder, and getting the film produced as an
antidote to the pain of her death.

How I was going to react was a different matter. No point
in raging against Pen, or ignoring it. I favoured phoning her.
Pen can be surprisingly helpful if she chooses. She usually
doesn't so choose.

'Hi,' she squeaked, when I announced myself on the phone.
'What d'yer think of the article?'

'Devastating, darling.'

Pen's sharp. She giggled. 'Always good to hear from you,
Jack, and don't say you don't return the compliment.'

'Touché,' I said politely.

'Want to be my man?'

I know Pen. No sex involved here, not even as a joke. She
must be in her early forties now and of her private life I know
and care little.

'Would if I could. But no way,' I answered. Be a temporary
tame poodle for Pen? Absolutely not.

'Pity. What's your take on Angie Wade?'

'No comment,' I replied. 'I've been quoted enough without my saying a word.'

To do her justice, Pen laughed. She always does. Criticism runs off her like water off a duck's back. 'Keep in touch, Jack.'

'I will,' I assured her. 'You might be able to help me.'

A silence as she rapidly assessed this. Then: 'OK.' A pause. 'Get me an interview with Louise Shaw and I'm yours for life. I hear there are wedding bells for you two.'

'Get lost, Pen,' I said less than amiably.

I dozed off again, lost in a nightmare in which I murdered Pen, but woke up when the doorbell rang. I didn't answer it. It might be Harry Prince. My caller came round the back of the farmhouse and appeared at the French windows, knocking gently. Fortunately it wasn't Harry. I awoke from another nightmare and saw Louise, clutching a box in both hands with a bottle tucked under her arm.

Every bone in my body cried out while I rushed for the door.

'Can you eat?' she asked anxiously.

'If I mash it up with a fork,' I managed to joke. 'I think so.' It occurred to me that I hadn't eaten all day save for the soup Zoe had heated up for me.

'Good. You just sit back there on the sofa.'

No further urging needed, as I watched her unpack an array of interesting looking dishes from their insulated box. 'Cooked by your own fair hands?'

'I wish. The catering staff packed it up for us.'

'What's happening up there?' I enquired once I had dispatched a couple of glasses of wine, a large portion of lasagne, salad, and strawberry mousse.

'Not going well. Bill is getting rattled. We did the takes of the hunting scene where we gather in front of the Manor and Julia makes her bid for Robert's attention. That didn't go well and we haven't got much time left at the Manor. The police say we can go back into the studios from this weekend, which in effect means Monday, but we might not be ready to leave Syndale by then. So Roger's rattled too.'

'And you, Louise?'

She hesitated. 'I'm not sure when I'm on all next week.' She looked at me hopefully. 'But I'm free on Sunday, if we don't have an emergency shoot.'

That was all I needed to know. 'Are you on call for Car Day?'

'Yes, briefly. Incidentally the news about us is getting around. Bill and Roger asked me to pass on their good wishes for your speedy recovery.'

'Fine by me, provided the *Kentish Graphic* doesn't print the story.'

She regarded me pityingly. 'It will. And it will spread further. Give it a day or two.' What she didn't point out, being Louise, is that she was a star and thus fair game everywhere.

'Do you mind?' I asked.

'Only if it stops us being together.'

'Together?' How long, I wondered. For tonight, for the duration, for ever?

'In the quiet places. Beside the still rivers, the green forests, and the silent meadows. With you, Jack.'

She did not return to the hotel that evening, but stayed with me for that quiet time in the quiet places of the night.

When I awoke on the Friday morning, Louise had already left. Bearing in mind that it was only twenty-four hours to Car Day, I experimented on moving like a human being. It was a tad easier than yesterday, and I reminded myself that I had a job to do that wasn't going to wait for those twenty-four hours. If there was indeed something amiss with the car situation, then tomorrow was crunch day, and as yet there were far too many unanswered questions.

I could understand the thief's annoyance with my finding the Auburn, but why should that extend to my returning to check out the rest of the car park? Two possibilities. Either my assailants had it in for me personally and the car park had been their choice of venue for making their point, or there was something in or about it that they didn't want investigated further. Or both could be true. So how did Car Day fit in with that, if at all? I could see why someone would not like a car detective prowling around, but what could be suspicious about an old Renault? There had been the Jag XK150, but that had gone. It had been worth quite a bit, and so of course was the Aston Martin DB4. That did not mean the cars were necessarily hot, because people often choose to keep their cars under wraps. It was odd, however, to keep such expensive pleasures in a car park like Gladden, although not unknown in such small ones. Was that significant, or coincidence? Nothing for it; I would have to take another look at Gladden car park – and it would have to be today.

As the old joke goes, it felt like déjà vu all over again as I drove into the car park. I've never been one for heroics and I wondered just how heroic I was being in hobbling in here one more time. Who was watching the CCTV cameras, for instance? Maybe no one was, because the car park was currently manned.

When I had been carted off to hospital, Zoe and Len had come over here to fetch the Alfa back to Frogs Hill and I had been agreeably surprised that it hadn't been ripped to pieces by my assailants. Zoe had reported to me that whoever was on duty it was not Nathan Wynn, judging by my description of a short, jolly thickset man. Nor had there been any interesting cars there, she said. That, I had thought, was odd. What about the Aston Martin? She hadn't seen it.

Nathan was not on duty when I arrived either. This guard was tall, thin and lugubrious. He didn't even blink as I drove in and drew a ticket. I decided to waive announcing myself with a police pass. I leaned my head out of the window and yelled conversationally, 'Where's Nathan, mate?'

'Gone,' came the sullen reply. There was a certain satisfaction in his voice.

'Where to?'

'Dunno.'

'Left the firm?'

'Dunno. Boss likes switching us around. Safer.'

'Who for?'

A pause. 'Business.' He did look rather puzzled, however, as if he too wondered why business was safer without job continuity.

I poked a little further. 'Best not to be guarding Stour Studios, eh?'

It got a reaction. 'What's up with Ken? Had another murder there?' He looked at me suspiciously.

'You know him?'

'Sure. Works for the same firm. Used to be here before Nathan.'

Did he indeed. I drove off to find myself a parking space, wondering whether this location turnover was an interesting fact or normal for a firm in a restricted locality. I parked on the lower level again, clambered ungracefully out of the car and walked over to where the Aston Martin had been. It wasn't there today. Nothing else seemed to have changed; it looked as it had when I came here last. A motley collection of modern and recent cars plus two under wraps. The Renault still greeted me, perhaps hopeful of an end to its solitary life here. Which was the second car? The Aston Martin had vanished, and the second car proved to be not Dave's missing Bugatti Type 57, but a Morris Minor.

Dave had had no record of a stolen Aston Martin on his list and presumably that meant the one I had seen was legit. Not necessarily, though, but with no proof to the contrary there was no use my wasting time on it. My wistful hope that Dave's Bugatti might have been the Auburn's successor in whatever scam was taking place was dashed. I would be driving into Syndale Manor on Car Day with a body full of aches and a mind empty of theories. Except, I grudgingly admitted, the possibly interesting fact that Ken Merton had once worked here. The car park where the Auburn had lain hidden.

NINE

I t was time to pay my overdue visit to Ken Merton. I can't say I was eager, as my body was crying out for rest, but with Car Day looming over me, I had to keep going. I had not seen him at Syndale Park and presumed therefore that he was still working at the Lenham studios, crime scene or not.

When I checked in at the studios the police presence was still strong, although it was over a week since Angie's murder. I could see vans in the car park, and police cars by the entry barrier, and the police had to clear me for entry. On the basis of Nathan's swift move, I had an uneasy feeling that Ken might have followed suit, but I saw him installed in his cubby hole, looking morose. I smiled at him genially as the police checked me through, but decided to view the crime scene activity first.

I walked unchallenged into what had once been a humble farmyard with chickens, dogs and the occasional pig. No one even looked surprised to see me. White-suited figures flitted to and fro like ghosts in a sci-fi film, mingled with one or two uniformed and several plain-clothes police. It made an odd contrast to the colourful scene here last week. This was the unvaunted side of policing, the careful painstaking work that few ever saw, the sifting inch by inch, the poring over every detail, any one of which might be the vital clue to the truth. Len Vickers could well have learned his trade here.

The farmhouse and the paved yard that continued beside it to the garden gate were still cordoned off. There was no one stationed there to repel unwanted entrants, but from the point where I was standing I could see all I needed to be sure this was no opportunist murder. It had been planned even perhaps down to using the same model of gun as Bill's, a Smith & Wesson .38, although that was a common enough model. Brandon would be following that up if he thought it had significance. I knew he'd established that it wasn't Bill's. The second problem I considered as I stared from the cordon tape down to that open gate. What was Angie doing in the garden? Had she been in Roger's office with him, or merely used that door because the regular one was locked? Unless the murderer was Roger himself, it was reasonably certain that the killer had come in through the garden gate, and since this part of the yard faced the post-production block, he was unlikely to be noticed by curious eyes there. The reason Angie had come down from her own office was still a mystery. It would be an odd place and time for a meeting. I remembered Clarissa's comment about 'a woman driving . . .' Connected? Too tenuous. The gardeners had been ruled out, and the most likely explanation was that someone had called Angie on her radio, with which all crew and cast seemed to be equipped.

I would get no further here, and so I walked back to have my word with friend Ken. He wasn't in his booth. Instead there was a lad who looked wet behind the ears, and the police on duty thought it suspicious that I wanted to speak to Ken in person. Their looks implied that being under contract to Dave Jennings was no guarantee that I wasn't the murderer come back to view the scene of his crime, especially when one of them remembered I was the chap who found the body. 'Always first suspect,' he told me jovially.

I replied equally jovially that in that case policemen must often be in the same position. Smiles promptly disappeared and no one wanted to tell me where Ken was. Luckily my powers of detection hadn't deserted me. I saw his car still in the car park and deduced that he was probably either in the loo or the canteen. I checked the first unsuccessfully and the second proved but a poor shadow of itself as I had first known it. All it offered was one lady to serve tea, coffee and some uninteresting buns and sandwiches.

I found Ken by the window, gloomily regarding a dry-looking sandwich. He must have noticed something odd about the way I was walking towards him – rather like the Tin Man in *The Wizard of Oz* – because he fixed distinctly wary eyes on me.

'Been in the wars, have you?' he enquired.

I joined him uninvited with my mug of coffee. 'Several of

them at the same time,' I told him pleasantly. 'Beaten up in a car park – strangely enough the one you used to work in.'

'Oh yeah?'

It was clear this was not news to him.

'Gladden car park at Charing,' I added.

'Yeah. Think I did once,' he said carefully. 'They shift us around a lot.'

'Nice cars there,' I observed.

I'd hit a nerve. 'That's what car parks are for,' he mumbled.

'It's where I found the Auburn.'

That wasn't news either, but he took it on the chin. 'I weren't there,' he said in an end-of-subject tone.

'Of course not. You work here now.'

That established, he became friendly. 'Our job's to guard cars from being nicked; we don't mind 'em being found.' He might have thought this dry wit would establish his honesty, but he'd have to work harder than that.

'The coincidence of your being here and the Auburn being found where you used to work is unfortunate.'

Not so friendly. 'Aren't many car parks like Gladden round these parts.'

I pounced. 'So you recommend it to people? Did anyone ask if you knew of one?'

'Not that I recall,' he said speedily. 'What's it to you anyway? The blasted car's been found.'

'The police haven't dropped the case just because it's back where it belongs.'

He took that on board. 'Word gets around in this place,' he said uneasily.

'Why should it? There's a car park here and transport laid on. Why should anyone be interested in one several miles away in Charing? Look, Ken –' I dropped out of the sparring match – 'do you recall mentioning Gladden to anyone – innocently of course?'

He looked relieved that he didn't seem personally in the frame. He was, in fact, but he needn't know that for the moment.

'Look, mate, I've been working here best part of a year,' he told me virtuously. 'How can I remember who I've chatted to? Anyone who's local is going to know about Gladden anyway, aren't they? And anyone who isn't has their own transport, like you said.'

That sounded reasonable enough, I conceded. Then I had some inspiration. 'What about Mr Biddington? He's the car adviser on the film. Did you talk about Gladden with him?'

'No reason to. He's local.' Ken pondered. 'He was in here a couple of weeks back with that Joan Burton. Nice piece of flesh that.' He leered. 'Something to get your arms round . . .'

'Nigel Biddington,' I reminded him as he went off into a lustful dream. 'And Gladden.'

'That's right, mate.' Ken looked pleased. 'He was talking about getting cars for Friday. I might have said there used to be some nice ones parked in Gladden on my watch. Expensive little estate that.'

I wouldn't claim total victory over this one. Nigel could easily have mentioned the car park to anyone he came across if the subject came up. It didn't even mean he was involved in any dirty work. After all, why on earth would he want to pinch the Auburn, thus giving himself a headache in his role as car adviser? Theoretically it was possible he might have a lucrative deal signed up with another Auburn owner to hire his car in the event of Bill's not being available but it was highly unlikely in practice. Nor did Bill's reaction to my suggestion of replicas imply Nigel would have an easy passage on that route.

No, not a victory, but one small step forward.

Saturday. Car Day. Why did I wake up with dread in my heart rather than a sense of anticipation at the prospect of seeing thirty classic cars or so gathered together, looking their best with their polish and glitter on, and surrounded by ladies and gents in elegant thirties' gear? I tracked the answer down to the fact that I didn't know what to expect. Furtive figures in homburg hats pulled down to hide their faces, exchanging bundles of pound notes for some scam to do with classic cars? Or that a hawk-eyed Jack Colby would stroll around and deduce what Angie's worry over cars had been, simply by studying the assembled cars and owners? For example: My dear Watson, it is surely obvious that the lady had noted that a crank handle for a 1935 Auburn would not be a very useful accessory. I'm no Sherlock, alas. I do believe you can tell a lot about the owners from the cars they drive, but I wouldn't bank on its counting as hard evidence in a court of law. Or did I expect to be able to clap my hands on Nigel Biddington with a triumphant 'son, you're nicked'? So far he appeared a perfectly innocent citizen, and I was forced in fairness to consider that he could be. On the other hand, he was in such a good position to be the organizer of some sort of classic car scam.

When I arrived at Syndale Manor at 5.30 a.m., it was hard to believe that a murderer was probably skulking here and that I had a job to do – catching a car thief at the very least. The early dawn in summer is a beautiful time. Birds are boasting of their good parenting in song, the flowers are unfurling their petals for a beauty contest, blades of grass are shaking off the dew and all in all the day seems full of promise.

What the day was promising me was still to come.

For this special day, I decided on a special car. I was wary of taking my Gordon-Keeble any great distance for fear it might meet with another accident, and in any case its heavy clutch would be tough going with my body still aching from its encounter with the heavies. That meant it was hats off to the Lagonda for this summer's day outing. At my suggestion, Zoe and Len had been roped in by Nigel to be ready to provide emergency help for any cars in need – and to watch out for spies, as Len put it. They were like kids at the seaside at the prospect of a drive in the Lagonda. Len was in the passenger seat and Zoe curled up in the rear seat. All we needed was a picnic basket strapped to the back and off we would motor into the idyllic summer sunshine depicted in Dad's Glory Boot collection of old railway posters.

It wasn't quite the idyllic scene I'd hoped for when we arrived. It boded well, but it was still damp and a bit chilly. Moreover there were nowhere near thirty classic cars drawn up in the compound allotted to them. True it was only five thirty in the morning but so far a mere dozen or so had arrived. I parked in the general car park, clambered out of the Lagonda – with some difficulty owing to my bruises – and saw Nigel in a floppy canvas sun-hat checking off cars at the entrance to the classics compound. I'd hoped that I could sneak my Lagonda in to join the other classics, but it was three years too young for a 1935 film. Nigel was looking worried, probably at the poor showing so far. I'd gathered that the cars were needed for two scenes. In the afternoon they were going to shoot a day for night scene of the cars looking lonely in the dark while the Jubilee ball was in progress in the bright lights of the Manor. This morning they would be allotted to costumed extras and shot in a series of scenes of cars arriving for the ball. The cinematographer and Nigel would be arranging them. The four star cars would also be taking part.

'Hi.' Nigel gave me a cursory look, as I walked over to him, and then he gave me a closer one. 'I heard about what happened to you. You look awful.'

'Thanks,' I said drily.

He grinned. 'My pleasure. Thanks for bringing your team over.' A pause. 'What do you plan to do today?' Was his question just a little too casual?

I had my answer ready. 'The police want me to make sure the thief doesn't have a second go at the Auburn.'

Nigel didn't buy it. 'Fairly unlikely, isn't it?'

'Very. But we detectives like nothing better than watching cars that *don't* get pinched.'

He looked at me doubtfully, trying to make sense of this. 'What were you doing in that car park to be beaten up like this? You'd already found the Auburn.'

'True, but with my job I have to keep a broad spectrum,' I said grandly and deliberately vaguely. 'Like you, I presume.' A good idea to pretend we were co-fighters against crime. 'Whoever took the Auburn,' I continued, 'either had local knowledge or heard about the car park from someone at the studios. You know Ken Merton used to work at Gladden car park?'

'So? Security's his job, not theft.'

If only life were that simple, I marvelled. 'Anyone could have asked him about local car parks.'

Nigel eyed me as though I were the idiot I sounded. 'And anyone could have driven around the area and found it for themselves.'

'That's true.' I tried to look crestfallen. From what I'd seen neither the cast nor crew had spare time on their hands to cruise around looking for opportunities. If they did, I reasoned, they'd be hunting for big Maidstone or Ashford multi-storey car parks, not ones that primarily served a smallish housing estate. I'd stick with someone having heard of it at the studios or who knew about it through living locally.

Like Nigel, I thought wistfully. I remembered Joan Burton lived locally and could well know about Gladden, and the 'female driver' angle popped into my head again. I pushed it right out. She had no reason to start a dirty tricks campaign or steal the Auburn and certainly I didn't see her as a murderer.

A 1934 Adler Trumpf Junior trundled in, with an elderly driver obviously relieved to have survived ordeal by Kentish lanes, and Zoe took over the marshalling duties.

'That Adler is a beauty,' I said admiringly to Nigel. 'From an agency?'

'Yup. Most of these are.'

'I've seen that one before.' I pointed to a 1935 Jensen-Ford Shooting Brake.

'Quite possible. It's reasonably local.'

'One of your clients?'

'Yes. John Pursey. He was bursting to get in on the film act, although he didn't like the news about the Auburn's disappearance. He'll be keeping an eye on it. By the way, I spotted your Lagonda coming in. Want to drive the charmer on film today?'

'Can't, alas. It's a 1938.'

'Might be possible. Insured are you?' When I nodded, he grinned. 'Hang around hopefully and I'll see if it thrills the great DOP's eyes. If so, he might use it. Louise told me there's a sort of valediction scene set in 1938.'

'Terrific.'

Fame at last. With this tempting prospect before me, I cheered up. Nigel was a good sort in my book – temporarily at least.

For the next hour or two I absorbed everything that was going on around me, starting off with the mouth-watering array of delectable classic cars ranging from the early to mid 1930s. It was exciting to see it all come to life, like the mythical village in Scotland immortalized in *Brigadoon*, shaking off the sleep of a hundred years and emerging out of the mist into glorious technicolor. I saw Chris wandering by as a stiff von Ribbentrop; Joan bustling past in her black outfit; elegantly clad extras strolling around in midnight blue or black dress coats and dinner jackets; chauffeurs with polished boots and caps chatting with women in close-fitting evening gowns and brocade wraps, all picking their way to the Manor forecourt. I saw Graham, currently an exquisitely tailored Prince of Wales, having a quick canoodle with a chauffeur, and Lord Charing arguing with Bill over something I could not hear. He must have seen me, because he came over when Bill had finished with him.

'I told Angie that line wasn't going to work,' Brian grumbled. 'Now even Bill wants me to keep it. I ask you. How can I say to Julia, "Come along and see me sometime, darling"? I'd sound like bloody Mae West. Bill just says try it.'

'Bill usually sees things straight,' I said sympathetically.

'Maybe. Trouble is Angie always had to know best, because she couldn't forget she was once a humble background performer like the rest of us. Once an extra, always an extra deep down.'

'That's not the image of Angie that came over to me,' I said.

'Of course not. But scratch the surface and there she was, quivering. You ask Tom.'

He wandered off, and I set off to admire a late arrival in the classic car line-up: a Delage cabriolet.

But then I saw her. The vision – the nightmare. The inimitable Pen, busy chatting up Joan and Chris at one of the tables in the catering field. She was wearing jeans, a tank top and a flowering hat. A typical Pen outfit. I strode over to her in the hope of minimizing damage.

'Morning, Pen,' I said dangerously.

She glanced up, nose twitching. 'Sweet of you, but no need to join us, Jack.'

'Thanks, I will,' I returned, sitting down at the fourth seat. 'My job is to look out for suspicious characters. How did you get in?'

Joan and Chris looked mystified, so I introduced them.

'Meet the Lady of the *Kentish Graphic*, Pen Roxton. You can congratulate her on her shrewd vitriol.'

Pen just laughed, looking as though butter wouldn't melt in her mouth. It probably wouldn't. She is the original ice queen when at work. As I had no doubt she was now.

'Bill Wade said I could sit in on the filming,' she stated.

'Did he know who you were?'

'Friend of his wife.'

'Were you?'

'Saw her once. Last week, I think. Nipped in to see whether there was any mileage in the Auburn theft. Told to see her, but she was arguing with that chap over there.' She waved a hand towards Nigel Biddington. 'I tried, but I couldn't hear much of it. They stopped when I came in.' She sounded aggrieved. 'Something about thirty, that's all.'

'Pieces of silver?' I asked sweetly. 'You'd know about that.'

'They must have been talking about the cars coming today,' Chris ventured as a pointless peace offering. 'Thirty's the magic number, isn't it?'

'Yes,' I said, storing the information about Angie away. It might be interesting if Pen could be relied on – and she could. It wasn't the facts that were the problem – it was what she did with them.

'Probably nothing,' Joan said. 'Angie often rowed with Nigel. I heard them too.'

I was about to enquire further when Pen barged in with all guns blazing.

'Then I went to see Bill. I asked him about Margot Croft.' Pen said blithely. 'He clammed up.'

'I'm not surprised.' Joan looked aghast. 'What did you ask him?'

'Whether Margot had killed herself in the Auburn – nice story if she did, with it going missing now and all that.'

All three of us sat stunned. Especially me. This was going it a bit, even for Pen. None of the reports I'd read of Margot's death mentioned the Auburn. 'Very tactful,' I replied at last. 'Did Bill reply, or did he get you thrown out?'

'He's a gent. Unlike you, Jack. Knows how to behave. He told me she killed herself in her own car, a Lancia.'

'Happy now?' I asked ironically.

'Not yet.' She grinned and I groaned.

'So what comes next? Whatever it is, I doubt if it will win you a free seat at the *Dark Harvest* premiere.'

'Maybe it's more fun not to have one.' Pen turned purposefully to Joan and Chris. 'You said you were around for *Running Tides*. You must have been extras, like Angie. And Tom Hopkins was there too. She sacked him last week, didn't she? Why? Knew too much, did he? Did Brian Tegg? Or that wimp Graham East? You knew Angie when she was an extra. Extras always fancy bigger parts. Wanted to play Ramble herself, did she?'

'Yes, but not—' Joan yelped, but Pen swept on.

'Jealous of Margot Croft, was she?'

'That's enough,' Chris shouted. 'Pure nonsense and it's not true. It's not. Margot was a star, a *real* star and Angie was a beginner. She couldn't—'

Pen shrugged him off like an annoying ant. 'Star? Because she slept with the producer, or in her case director, maybe both, to get the part?'

Joan rose trembling to her feet. 'I will not listen to this. I *will not*. Come on, Chris.'

Chris needed no urging after this attack on Margot's integrity, and followed her, leaving me poleaxed with a complacent Pen. 'Touched a nerve, didn't I? I've got a theory, Jack,' she said confidentially, although that isn't a word that sits easily with Pen.

I struggled to keep listening, on the basis that I have – odd though it might seem – respect for Pen in some ways. I like the way she pulls no punches; I hate the way she prepares them. On one level she's trustworthy, but on all the others, put on your hard hats because concrete rain's going to fall.

I put on the hard hat this time. 'What is this theory, Pen? Tell me the worst.'

'Bill Wade killed Angie.'

'*What?*' This was worse than even I could take, much worse. 'You can't go with that.'

'I can go with what I like,' she said with dignity. 'I put two and two together.'

'And made forty-nine,' I whipped back. 'What on earth makes you think Bill would kill Angie? He adored her.'

'Granted. At one time. Suppose dear Angie was involved in Margot Croft's death? Plenty of extras have it in for the stars, especially if they're turned down for the big parts. And I bet that's what happened. Angie thought her career path should go straight up, but she wasn't good enough.'

I was hypnotized by the ludicrousness of Pen's suggestion that Bill had murdered his wife. 'Where does Bill come in?'

Pen gripped me by my bad arm, the darling. 'Revenge is a dish best served cold, you know.'

'And what does that sinister remark mean?'

'*Dark Harvest*, the Auburn and Angie Wade. They all add up to Bill Wade's revenge.'

'For what, for heaven's sake?'

Pen was on a roll now. 'He discovered the truth about little Angie and Margot Croft. Suppose Margot did die in the Auburn? He might even have moved the body himself. He might have felt responsible in some way. Or maybe, yes, this is better, suppose he just found out recently?'

'Found out what?' I hissed, conscious that others were in earshot.

'That Angie murdered Margot Croft.'

I was no longer mesmerized. Voice and brain got together at last. 'Do you have one scrap of evidence, be it hearsay, third party, a loose thread – or better, DNA – to back this up?'

'No.' Pen grinned. 'But I will. It will make a damn good story.'

'Pen,' I said through clenched teeth, 'you print anything like that and I'll personally see every libel lawyer in town will be at your throat. *Get lost.*'

TEN

Pen did get lost – or at any rate appeared to do so. I saw her marching to the car park, so I hoped for the best. Her daft 'theories' dreamed up out of nowhere could do real damage if spread around and I was glad that Chris and Joan had left by the time she really got into her stride. Should I even waste time in considering what Pen had so cheerfully suggested? Reluctantly I supposed I should, but first they needed digesting. Pen could whistle down the wind for a while.

Luckily Nigel appeared and asked me to move the Lagonda out of the general parking area to a position nearer the compound. Zoe would guide me there. Would she indeed, I thought. Zoe was clearly rising in the ranks from park attendant to film crew. The Lagonda couldn't be in the compound itself because that was where the overall shots of the Jubilee guests' cars were to be filmed. The idea was to indicate that all nations were together – temporarily. 'One of Bill's crazier ideas,' Nigel said vaguely.

Looking at Nigel, I decided my money was on Bill. Many ideas sound wacky when spelled out, but in the hands of a master prove to be magic. I couldn't make Nigel out. He had one of those pleasant faces that tell you nothing. The English when they choose can be every bit as inscrutable as the Chinese. If Angie had been right and there *was* something going on with these cars, then it would be hard to believe that Nigel wasn't involved, simply because of his advisory role here combined with his day job. To me he didn't look as if he could organize his way into an empty garage, but I've had enough surprises in my life not to bet on it.

Zoe duly ushered the Lagonda to a parking spot at the side of the house, beyond Roger's temporary office, and the first person I set eyes on when we returned to the compound was Dave. He isn't really a classics man so seeing him here was surprising. He was talking to Nigel, but broke off to walk over to greet me. 'How's it going, Jack?'

'Still aching.'

He regarded me pityingly. 'Talk sense. I can see you're back on your feet. I meant how's the job?'

He already knew about Angie's words to Bill, so I told him that both Pen and Joan had indicated there was trouble between her and Nigel and that I would be following up that lead. So far, I told him, the insurance angle seemed OK, so assuming that was the case there must be something I or we were missing.

'With Biddington involved?' he asked.

'Jury's out. He seemed ecstatic over seeing the Auburn back, which doesn't suggest funny business on his part.'

'Unless he forgot to insure it. Inverted commas round the "forgot".'

'According to Roger Ford, he didn't. And don't forget I was attacked *after* the Auburn was found.'

'Coincidence. Opportunist mugger or a righteous owner thinking you were up to no good,' Dave retorted.

'If so, there were two righteous owners and muggers. Anyway, I don't believe in chance. Nathan Wynn has vanished, posted elsewhere.'

'Right. My info is that he's still with Shotsworth Security, but at an estate car park between Faversham and Whitstable, called Helsted.'

'I'll follow that up.' I had a feeling there was a loose connection that I wasn't making. 'Harry Prince might be owner and Mark Shotsworth doing the dirty work.'

'Maybe, but I don't see how that ties in with the attack on you. Still looks like a straight mugging to me.'

'Nothing straight about it,' I said with feeling. 'They didn't pinch anything for a start, except maybe my mobile.' Then I grasped the loose connection. 'Missing classics, Dave. Remember that Jag XK150 I told you about?'

'I do. Nicked from outside a posh house near Tunbridge Wells. No sign of it. Insurance paid up like gents after the thirty-day limit for finding it expired. But that Aston you mentioned—'

'Too late. It's gone.'

'Don't tell me. One came on the books today, and the number you gave me for the one you saw was false. But we've double-checked Gladden and you're right, not a sign of it. Nicked from Brentwood in Essex. Owner away, only just discovered it missing.'

'Have you tried the Helsted car park? The Aston might have taken it into its head to chug after Nathan Wynn.'

'Not there either. But, guess what, all by ourselves we thought of trying the other car parks guarded – if that's the right word – by Shotsworth Security. I'll keep you posted.'

'Thanks. Any instructions?' I called after him as he left.

'Yes. Keep on taking the pills.'

I would, if I knew which pill to take. I went to the catering area in the hope of finding Joan, but there was no sign of her. I caught a passing runner, who said Joan was on call for Scene Seven, whatever that might be. The good news was that I could legitimately sit down and eat lunch. From here I had a long-shot view of what was going on. There were crew, cast, noise, lights, cameras mounted on cars, cranes, various sound effects, but nothing actually *happening* in terms of filming, even though I could see two or three of Nigel's classics moving slowly towards the gates. I thought about their insurance again, although just as with the filming nothing seemed amiss. Roger would hardly be part of any conspiracy to diddle his own company, but there must surely be two insurances involved, not just Oxley Productions'. They would insure the Auburn and other cars for the filming, but there was the private insur-ance too. Suppose there was an angle to that which had stirred up Angie's rage.

I could not collar Bill yet awhile. He was currently cheering on his troops like Montgomery at El Alamein. Like him, Bill was quiet, determined, indefatigable. Did Pen's wild ravings fit in with that? I couldn't see it. Nor could I see her around anywhere, although that might be a bad sign. It would be unlike her to abandon enticing fruit here for the picking.

Baulked of speaking to Joan for the moment, and with Louise, wherever she was, beyond my reach, I looked around for Tom as soon as I'd finished lunch. As well as being in the firing line for Angie's murder, he was a firm part of the 'old gang' and I needed to warn him about Pen's probable presence, the worm in today's apple. It wasn't hard to find him – he was in the ops caravan, admiring his precious storyboards.

'Good, eh?' he said, justifiably admiring his comically inaccurate sketches of the Auburn and its three companions. He was right to do so because despite their flaws they worked. There was a feeling of threat both in his sketches of the massed cars and in those still making their relentless way up the drive. There was even one of the last scene – *my* scene as I thought of it, although I hadn't yet been called. There was a sense of finality in the sketch with a car making its way along the drive alone and somehow isolated in the vast expanse of the 'Tranton Towers' estate, representing, I guessed, the false 'peace' of Munich and the isolationism of the USA. That car, I thought hopefully, might be my Lagonda.

'I came to warn you there's a journalist at large,' I told Tom. 'She's digging up old leather and trying to make new shoes out of it. Old leather being *Running Tides*.'

'Oh?' He was looking away from me rather too obviously.

'She's working on a theory that Angie's murder was connected to it.'

Very wary now. 'How's that then?'

'The crazy idea that Angie killed Margot Croft. That it wasn't suicide at all.' I decided not to mention Bill's inclusion in Pen's theory.

Tom merely looked astonished. 'She shot herself in a car on the cliffs near Folkestone. Everyone knows that.'

I tested him. 'Bill's car?'

'No,' he said, again surprised. 'Her own. An Italian job, I think. So how does this Pen woman figure Angie killed her?'

'No idea.' I didn't add the word 'yet' but I was getting an uneasy feeling that this theory wasn't going to go away.

Tom frowned. 'Angie was a pain in the neck, but it's rubbish that she could have killed Margot. For a start Margot did not die until after the shooting was finished. Angie wouldn't have been around.'

'Did you see Angie with Bill while the film was on?'

'Wouldn't have mattered if I did.' Tom seemed to find his drawings even more fascinating. 'She fancied Bill, no doubt about that, and she might have stalked him a bit, but Margot was the one.'

'Was the split his doing?'

'It was. Absolutely.'

Not quite the story as I'd heard it from Roger, from whom there'd been no mention of Angie being in the picture at all, let alone stalking Bill. 'Did Margot still want Bill?'

''Course she did, but she came first in her own mind. Margot was always totally wrapped up in what she was doing and with herself. She loved Bill, no doubt about that, but Margot was her main love. She was another Garbo in a way. She was the flame, Bill was the wick she needed, and, believe me, Bill had to melt wax all round her.'

'If she believed in herself so much, why kill herself?' I asked.

'She needed Bill. It's not so simple. Margot needed her husband too.'

'Does that fit with her being wrapped up in herself?' I wondered for one mad moment if Pen could be right, and that Angie saw the threat as ongoing because Margot would never let go her hold over Bill.

'No, it doesn't,' Tom said savagely. But with someone like Margot anything goes. You don't have a plan. You have a mood. And in the mood she killed herself, shot herself with the gun like Bill had.'

'Any doubt it was her gun?'

'None. The coroner went into it thoroughly.'

'How long after filming finished did it happen?'

'A month or so. The cast had scattered and we were in post production stage. Heads down editing. I was involved in that.'

'But not Angie of course.'

'No way. She was background and had gone back to London. On set Bill would have brushed her off like an annoying fly if he'd even noticed her. It was only after Margot's suicide that she must have come back into the picture and helped him pick up the pieces. I think she got a job in his next film – another extra, and I doubt if Bill had anything to do with that. It took a mighty long time for him to get over Margot's death. He and Angie didn't get hitched for another three years.'

'Did you dislike Margot?'

Tom looked taken aback. 'Dislike? You've got me all wrong. We all loved Margot. You'd have to have met her to understand. She had her head in the clouds one minute, the untouchable Garbo the next, and suddenly she'd be with you, and you were the most important being on earth for her. All genuine. She was charming to everyone, Angie included. She knew Angie's sort was no threat to her.'

'Was she easy to deal with on set?'

'Always and for all of us. Margot wasn't an interferer. She wasn't an angel either. She was wrapped up with her own role and the film, but she left everyone else to get on with their own jobs. She took Bill's direction like a lamb, she didn't quarrel with Roger's handling of the production, she never demanded star's rights. She loved my storyboards. She was a . . .' Tom struggled for words.

'A hard act to follow,' I finished for him. 'I can see that.' Now for the 'innocent' question. 'So why did Bill walk out on her?'

Tom sighed. 'None of us knew. Probably because she wouldn't leave her husband.'

'What happened to him?'

'Manning? I don't know. He wasn't in the film business. Geoff was his name. Geoffrey Manning.'

As I left, history repeated itself. I ran into Bill again. He seemed to have aged twenty years since I first met him. The strain of the day's filming on top of everything else was showing.

'Nice car that Lagonda, Jack,' he said. 'You're called for six o'clock. The shadows are right then.'

'Thanks,' I said. 'I'm looking forward to it.'

He grunted. 'Not so fast. Lord Charing takes over for the close-ups. OK?'

I gulped. 'Sure.' As far as I would trust anyone but myself to drive it, Brian would do. 'I need a word with you, Bill.' I saw him flinch and quickly added, 'Some other time?'

'*Now*,' he said. 'My van.'

This looked as Spartan as a bachelor's flat. Functional rather than a retreat. Bill sat there with folded arms and waited.

'I need to know the exact words Angie used about the cars

that morning,' I explained. Bill was a pro. If he couldn't remember, he would tell me. If he spoke, the words would be accurate. There was a silence as he reconstructed them in his mind. 'I was pulling into the lot,' he said at last, 'thinking about the scene I was about to shoot. I heard her say, "You go on set. I'll see Roger first and tell you later." Yes, I'm sure that's right. Then I said, "What about?" She said, "It's the cars. There's something odd—" no, "*fishy* about the cars. That's why I need to see Roger right away. See you, darling." That help?'

He was obviously relieved to be finished and when I nodded, he couldn't wait to leave and we went our separate ways. This time I noted the words down before I went to find Joan to follow up what she had been intending to say about Nigel and Angie. Or should I track down Pen first, to see what harm she was wreaking? I was fairly sure she hadn't gone away, and shuddered to think that Bill might get to hear her theory about Angie and, worse, the one that he might have murdered his own wife. Was Pen even now ferreting out the little cogs and screws which she would chuck willy-nilly into an engine of her own making? Knowing Pen, she would have no hesitation in throwing away any that did not suit her purpose – such as that Angie was innocent, for instance.

I chose Joan in case she was on call again later and found her still costumed and talking to Brian Tegg on seating that had been provided on the lawns at the rear of the manor. Brian was looking very lordly in plus fours, smart Norfolk jacket and cap. When I told him about our rendezvous with the Lagonda, he groaned.

'Have you got something against Lagondas?' I asked mildly.

'Means another costume change – back into city gear if I'm coming down to Tranton Towers for the weekend. Can't appear in plus fours and brown shoes. Not done.'

'What part did you play in *Running Tides*?' I asked. 'Officer?'

'Nothing so grand.' He grinned. 'I was a waiter in a Lille *estaminet.*'

Joan eyed me suspiciously. 'You look very purposeful, Jack. I'm sorry I had to leave that delightful journalist so abruptly, but I really couldn't take any more. You want to ask me about that "more", I suppose.'

I glanced at Brian, thinking she might not want to speak in front of him, but she said calmly, 'We all know now what that journalist is proposing to write.'

'Don't worry,' I assured them. 'I'll see Pen Roxton off.'

'Do so,' Brian said with feeling. 'I have an idea I shall be in her sights soon. I too was in Margot's toils. We all were. I wasn't a fan of Angie's though, as you've probably heard, but I don't see her as a killer.'

'It's just too bad,' Joan said vehemently, 'that woman trying to make a story out of Margot's death.'

'There must have been something special about that production to keep you all in touch for so long afterwards,' I said.

Joan and Brian exchanged glances. 'It hasn't been because of Margot's death,' Joan answered. 'That was a private tragedy for me because I was a friend of hers since schooldays, and it was a sadness for us all. In fact the cast dispersed after the wrap party in Chilston Park.'

'But you kept together off and on after that?' I asked.

Brian hesitated, then explained, 'Usually the glue that holds a cast together during the shooting melts pretty quickly afterwards, but when one meets again there's a shared mutual experience that brings you back together. That's what happened after *Running Tides*.'

'And that explains your closeness on set here?'

Joan answered this time. 'We're close, but not because of mutual nostalgia.'

'Shared tragedy?'

'No,' Brian said vehemently. 'Call me crackers, but it's more like Bill's mood for the film. Menace.'

Joan went very white. 'What *do* you mean?'

Brian gave a nervous laugh. 'Almost as though we're herding together for protection. Don't you feel that, Joan?'

'I suppose I do. It must be the practical jokes that kept happening. And now this terrible murder. Do you think we're harbouring some deep dark secret, Jack?'

'Not consciously,' I said. 'But I still believe there was something out of the ordinary about *Running Tides*.'

'Margot,' Joan said flatly.

I could see tears in her eyes, and hastily changed the subject.

'Joan, you implied you'd overheard a row between Angie and Nigel.'

Joan looked uncomfortable. 'Angie had rows with everyone.'

'I know, but do you remember what you heard and when over this one? It's important.'

I thought she wasn't going to answer, but eventually she did. 'It was the Tuesday evening before she died,' she said after a while. 'I was in the canteen, in the part that extends into the foot of the L shape. I wouldn't have been visible to them, and I didn't like to announce my presence. I'm not sure if I can remember what was said.'

It was bad practice but I had to prompt her. 'Was it about the Auburn?'

Joan looked more hopeful. 'It was mentioned. She said something like, "It's more than the Auburn involved, isn't it? You didn't bank on it going missing, did you?" Nigel sounded alarmed, and said, "You're barking up the wrong tree", to which she replied, "Maybe, but I'm going to chop yours down".'

If Joan was right, I thought, that implied the Auburn wasn't the main issue, which might explain why he could have been genuinely excited when I found the car. But what was the 'more' – and was Angie's threat serious enough to have brought about her death?

With this new scent to follow, at least I had more cogs of my own to work on, and my engine was going to be one that worked, not a mad design by Pen Roxton.

At about five thirty I slid into the Lagonda barely noticing my aches and pains in my excitement over being immortalized on film. I'd given Brian the instruction he needed for the Lagonda, and was pleased that at least I would get to drive it through the Syndale Manor gates, as this was to be filmed in longshot. After that Lord Charing would take the wheel for the approach to 'Tranton Towers'. Even so I was provided with headgear identical to Brian's just in case the camera picked me up.

Actually being in the film for a modest moment was giving me a whole new dimension on the day's proceedings. I was no longer an outsider, but a minuscule part of the gang. I wondered hopefully if I'd get paid, as some paperwork had been whisked before me and details of the Lagonda hastily recorded. I decided not to press the point, and to wait to see if I had a happy surprise.

Brian and I remained outside the gates for some while as the camera crew fixed angles in the drive and the gaffer's team and sound technicians prepared for shooting. Eventually my great moment came. I was told to drive some way back, turn and be ready for the shot. Then I heard 'master', the clapperboard snap shut and then came the magic word 'action'. I was Hastings in his Lagonda in the Poirot series, I told myself, trying to adopt his look of grim devotion at the wheel, as I drove the Lagonda back towards the gates – the idea was that the engine should be heard before the car actually turned into the gates. I liked that touch. The Lagonda's engine is one sweet purr. And then I made my triumphant way through the open gates. I was on film. The cameras were rolling.

Not for long, I have to admit. The word 'cut' rang in my ears, and Bill demanded a retake. Then another. And another. The Lagonda was beginning to baulk at yet another turn in a bumpy gateway, but at last Bill was satisfied and Brian came forward to take my place. I kept pace with him and the crew as they advanced up the drive, in case Brian had difficulties, but he managed well (albeit with two or three extra takes of his own, which made me feel better).

Divorced even so temporarily from my outsider's position I could appreciate better the unity that held cast and crew together. I could understand the spell that *Running Tides* might still be casting over those involved in both films, no matter whether they were stars, management, actors, extras or crew. But Angie had been murdered, and it was possible that that unity had been broken.

The consensus was that the day's filming had gone well. The Lagonda scene was the last to be shot and by a mere seven p.m. I was free and so was Louise, which left the evening for us to share – or so I hoped. I had still not yet managed to speak to her in person and finally resorted to calling her mobile to leave a message. Luckily she happened to be in her caravan, and so the evening, and night, lay ahead.

I drove Len and Zoe back to Frogs Hill in the Lagonda, and then came back to meet Louise, assuming that we would eat at a local pub without the hordes watching our every move. 'We could get a takeaway and eat at Frogs Hill,' she suggested.

'You're a dream.'

'No, all too real. Are you on?'

'Eat at a pub near Frogs Hill?'

'Done.'

There was no one around in the car park to be remotely interested, and so I took her into my arms and kissed her. It was a fairly long kiss and it was being returned with enthusiasm when I came briefly up for air and saw we were no longer alone. I groaned. Pen was studying us with great interest, nose twitching, the dear little ferret.

'Pen—' I began.

'Jack,' she interrupted. 'I hope I'm the first to hear your happy news.'

The last thing Louise needed was this kind of publicity. There was no reason she and I shouldn't be a couple, as we were both single, but I have a funny preference for keeping my love life to myself. I imagined that Louise shared this view and with much more reason. I'd never seen anything about her private life in the press and was certain she would want to keep it that way.

There was only one way out, and I was forced to take it. 'I'll swap you, Pen. Collaboration for letting Louise and me off the hook.'

To my astonishment Pen had no chance to reply and I was physically and vocally pushed aside as Louise took to the battlefield. 'No deals, Jack. No need for them. Pen and I understand each other very well, don't we?'

Pen was knocked off course – for the first time ever in my experience. 'Do we?' she asked cautiously.

'Certainly we do. You go ahead and print a photo of us – I'm sure you've already taken one or two on your mobile. And do please print an outrageous story about us in your newspaper.'

I gazed at her, wondering whether I'd figured Louise out correctly, as she continued, 'I shall be interested to read it.

Especially as on the day before you will be reading a similar story written by *me* in the *Kent Evening Star*, and possibly in all the tabloids too. You publish on a Wednesday, so I can give my exclusive to the *Star* for their Tuesday edition.'

Pen got the message. Oddly she didn't seem to mind. 'You're ace, Louise,' she said admiringly. 'I could give it to the tabloids right away, but I think I'll keep it on file, OK?'

'Any point saying no?' Louise asked.

'No.'

'I'll bear that in mind,' Louise said casually. Pen looked suspicious but Louise refused to elaborate – even to me, but then we had better things to think about than Pen. Not only think, but do. I didn't consider what might lie ahead for us in the future, and I doubt if Louise did either, but whatever it was the present was enough.

The next morning Louise had again vanished by the time I woke up. Bill had called the cast even for today, and our quiet planned Sunday was doomed. Which made it all the harder to remember that I had to speak to Harry Prince and I might as well get it over with, Sunday or not.

I drove over to Charden, without much idea of how to approach the matter of Shotsworth Security. I rather fancied Lewis Carroll's method in his poem about the old man a-sitting on the gate. 'Come, tell me how you live,' orders the narrator, 'and thumped him on the head.'

Somehow though I didn't think Harry would appreciate this. When I arrived, his wife opened the door. Jackie is a peach, and I like her very much. 'Afraid he's out, Jack.'

'Odd. I did ring,' I said pleasantly.

'His memory's getting *awful*.' Jackie giggled. 'Want a coffee?'

I was tempted, but decided against. Harry undoubtedly *was* here and it would be fun to make him cool his heels wherever he was hidden, but pointless. Instead I pondered over just why he didn't want to meet me. It was strange. Usually he's very keen indeed to see me, hoping I want to throw myself on his mercy and ask him to take over Frogs Hill. It didn't take Sherlock Holmes to work out therefore that Harry must be edgy over Shotsworth Security. I'd like to think he had objected to the way I was duffed up but I doubted that very much. What it did mean was that tracking down good old Nathan in his new assignment should be priority.

Dave had given me the details and I found it quite easily. Helsted was a larger affair than Gladden with four parking levels, and was so called because it was on an eighteenth-century smuggling route from the Seasalter coast. I was looking forward to my reunion with Nathan, and relished the look on his face when I pulled up at his booth. I'd like to say he looked as jolly as ever, but today he was distinctly sullen, as though the old amusement arcade attraction the Laughing Sailor had suddenly turned into Captain Hook.

'What do you want?' Nathan snarled.

'First to show you my police badge.'

He didn't even bother to look at it.

'And then to park my car,' I told him amiably.

'Then what?'

'I thought I'd just wander round. Want to come with me?'

He didn't accept my offer. There were quite a few classics in the car park, but mostly they looked in use and without that forlorn look that unloved cars (and people) can acquire. To my pleasure I spotted several under wraps – cars, not people. Before I began to investigate them, however, I returned to friend Nathan.

'Got a list of the cars under wraps?'

'No,' he snapped. 'Permanents. Ring Mr Shotsworth. He'll have the details.'

'Have any arrived or left since you've been here?'

'I have to sleep some nights. Might be whizzing 'em in and out all the time when I'm off duty.'

'They wouldn't be under wraps then, would they?'

Nathan found logic too hard to deal with, so I returned to my prey. I didn't find the Aston Martin, but I did score a bullseye. Securely wrapped up was a pearl cast amongst the mundane swine.

It was Dave's missing Bugatti and it made my day.

ELEVEN

Dave fastened on to my phone call like a seized wheel-bearing. No long wait this time. His team was at the car park within thirty minutes and I left them to it. Back at Frogs Hill, I basked in my own glory for a while, then remembered that although this move might or might not be a step forward in my assignment for Dave, it was no indication that it had any connection to Angie Wade's death or to Nigel Biddington, save that the same security firm was involved. Consequently there was unfinished business.

I was cheered by the signs of Louise left from her snatched breakfast – the half grapefruit left in the fridge, the banana skin in the composting box and the crisp packet wedged under the rubbish bin lid. Hardly romantic memorabilia, but they served as welcome signals. The filming of *Dark Harvest* was soon going to come to an end and what happened then between Louise and myself would be up for grabs. So would my present assignments. I could not claim the Auburn was an ongoing case much longer, and I doubted if my hunt for Angie's killer would outlast filming. Still, there was no point looking at the chequered flag while taking a tricky corner at speed.

Speed had to wait until Monday, however. Nothing was going to move on the car front until then at least, and I knew that Oxley Productions was frantically trying to catch up with the schedule.

On Monday, while I was in the Pits endeavouring to sort out where Len and Zoe were with the work load there, my mobile rang and I took it into the yard where the reception is better. It was Harry Prince.

'Jack, my old mate,' came his booming voice. 'Sorry to have missed you yesterday.'

Something was up. For Harry, yesterday was yesterday. He wasn't into politeness where business was concerned, and I was definitely considered business.

'I'm sorry too,' I said cordially. 'No problem though. I paid an interesting visit to Helsted car park. Met one of your employees. Nathan. I think he's the man—'

'Wouldn't know about that, Jack,' he told me hastily.

'Pity,' I remarked. 'It holds the most interesting cars. The Kent Police Car Crime Unit dropped in later to take one away. Fancy finding a stolen Bugatti there. And so recently after their visit to Gladden, also guarded by Shotsworth Security.'

'Nothing to do with me.' His voice had risen a note or two. 'That's what I wanted to tell you.'

'Really?'

'Me and Mark Shotsworth had a talk,' Harry pressed on. 'The long and short of it is that I'm cutting loose from the firm. Can't keep my eye on every ball to see where it's bouncing. I drive on a straight road. You know me, Jack.'

I admitted that I did.

'I'm a garage man, not security and all that stuff. I've decided to leave that to those who know the business. Hands on, not off. Understand me? Mark did. All friendly.'

I hoped Harry was right for his own sake. I was still suffering from the results of a non-friendly encounter with Shotsworth Security. 'Is that all you wanted to tell me?'

'Sure. Didn't want you to get the wrong idea.'

'Don't worry, Harry. I never do. Not with you.'

The message was clear. Harry Prince was clambering as fast as he could out of dangerous waters. Any fish he wanted to fry, dirty or clean, would come from safer ponds. 'Now you're no longer part of Shotsworth, Harry,' I continued, 'I'm sure Dave Jennings would like to have a word with you about it.'

'Rather not,' came the instant reply. He'd obviously foreseen that risk. 'That's why I rang *you*, Jack. There's still the paperwork to do, and all that stuff. All going through quickly. I've no active part any more, but I'm still tied up with it. See what I mean?'

'I do. What active part *were* you playing, Harry?'

A split-second pause. 'Only a manner of speech, mate.'

'I'll explain that to Dave.'

Harry then got very ratty for some reason. 'Let's talk plain,

Jack. I didn't know what was going on, and I still don't. That clear?'

'So you don't know who kicked me senseless at Gladden last week?'

Harry grew very silent, and then said, 'No I bloody don't and that's what sent me to Mark. Not that he had anything to do with it,' he added hastily, 'but I believe in being safe.'

'Of course. Any help you can give me on cars and Stour Studios, Harry, to show your good intentions?'

A long pause. 'Nothing, and that's the truth.'

In case the phone was tapped, I didn't comment, but I was prepared to give Harry some credit.

Whether Dave Jennings would was another matter.

I heard nothing further from Dave on what had transpired after my visit to Helsted car park. Stour Studios was now cleared, but filming was still continuing at Syndale Manor and Louise told me they were now shooting in the gardens, in particular by the lake and temple. The latter was an eighteenth-century folly and had at first been deemed too decrepit for use. Bill, however, egged on by Tom, had been seized by its possibilities. There might be secret meetings between guests in the folly, Tom told me, giving a sense of old ages passing away and politicians oblivious to the new trends in Europe. The DOP had been working overtime to get the necessary repairs carried out to meet H & S standards.

As for us, when Louise had time between calls and in what was left of the evenings, we went walking in the Kentish countryside, through apple orchards and strawberry farms, through meadows and woods, beside rivers and ponds. We followed the Jane Austen trail around Godmersham, as Louise took a fancy to seeing where Jane Austen used to stay on her visits to Kent, then drove to Godinton and Goodnestone, which were quietly slumbering off the beaten track and looking much as they must have looked in Austen's day. I murmured about Julius Caesar and his camp on the Pilgrims Way, but battles didn't interest Louise so much. We ate in pubs so remote that even Pen Roxton would never find us.

On Wednesday however Louise returned too tired even to go out and brought an Indian takeaway with her.

'Filming not going well?' I asked, concerned.

'Superficially, it's fine, but the pressure is beginning to get to Bill. The ideas are all there, but then his mind calls wrap. He's trying hard, but the soul is missing.'

'Couldn't that be down to the police investigation?'

'Could be. DI Brandon came to see him yesterday. After that, Bill was closeted with Roger for an hour. Don't know what that was about. The sergeant was whipping around everywhere with questions for everyone. It's throwing us off course, naturally enough. We try to live completely in the nineteen thirties and are dragged back to the twenty-first century just as we're settling in. Don't get me wrong, Jack. We want Angie's killer caught, and the police have to find him, but it's hard to concentrate on work.'

I tried to put myself in her place. 'Would it help if you thought of the thirties and the police investigation as being on parallel lines? In the film you're living in the shadow of the First World War and of what might happen in the future. Isn't living with the police around the same – with the shadow of Angie's death and the unanswered questions of what will happen next?'

Louise considered this. No instant answers for her. 'You mean we should apply our current situation to the film, not fight against it.'

'Yes. Is that psychological claptrap?'

She put her arm round me. 'No. There *is* a dark edge to what's happening to us, like the one Mosley and the Nazis created. It's a shivering thought though. Is Angie's death part of that? Does it mean there's still something worse to come? Even that Pen Roxton's theory might have something to it?'

She looked so upset that I hastened to reassure her. 'There were plenty of motives for Angie's murder, without accusing Bill.'

It didn't help. 'Tom?' He wouldn't, Jack. He really wouldn't kill Angie, and anyway he's one of us.' Her voice rose.

And so was Nigel Biddington, I thought, aware that I had not heard from Dave.

*   *   *

The next day I did. He asked me to come over to HQ in Charing. That meant it was serious. I was torn between wanting to believe Nigel was involved in some dirty work and finding it hard to reconcile with the Nigel I'd met.

Charing village is cut in two by the A20, and the police HQ is on the far side from the main street, as is the railway station. This is convenient for me, as they are both on the Pluckley road from which I turn off for Piper's Green. It's not so convenient if you want to see Charing itself, however. It's an ancient village on the way to Canterbury with the ruins of a medieval bishop's palace and a lovely old church, nestling in the lee of the downs. I always expect to see Miss Marple popping out of one of the timber-fronted cottages and shops. Police HQ is not a timber-fronted cottage, alas, nor does it house any Miss Marples. It's a modern purpose-built block. Dave's office is on the first floor so there is a good view of the Downs in compensation. Not that I get much chance to admire them.

'Good news,' Dave greeted me. He was in his breezy mode which sits oddly with his academic and organized appearance.

'I've still got a job?' Good news depends on the angle from which you're looking.

'You have. You're high on my list of favourite people.'

This sounded really good. 'I try my best,' I said modestly.

Dave snorted with laughter. 'Luck, that's all it is. Now look, remember that Aston Martin you saw, the DB4, which then vanished?' And when I nodded, he told me, 'We've found it. Stolen all right, and false plates, but its chassis number doesn't tie in. It's not the one we were after.'

'And that's good news?'

'Give me a break. That's coming. There's no sign of the Jag either.'

Nor of the promised good news yet. 'And?' I asked.

'We did a check on the car parks guarded by Shotsworth Security, eight in all over our neck of Kent, and lo and behold we found six more classics in six different car parks. Not a lot, but this particular crew doesn't seem to deal in numbers. It deals in quality and not getting caught. Until now, I trust.'

'I take it the six were all stolen?'

'Yes. But,' Dave said complacently, 'the interesting thing is the time they've been in their present car park homes since the thefts took place. The Bugatti was only nicked two days before you found it. The DB4 only one day, but the others between two and six weeks max – quite a time, don't you think? The Jag had been there thirty days before you found it gone. And all of them under the guardianship of Shotsworth Security. Conclusion: there's a plan.'

'Any links to Stour Studios and our chum Biddington, apart from Ken Merton working there?'

'That's the bad news. We can't find anything on Biddington for you. There was an insurance hitch over the Auburn and Oxley Productions but it got sorted out.'

'What sort of a hitch? Roger Ford didn't mention one.'

'He was right. It had been sorted. The Wades' private insurance on the car turned out to be nowhere near high enough, and Oxley Productions was therefore suddenly presented with a whacking extra premium. That meant there were about ten days when it was insured privately, but not yet for Oxley's use while it was under negotiation. The Oxley insurance for the film didn't kick in until the Friday morning before filming began at Syndale Manor, two days after Angie Wade's death.'

I saw immediately. 'But on the Thursday before it was pinched Eleanor Richey went for a drive in it with Angie.'

'Right. Before they left, Angie checked the insurance situation either with Roger's office or with the company and must have been told it wasn't yet insured for film work. That didn't matter since she and Bill were privately insured for the drive with Eleanor. Nevertheless when she next saw Nigel, she tackled him about it, since she knew the car should have been covered by Oxley from the day she and Bill first brought it there. In her book, that meant Nigel had been paid.'

'Expletive deleted,' I commented. 'That can't be laid at Biddington's door. Even if he mishandled the private insurance, it doesn't add up to a motive for killing Angie.'

'Looks as if you'd better get your skates on finding out who pinched that Auburn. I can't hang on forever, Jack. There's the—'

'Budget,' I finished for him gloomily.

*   *   *

My theory had exploded in my face. I was not in the business of concocting theories without evidence – that was Pen's province – and I was forced to admit that over Nigel I had come a cropper at the first fence. Angie had been rampaging with Nigel about some trivial point she had misconstrued and I'd blown it up into a major incident. Nor was I doing much better over Angie's death. Only Tom had any motive as far as I could see, or possibly Brian Tegg – excluding Pen's daft notions. I forced myself to wonder whether they were so daft. Should I begin looking into the *Running Tides* angle more deeply? Over ten years still seemed a long time to wait for a boiling pot. Revenge would not only be cold, but icy. My time was running out though. The end of the filming couldn't be more than two weeks or so away, and then finished or not, the stars were going to have to take up previous commitments.

Including Louise.

Wild thoughts raced round my head. Were there hidden financial difficulties with the film that gave Roger a motive? Was the film planned to make an enormous loss, as it was insured against failure? No, that was ruled out because Roger's wife was financing the film. The dirty tricks campaign, Angie's death, the theft of the Auburn, Tom's sacking. Nothing fitted. No one fitted the role of murdering maniac, but then how many murdering maniacs had I met?

When I arrived at Syndale Manor on Thursday afternoon, security told me that filming was going on in the grounds behind the house, but I could hear something happening much nearer than that. An interested crowd had gathered around a slanging match going on through the open sash window of Roger's office. Pen – for of course it was her outside the window – was conducting her own form of interview with Roger. Today Pen had been clever. She was dressed in 1930s costume, obviously hoping to be taken for an extra. Roger had not been fooled. He, as everyone else, had been forewarned about Pen.

'Out,' he was shouting to her, as I approached to join the fun.

'Don't you want publicity, Mr Ford?' Pen sounded hurt. She was in her element.

'Not your kind,' he retorted.

This was a new Roger Ford to me. Gone was the smooth businessman, the caring fatherly figure and pacifier. His angry face showed the gritty determination and prize fighter qualities that must lie behind his rise to the top.

'There's a hate campaign going on, isn't there?' Pen cried gleefully. 'It will make jolly good reading. Especially after Mrs Wade's death. Who did you think did it, Mr Ford? Does it go back to *Running Tides*?'

There was a commotion at the window and an attractive dark-haired woman in her forties pushed past Roger. 'No, Miss Roxton, it does not,' she said coolly. 'That is your name, isn't it? I hope so because I've been on the phone to your editor.'

Pen laughed. 'You terrify me.'

'I hope I do. I've also spoken to the police. They take seriously the fact that you are masquerading as one of our cast.'

'I'd willingly leave,' Pen said plaintively, 'if only someone would tell me the truth.'

'And what,' Roger said quietly, 'would you accept as the truth?'

Pen immediately sharpened up. 'Something that makes sense. The police line is *still* that they're following up lines of investigation. What are they? Is Bill Wade chief suspect?'

Time for me to intervene or Pen was going to get into serious trouble. I moved forward, put my arm round her and practically lifted her, still fighting, away from the scene of action. 'Enough, Pen,' I said as she dug her elbow into my sore abdomen.

I promptly dropped her and she flew at me, but I managed to catch her flailing arms. 'Wrong target, Pen. Remember me? I'm the good guy.'

'Judas,' she hissed. 'I'll sue you for assault.'

'That won't save you if the police come. And the *Graphic* isn't going to like the publicity.'

'They will if the story's good enough,' she shouted at me. 'You'll see. They're all hiding something.'

'Possibly. But, Pen, just trust me. *Go*.'

This time she took some notice. 'Look, Jack,' she began, in a voice carefully designed for everyone to hear, 'there's something weird going on here. There's a story and it's one I'm going to get with you or without you.'

'Without,' I said firmly, marching her away without too much injury to myself. I escorted her through security and then over to the car park. 'Pen,' I continued, 'you must see you have no evidence for this cockeyed idea of yours.'

'I never will have if I don't have a chance to look, will I?' she said, reasonably enough, and I had to laugh.

'Look, Pen, if I find anything to help and it's not under police confidentiality, I'll tell you.'

'By the time it's been through that mill it'll be mush. Thanks, Jack, but I prefer my own methods.'

And what they might be I didn't dare to think.

When I returned to the Manor, I was asked to step into Roger's office by reception, which was usefully sited next door to it. I half expected expulsion myself but he was surprisingly cordial. He wanted me to meet his wife, Maisie, the dark-haired lady who'd faced down Pen.

'So you're Jack Colby.' Maisie welcomed me appraisingly. Luckily she didn't look another Angie Wade, which was something. 'Roger says Bill wants you to help find Angie's killer. We wanted to ask you if there was any news?'

Bearing in mind that she had been a close friend of Angie's, I went cautiously. 'There's progress on what Angie meant about something fishy going on with the cars. Whether it has any bearing on her death, I don't know.'

'Don't tell me. Insurance.' Roger groaned. 'I had the police crawling over our house, the studios and even here, looking at every blasted computer and bit of paper we have.'

'But what they found or didn't find seems to eliminate that as any kind of motive for her death.' I hesitated. 'Do you know what Pen Roxton's line of investigation is?'

'I do.' Maisie flushed red with anger. 'The woman's mad. She thinks Angie killed Margot. It just is not true.'

So even Pen had not dared go the whole hog and accuse Bill of murdering his wife. Perhaps she was keeping that back as a nice surprise.

'It's pure fantasy,' Maisie continued. 'For a start Angie and

I were lowly extras. Margot was light years above us in the pecking order, and we didn't even know her to speak to. The idea that after the filming was over, Angie was so keen on Bill that she went out and killed his ex-lover is ludicrous. Angie wasn't so tough in those days.' She grimaced as she realized that even she had acknowledged Angie's imperfections. 'Sorry.'

'She changed, honey,' Roger said. 'Recently she was hell to deal with. But you know we needed Bill and Angie came as part of the package.'

'Were you still very friendly with her?' I asked. 'Or did the friendship cool?'

Maisie took this on the chin. 'Good friends never cease to be otherwise. Roger and I helped Angie whenever we could.'

I think she meant it. She seemed a nice woman. 'Helped by giving way to her?' I asked bluntly. Too bluntly judging by Roger's expression.

'Where reasonable, yes.'

'Didn't it get beyond reasonable?'

'No,' Roger said flatly. 'I know what you're thinking, Jack. Angie was out of order over Tom, but Bill and I saw he kept a job here. She knew she couldn't push us too far.'

And nor could I push too far. I retreated to safer turf. 'Did you both get on well with Margot Croft?'

'Yes, both of us,' Roger shot back at me.

Maisie however hesitated. 'I didn't *know* her and nor did Angie. We just saw her as extras do stars. She was kind to us, when she noticed us at all. That's not meant to be brutal. It's a fact of movie production. She and Bill were inseparable and Angie knew that. Angie and I were both horrified at the news of her suicide. Roger was still at the studios in post-production stage then and I'd hung around in some menial role. Angie had gone back to her home in London, but we stayed in touch.'

'It was impossible not to like Margot,' Roger joined in. 'She was a dream star. Interpreted what Bill needed on screen and gave it to him. Didn't throw her star weight about, just got on with the job.'

'Did you know her husband?'

Roger again took the lead. 'Not well. We knew him of course, but once the funeral was over we lost touch. Like Bill, we live about half of the year in the States so it's easy to do so.'

'You told me Margot wanted to have a happy threesome with her husband and Bill but Bill wouldn't have it. Any idea what her husband thought about that?'

'No,' Roger replied. 'What I do know is that Bill was beside himself with grief when she died.'

'But if it was his decision to leave her . . .' There was something wrong here but I couldn't get at it.

'It was,' Roger said.

'None of us knew the whole story,' Maisie broke in. 'Joan Burton probably knows most. She was closest to her, so talk to her about it. Look, is all this relevant?' she asked impatiently.

'It is if it helps me ward off Pen Roxton,' I said firmly.

I felt crunched between pillar and post as I went to find Joan again. Not that I felt I would get much further. I was flailing around in a place I didn't understand, although Joan was clearly unhappy about something more than classic cars and Nigel Biddington. I didn't at first find Joan, but I caught sight of Pen, although luckily she didn't see me. Thinking she was out of sight, she was eavesdropping on Eleanor Richey who, from her body language, was intent on seducing Justin Parr, poor bloke. I decided not to interfere. Neither was in *Running Tides* and neither as far as I knew had any reason to kill Angie, so Pen could do her worst.

Someone told me I'd find Joan with Bill in his caravan, so I went over there hoping she might be on her way out. She wasn't. It seemed to be my day for busting in on rows, however, because I could hear Bill and Joan arguing. Had it not been that the name Pen Roxton reached me, I'd have crept tactfully away, but it glued me to the spot in frozen horror.

'Margot, Bill.' Joan sounded as if she was crying. 'That dreadful woman Pen Roxton wants to know about Margot.'

'For God's sake, Joannie, give me a break.' Bill sounded furious. 'It's Angie who's died. Margot died more than ten years ago. Why rake it up again?'

'But she thinks Angie killed Margot.'

An awful silence, then an explosion. 'She thinks *what*? The woman's crazier than I thought. There's never been any doubt that Margot killed herself.'

'I know she did.' Joan was clearly weeping. 'But you know how it was. Margot was one of those people who stir up passions without meaning to.'

'Joan, stop,' Bill said more quietly. 'Are you telling me that *you* think Angie killed Margot?'

Joan was really breaking up. 'No, Bill, *no*. But Margot never realized how strongly people felt about her. She created lasting emotions. That's bad, because it can fester.'

There was a silence, then the door was pulled open, Bill came down the steps, saw me, realized that I must have overheard, but brushed past me and walked away. I rushed up to see how Joan was. I found her ashen faced and she hardly seemed to recognize me.

'He doesn't realize,' she blurted out. 'It was always just him and Margot. Margot said he never noticed anything else, he just went blindly on, as he always does, regardless of other people. I'm afraid . . . one day . . .'

I wanted to take her somewhere quiet to recover but she refused my help and said she could cope. They were about to do some outside shots and she wanted to be there.

'It's Nemesis,' she added.

'Revenge?'

She looked surprised. 'Perhaps. I don't know. I hope I'm wrong, Jack.'

I could see one or two of Tom's storyboards propped on Bill's table – he must have brought them over from the ops caravan. They were new ones – and they were dark. In these the charcoal helped create Bill's mood for the film better than in any of the earlier ones I'd seen, and I could understand why he liked the storyboards to be around all the time, not only as a pre-production tool. In these, clouds and shadows hung over a Greek temple – of course, the temple in the grounds. No wonder it had caught Bill's imagination. All it needed was a few bats flying around and it would seize the imagination of Dracula himself.

*   *   *

I returned to Frogs Hill and the Pits, hoping that a dose of reality there would help sort my mind on Angie's murder. For once Len was the talkative one; Zoe was deep into a dynamo overhaul and I was lost in thought. Then I began to listen to Len's unusual chatter. 'New customer with a Daimler Dart SP250, needs a gearbox rebuild. You went to the Wealden car show, didn't you, Jack?'

'Sure, but I don't remember the Dart.' Or did I? I go to quite a few car shows. I searched my mind and one salient fact came up. I did go, and that was one of the shows at which I remembered seeing Nigel Biddington. I'd gone with Liz Potter, but the idea of jolly jaunts with her now is right out. The trip had been before we'd split up and she'd married the nerd Colin. It wasn't surprising I'd seen Biddington there, I supposed. Not only was he relatively local but his job would take him to car shows.

Had I slipped too quickly over something important? I scrabbled for the notes I had made on Angie's words, which were: 'something fishy about the cars'. Suppose good old Nigel had misinterpreted them not as applying to the Auburn or the other cars he'd hired for the film, but as something with a much wider application? More than the Auburn, more even than the cars here on Car Day. If he was mixed up in something shady, however, Dave would surely have picked up on it.

Or would he?

Dave was investigating insurance, theft and stolen cars. Angie was referring to the Auburn and by 'more than the Auburn' she meant the other cars Nigel had hired. But if her words had been taken by Nigel to refer to some far wider crooked scheme in which he was involved, something for instance that did involve those cars under wraps, Dave might not yet have thought of looking for a link between Nigel and Mark Shotsworth.

What scheme, though? Could we be back to insurance? Some of the cars Dave's team had seen under wraps were there for an unusually long time for stolen goods. As policies usually carry a time limit beyond which the company has to pay up if the car is still missing, the Jag I had seen might have been in Gladden car park waiting for the necessary time to expire. It would be out of the limelight while the hunt was at its hottest and the insurance investigating team was on the trail. Once the owner had been paid off, there would be less chance of its being spotted and thus it went on its merry way to a new owner across the Channel, probably in Holland or Belgium, suitably disguised. Cars like the Jag that were still lying low however needed to be kept somewhere safe and sound. Such as in a small car park guarded by Shotsworth Security.

I allowed myself the luxury of feverish excitement. Could that be it? If so, what part might Nigel be playing apart from his day job as broker in placing the insurance and processing the booty? Answer: he could be the middle man knowing when it was safe to move the cars on. Also – I clung on to my mental seat belt in case I went through the roof with this – he could be a *spotter* for the organization. Maybe that was too simple. Gang leader? Regional organizer?

I thought of Pen, with her love of theory built on air. For once I didn't care. All I could think of was that if Nigel had taken Angie's words as an accusation of his role in a major classic car ring, it could well give him a motive for her murder. Trouble was, I was almost sorry.

TWELVE

Dave did his best to be interested in this new theory, but there was a definite touch of a damp squib about his response. He would, he promised, check into it – and he would keep Brandon posted. The more I thought about it, however, the more it seemed to me to fit, although I was forced to admit that finding proof was another matter. Dave might nail Nigel on the car theft front, but proof for murder was a very different matter. The message Dave put over was that I should keep my nose firmly glued to what I was paid to do and leave the clever stuff to the professionals. Fair enough, I conceded, but there was *something* I could do on home ground.

Len and Zoe should have been slaving away in the Pits on my behalf when I reached home, as there was a Riley RME to finish by the end of the working day. In fact only Len was there. Zoe was going to be late as she had to run Rob somewhere. Luckily she and her Fiesta arrived in a haze of blue mist before I got too involved in my story.

'Physician, heal thyself,' I remarked drily to her.

She looked puzzled. 'I'm fine.'

'But your car isn't,' I said patiently. 'So why not fix it?'

She wasn't fazed. 'I would if I knew a good garage. What are you doing here, anyway? We thought you were set on a movie career.'

'I am, but I've had an idea about why I was duffed up the other day.' I proceeded to tell them my Biddington theory, but they both looked unimpressed.

'Soooo . . .' Zoe began doubtfully. 'What do we do?'

'Keep your ears open when you're out and about in car circles,' I said firmly.

'For what?' Len grunted. He isn't exactly a socialite.

'Who the big hitters insure with. Who's had cars nicked.

Possible spotters. Anything that might tie in with Shotsworth Security.'

Len grunted again, from which I understood that he was far too busy doing things that mattered, such as adjusting a throttle linkage. Zoe looked distinctly disapproving.

'What about Rob?'

'Rob?' I couldn't remember mentioning him.

'Are you suggesting he's bent too?'

I'd clean forgotten lover boy was a chum of Nigel's. 'No,' I said firmly, hoping to goodness I was right. I have little time for Rob but even so I couldn't see him being energetic enough to be a crook. Then I remembered that it had been Rob who first offered to take me to see Clarissa at her Gladden home, and that had led me to finding the car park and the Auburn. Had he had some sneaky reason for doing so? Or was it yet another case of Rob blindly barging into trouble? I was prepared to go with the latter – for the moment.

'You might be doing him a favour,' I pointed out. 'If Nigel's clean no problem.' (And Ferraris can fly, I thought meanly.) 'If he *is* mixed up in this racket then Rob would be well out of it.'

Zoe thought this through. 'OK,' she said reluctantly. 'You're on.'

'Len?'

A further grunt which I took as a yes. 'Good,' I said. 'Remember, folks, it's all in the cause of our classic car heritage.'

A wet cloth flew over the Riley RME and caught me mid-T-shirt.

Somewhat cheered by this partial success, I drove up to Syndale Manor the next morning in happier mood not least because it was Friday and the weekend offered some promise of time with Louise. As I turned in through the gates, however, the mood began to evaporate, for no reason that I could deduce. I parked the car and began to walk up to the house. There had been few cars in the car park, so I guessed that meant that today we were down to the cast, crew and catering staff without extras.

It felt somewhat creepy on my own, as though I were in one of those old ghost films where buildings suddenly vanish and trees close in for the kill. True, it was early morning, damp and even drizzly, but that did not fully account for it. Even the catering area was deserted as I passed it, and there was no one around on the manor forecourt. No, I was wrong. The front door was opening and out came my old friend Nigel, who looked as pleased to see me as though I were a long lost friend come for the weekend. It was good to see me, he told me, and even looked as if he meant it, which made it hard to remember that this was the man whom Dave and I were investigating as a possible major player in a car-theft gang.

'Where is everyone?' I asked. 'Filming inside?'

'No. Up at Nemesis.'

'*What?*'

He laughed. 'Sorry, that's our family name for it. The old folly built like a Greek temple – it's behind the house up on the hill.'

So that's what Joan had meant when she referred to Nemesis. It was I who had put the thought of revenge into her mind.

'Why Nemesis?' I asked. 'Is it dedicated to him – or is it her?' I knew the old myth of course, but had never associated a sex with the name. Perhaps that was as it should be. The avenger of the gods, the child of night, needs no further identification.

Not Nigel's field, either. 'No idea,' he replied. 'It was built ages ago. Want to join the fun? I'll take you over.'

And so we set off together, the best of chums, through the gate leading to the gardens and lake at the rear of the house, which I had not yet fully explored.

'Perhaps it got its name from dark doings in your family way back?' I joked.

Nigel looked unconcerned. 'Maybe. My father is a bit of a stickler for kids obeying the rules – maybe his father was too. The temple seemed to glare down at us as it's fairly high up on the hillside, so Dad used to say that Nemesis was keeping an eye on us making sure we were good, otherwise we'd reap the gods' vengeance.'

Some way of parenting, I thought, beginning to dislike Sir John Biddington, even though I hadn't yet had the pleasure of meeting him. 'Nemesis' reeked of medieval discipline. Be good or be whacked by the Devil – or alternatively in this case by your father. As we reached the terrace of the house overlooking the gardens, I could see Nemesis far off on the hillside to our right. It looked harmless enough from here, just another small stone building with a few pillars, like the one at Godmersham Park, in which Jane Austen must once have enjoyed sitting. There was something off-putting about Nemesis's position, however; it was surrounded by guardian trees that looked ready to march in force to repel invaders. I could see figures moving around up there, but at this distance they looked dwarfed as if conceding that nature had the last word.

'Is the name one of the reasons Bill was so taken with it,' I asked, 'as the theme for his film is revenge behind and darkness ahead?'

'Louise thinks so. Not my field,' Nigel said dismissively. 'I hate the place. I know it's only a building but I'd pull it down if I got a chance.'

Only a building, I thought. But buildings have atmospheres, and atmospheres often have good cause behind them. I was still battling to consider that Nigel might be mixed up with major car crime, and had to bear in mind that I might be *his* Nemesis. Liking him was an increasing nuisance, although I reasoned that even Al Capone must have been liked by someone.

'Maybe we'd better forget revenge and talk cars,' I said lightly. 'What's your car at present?'

He brightened up. 'A Merc 280SL.'

'Great. Did you know there's a good parts supplier in south London?' Then I broke off, as I could see Louise coming to greet us. She was costumed, clad in a shimmering slinky green evening gown and her evening make-up shouted at me, but apart from that she was Louise, not Julia Danby. Either way, she looked worried.

'Did Nigel tell you?' she asked.

I didn't like the sound of this. 'About what?'

Nigel had been caught on the wrong foot. 'Thought it better not,' he muttered.

'It's no secret,' she said impatiently. 'One of the cars was vandalized last night, Jack.'

I definitely didn't like what I was hearing. 'The Auburn?'

'The Fiat,' Nigel said.

Louise's car in the film. 'What happened?' I asked sharply. Another in the dirty tricks campaign, I wondered, or some new problem? There could be no question of its being merely passing vandalism here.

'Nothing much. Just graffiti,' Louise said. 'Nigel cleaned it off easily.'

'*What* graffiti?'

'In lipstick. It read "whore",' she told me evenly, then as she saw my expression added, 'Nothing personal, Jack. Don't worry about it.'

Personal was exactly what it sounded like to me. Very personal. Not just a general expression of dislike. It could be very much directed at Louise and me, now that news had crept out, no doubt given a hefty shove by Pen. It was either another episode in the dirty tricks campaign showing that it had not stopped with Angie's death, or it was someone who disliked the idea of Louise and myself as a couple. Such as, I couldn't help thinking, Nigel.

I glanced at him, and caught him off-guard. The hail-fellow-well-met look had vanished from his eyes. 'Pointed eh?' he said.

Louise considered him only a friend, but how did he think of her? And what might be coming next in the way of dirty tricks.

'Here,' Nigel said, waving a hand at the temple ahead of us. 'Welcome to Nemesis.'

I watched the filming for the rest of the day, chiefly because Louise was on set much of the time. It was a scene between Julia Danby and her former lover Lord Charing, in which he has soused out Julia's plan to seduce his son away from his fiancée Cora, but his fury turns to passion and they end up in each other's arms. Lucky chap. I could do with more of that myself. There were more people here than I had expected from the number of cars, and I could even see a few extras. Von Ribbentrop (Chris) was having a quick smoke with the Prince of Wales (Graham), and Joan was chatting to Tom and Eleanor.

Nemesis itself consisted of one small room, presumably the 'temple', and a columned platform outside with stone seating along the wall by the entrance to the room for people to admire the view. The love scene was taking place inside the temple but Bill was filming outside it as well. There were clearly lighting problems with both, judging by the deteriorating tempers as the day wore on. Particularly Bill's. He never lost control, but we were all aware of rising tension, especially in him. There was take after take, and even Tom came in for criticism over the storyboards which Bill said were misleading, even though he must have passed them in the first place. He ordered Tom to adjust them and bring them to him before the end of filming that evening.

I found it hard to watch as Louise's performance, which seemed perfect to me, was torn to shreds time after time and then painfully reconstructed. It wasn't just her. When at last Bill was satisfied, the next scene went just as badly. This one featured Lord Charing and his son, but with a glimpse of von Ribbentrop, the Prince of Wales and an attractive woman no doubt playing Mrs Simpson behind them. None of the trio had speaking lines and Lord Charing and his son had come upon them unexpectedly. It worked for me, but Bill found fault with all of them, demolishing the performances of all five.

'Don't worry, Jack,' Louise said, seeing my set expression. 'It's pretty routine.'

'In that case, I'm glad I'm not in the film business.'

As the day wore on Brian and Joan also came in for the full Wade treatment. Joan seemed the most relaxed, but also distracted. At the brief break after hours of filming, she sought me out at the canteen to ask whether there had been any follow-up on Pen.

'Bill seems out of sorts today,' I said once we'd put that subject to rest. 'What's wrong?'

'The attack on Louise's car, I expect,' she said.

'Louise herself doesn't seem worried.'

'Maybe not. But Bill is.'

'Why should that be?'

Joan hesitated. 'It meant something to Bill. Someone

scrawled "whore" on Margot's car during the filming of *Running Tides*. Her husband we thought. It caused a stir, and it was after that things seemed to go wrong between Bill and Margot. So he might . . . You see—'

Whatever she was going to say she thought better of, however, as the runners recalled the cast to Nemesis.

'Will filming go on much longer?' I asked, as I walked with her back to Nemesis. I hoped not, for her sake. She still looked under strain.

She shivered. 'I hope not. I really do. It's that place. Nemesis. Bill's got us in such a state that we're all beginning to think in terms of revenge and footsteps in the dark.'

Bill eventually called it a day about seven thirty and Louise rejoined me in the catering area after changing. She was tense and so was the rest of the cast. I tried my best to soothe her but without success.

'I hate that place,' she said. 'We all do. It seems like stepping into a nightmare from the past. I know that's ridiculous, because I wasn't even in *Running Tides*, but I can't help feeling it's there all the time.'

'Sweetheart, remember how you told me that what's going on now couldn't be relevant to something that happened over ten years ago?'

'I do remember. But suppose I'm wrong? All I know is that the sooner this film's in the can the better.'

'For us as well?'

She looked at me appalled. 'That's a separate issue. You're the one good thing that's come out of this job.'

That shook me, not for myself, but on behalf of *Dark Harvest*. 'Don't you think it will be a success?'

'I'm sure it will be,' she said bitterly. 'One can never tell during the filming itself. To me it seems as if it's all ragged, no unity, as though we're groping our way through but only towards something that seems to disappear as soon as we get anywhere near it. But Bill seems happy with it that way.'

'Can he see things straight, given what's happened? The film is an escape route.'

'Granted, but I don't think that affects his judgement. And nor does *Running Tides* or Margot Croft. They really are in the past for him. Bill has this new dream in his head now, and he has to get it on film. It happens with every film of his, not just this one, according to Joan. What I'm afraid of, Jack, is that . . .'

'Tell me,' I urged, when she paused.

'That it will catch up with him, and that he'll collapse.'

'His own Nemesis?'

'No, just the effects of both Margot and Angie dying at the point of success.'

'Even though Angie's death has nothing to do with Margot's?'

'Yes, although we can't be sure of that. But if the motive is rooted in today, not yesterday, who has one?'

The name Tom hung between us but wasn't voiced. There were other people around us now. Living human beings, not names on a list to be shifted from innocent to guilty at will. 'Shall we get out of here?' I asked her abruptly, as I realized that was exactly what I was doing to Nigel. 'Leave right now?'

She looked at me despairingly. 'I'd love to, Jack, but I can't. We or I at least have to stay.'

I knew she'd say that, but I had to push on as gently as I could. 'Why? Can you explain? The filming's finished.'

She hesitated, then said, 'Yes, I can explain. We've been through such a ghastly day that I feel I should remain with the others for their sake, for the film's sake. Who knows whether it matters or not, but I think it does. Do you understand?'

Of course I did. I felt the same about Zoe and Len. If either of them go through troubled times I try to help. I looked round at the assembled company of which Louise was so fiercely protective. Conversation was muted; there was no sign of Bill, nor any of the other familiar faces, except for Justin and Eleanor. And then I saw Tom. He had only just arrived at the catering area, looking so unlike his usual self that it wasn't only Louise who was worried.

'Everything all right, Tom?' she asked. 'You don't look too good.'

'No one would after a bollocking like that from His Majesty. I got the storyboards back to him at Nemesis long before he finished for the day, and he still didn't like them and let everyone know it. "Bring them over to the Manor before eight thirty," he roared. Then I get a radio call telling me he and Joan were checking lighting up at Nemesis and don't bother coming to the Manor.'

'That's odd,' Louise said.

'*Too* macabre, he told me. I should be keeping the dark stuff in the background, not pushing it to the front. He threatened to go digital again.'

'He doesn't mean that,' Louise said comfortingly. 'He's been iffy all day long.'

'We all have,' Tom grumbled.

'True enough,' she said. 'Don't you feel the same, Jack?'

I nodded. I couldn't wait to get moving and yet was anything so very different to other days on which I'd been present? I decided it was, but in a way I could not define. Perhaps that was how Nemesis worked.

'Are you sure you can't leave now?' I pleaded with Louise as Tom went off to get some food.

'No. I have to stay.'

She looked past me, and I turned round to see Roger advancing on us – which perhaps explained why Tom had retreated so quickly. Wise move, I thought. Roger might have joined forces with Bill and banished his storyboards for ever. He didn't look in a mood to take Tom's side against Bill's.

'You seen Bill anywhere?' Roger asked.

'Sorry. No sign of him,' Louise answered. 'Ask Nigel.'

'No point. Sir John was holding dinner for us, but Bill hasn't turned up.'

'Trying to sort out what went wrong today,' Louise said perhaps unwisely.

Roger immediately turned on her. 'Wrong? What did?'

Louise hastily backtracked. 'Nothing serious. Just one of those days when you don't quite hit top note.'

'Bill doesn't have those days,' Roger said dismissively, which made me think the less of him. Everyone has *those days.*

Louise tried again. 'He told Tom he'd see him at the Manor but he cancelled it, so he might be up at Nemesis thinking about the blocking or lighting for tomorrow.'

'Could be.' Roger seemed unwilling to go alone and Louise offered to go with him. 'Odd he didn't let Sir John know though.'

Something made me tag along too, and not just my love of Louise. On any other day it would have been a pleasant walk through the gardens at dusk. The lake was calm, the water lilies closing up for the night, and the scent of roses was in the air. Ahead of us, however, Nemesis looked ominous in the dying light and even threatening. Stupid, I thought. This was just another evening.

It wasn't.

The quiet was shattered by shouts. Startled, we looked up to see Chris Frant hurrying, almost running, down the hill towards us and even in that light we could tell that something was wrong and rushed to meet him.

'Graham's rung,' were the only words I made out in his gibberish.

'What for?' Roger hurled at him.

'Ambulance, police . . .' Chris looked close to tears.

'Bill?' Louise cried out.

'No. It's *Joan*.'

THIRTEEN

Sitting at tables on chairs already damp with the evening air, we were unable to cope with this new horror. We all seemed to be groping in the dark for handholds to pull us back into a world we recognized. Dusk was hurrying to meet night, and the flashing police lights as vans and cars drove past the catering area to the manor forecourt only served to heighten the impression that this was yet another film set.

I knew I had to force myself to think of Joan, if I was going to be able to contribute anything to find her killer, but it was hard. She had been strangled, Chris had told us in his first gasping words. Graham had stayed with the body, while he sounded the general alert. He and Graham had been looking for Bill to check if they were needed for the next day's filming, and Tom had told them he thought he was up at Nemesis with Joan. When Graham and Chris arrived there, Joan was dead and there had been no sign of Bill.

I had persuaded Roger and Louise to return to the house to await the police and gather everyone together, but I had known I would have to go to Nemesis. I had enough experience in such situations to check whether there was any chance of saving her. Neither Chris nor Graham had first-aid training. I did.

Joan had been lying in front of the temple door. I checked, but I had seen at once she was beyond anyone's help. Graham was still green with horror when I arrived, but I insisted he stayed until the police came, not least because I needed him as an insurance policy against my being alone at a crime scene. Having witnessed the terrible sight of Joan's body, I also needed company. The sight had made me want to throw up, and Graham was in a similar state. Chris, who had by then ventured part of the way back to Nemesis, volunteered to stay with me while Graham took a breather.

While we waited, Chris and I had sat on the grass close

enough to Nemesis to ensure any other arrivals would be
noticed. There was no sign of von Ribbentrop in the trembling
man beside me. It had been a weird time, a silent time, because
there was nothing to say. Neither Chris nor I had wanted to
face this nightmare head on by putting it into words, and the
arrival of the police had been welcome. Responsibility had
been passed over, and there was at least something we could
do. We could answer questions. The full team was on the way,
including Brandon as senior investigating officer, so the police
advance guard had told us. I presumed that the location had
immediately indicated to HQ that this was no practical joker
at work or a false alarm. Graham had rejoined us, and one of
the two PCs remained with us. By the time we had talked to
Brandon and then returned to the catering area where everyone
was still gathered, it was getting on for ten o'clock and the
ranks had been reduced to about twenty. Thankfully I had seen
Louise amongst them, sitting with Nigel and an older man,
probably Sir John.

'What's going on, Jack?' Louise had asked as Chris and I
joined them. She didn't mean the police procedure. I knew
she meant the frightening scenarios that must be opening up
for her, as well as for me.

I hadn't been able to reply properly because I had no answer
to give her, and we sat there, numb with shock as the crime
scene established itself. There seemed no rhyme or reason to
Joan's murder. If Bill had been the victim or Roger Ford there
might have been some obvious pattern to this horror, but why
would anyone want to kill Joan? Unless this was entirely
unrelated to Angie's death, which was highly unlikely, there
was nothing that could have occasioned this terrible response.
The quarrel between Angie and Nigel that Joan had overheard
was surely too trivial for murder. Had I missed something? If
so, it was the wrong place and the wrong time to brood over
it. I was too close to tragedy to see its context.

Sir John and Nigel were shortly called for police interview
and Chris and Graham had gone to join Brian, so Louise and
I were alone. I reached out to her, but then Roger came over
to us.

'Have you seen Bill?' he asked worriedly.

'No. Isn't he with the police?'

'Maybe.' Roger looked so shell-shocked that Louise insisted he sat down and then went to fetch a strong coffee for us all. It was going to be a long night – not that the police would keep us out here in the damp much longer. As if reading my thoughts, Nigel came back to announce we were all moving into the Manor, catering staff and all. And so we sheep – for that's what it felt like – were led into the warm house where we sat in more comfort, but still uneasily, in an eighteenth-century drawing room. We'd been there for fifteen minutes or so when Brandon himself came in, scanned the room and fixed on me.

'I need to speak to Bill Wade, Jack. Is he here?'

'I haven't seen him.' I called Tom over. 'Seen Bill?' I asked him. 'Chris said you told him Bill and Joan might be up at Nemesis together.'

'Right.' Tom looked worried. 'I told you I had a radio call to cancel the storyboards meeting because he was going up to Nemesis with Joan. He's always a demon for wanting the shadows right.'

'That's for the scene where Joan trots out to the folly and finds me and Lord Charing together,' Louise explained. 'Bill has in mind a sort of Mrs Danvers revenge scene as in Hitchcock's *Rebecca*.'

Brandon was no film buff so this clearly meant nothing. 'Mr Wade himself rang you?' he asked Tom, his gimlet eyes fixed on him as if they could nail him to the spot.

'Message from him,' Tom said.

'So where the hell is he?' Roger muttered.

'That,' Brandon said drily, 'is what I'd like to know. *Quickly.*'

'Is his car here?' I asked.

No one knew. 'Check it out, Jack,' Brandon told me. His tone told me 'at the double'.

At least the way to the car park was lit, albeit dimly. Even so, it was a lonely walk, or rather run. There were a couple of dozen cars there, including, I saw with misgivings, Bill's daily driver, a Porsche Boxster.

All sorts of crazy ideas went through my mind. Standing alone in a dark car park on a summer's night is not conducive

to logic. Especially with a murderer at large. Where was
Bill? Another corpse? A murderer who'd fled the scene in
remorse? Stop, I warned myself. Brakes on. The next step
would be a search of grounds and house, which meant
involving Sir John or Nigel – a man whom I'd once cast as
chief villain. Brandon might want to do the search himself,
but I'd offer. He compromised. Nigel, me, and two PCs to
search the house. I did make a feeble suggestion about the
room in Nemesis – had that been checked? Brandon looked
at me pityingly. Yes, it had.

My morale was lower at that point than I had ever known
it. I seemed to be standing in the middle of a tornado whirling
around me and I tried to clutch on to at least one firm objective. Bill had to be found. On a normal day I would have
jumped at the chance of touring Syndale Manor, but this was
not a normal day, and both Nigel and I were – to be honest
– terrified at the prospect of possibly finding yet another corpse.

'There are only a few places where he might be,' Nigel
said, producing a mass of keys. 'We'll try them first – Roger's
office, my study, my parents' studies, bathroom and so on. He
might be locked in, or taken ill, or both.'

Tension levels rose as one after the other possibility brought
no sign of Bill. Was that good or bad? Keep going, I told
myself. I still felt dazed, as though I were on some crazy
National Trust tour. When none of the obvious locations
produced a result, we broadened the search to the private parts
of the Manor, again without success.

'We could try the garages,' Nigel suggested. 'The police
might not be covering them.'

Even though Brandon's men might have covered them, it
was such an obvious solution that I became convinced it was
the answer, and we rushed straight out to them.

'Bill's been worried about the Auburn ever since it came
back,' Nigel said. He explained that the garages were converted
stables that Roger had had specially fitted up for the four
classics. When we reached them, all of them looked securely
locked, and security lights flashed angrily out at us.

'Bill?' I yelled.

The string of expletives that answered me from within left

us in no doubt that he was locked in with the Auburn. 'We'll get you out of there,' shouted one PC encouragingly. It took a while to find the right keys, especially with Bill ranting his fury at us. When we were finally successful, he shot out of his prison like Nemesis itself.

Brandon had by now joined us, which made Nigel and me redundant. 'What happened?' he asked Bill, in his quiet voice.

'Had word there was trouble down here,' Bill growled. 'Message to the Manor phone. Came over to check, door slammed, never carry radio or mobile so that was it.'

The door was, I couldn't help seeing, self locking, so it could have been accidental or intentional.

'Message from whom?' I asked, not to Brandon's pleasure. Bill glared at me. 'Security. OK by you?'

Bill wouldn't yet know of Joan's death, but Brandon swept Bill off with him, making it clear that my role was over, and Nigel and I returned to the communal room. It was by now past midnight, and the strain was evident on everyone's face.

Eleanor Richey was in full flow. 'Joan of all people,' she wailed. 'Surely it was an accident, or if not . . .' She stopped short of the proverbial tramp or sex maniac and finished feebly with: 'Someone who climbed over the boundary wall.'

No one commented, and she didn't look as if she believed it herself. The next person to produce an unlikely scenario was Tom. 'I reckon it's one of the caterers. Get some odd people nowadays.'

No one commented, especially as I could see one or two of them present, and Tom relapsed into silence.

'Her ex-husband?' Chris ventured. 'He lives down this way.'

'No,' Brian contributed. 'He moved to the States.'

There were several other attempts but then silence reigned. Louise looked exhausted and I felt it. I was glad when Bill put his head round the door and summoned me to Roger's office, which was guarded by two PCs – I wondered whether this was to prevent a murderer bursting in, or Roger and Bill from making a bid for freedom. At least Bill was freed from Brandon's tender mercies, which was a good sign.

'He's OK,' Bill told the guards, indicating me. 'Check us over if you like. Just need to talk.' The strength of Bill's personality achieved its object, and the door was opened for us without a murmur. Roger was already there, and barely seemed to have the strength to acknowledge our arrival. 'Any ideas on this nightmare, Jack?' he asked. I shook my head. It was still too new, too raw. Bill took over. 'You any further on with Angie's murder?' 'Several trails to follow,' I said diplomatically. 'The trouble is that it's never a matter of following clues up to the finishing line. You start off with a whole range of trails, some of which lead somewhere, some of which don't. I'm eliminating the don'ts.'

Roger grunted. 'Was Joan part of the joker's trick box?'

'How can I know yet?' I said wearily. 'She could have been getting too near the truth for comfort.' And perhaps that was true. I remembered her words to me: 'I'm afraid . . .'

Roger nodded, more to himself than to me, as though this confirmed his own thinking. 'Bill and I don't think that line about the cars is leading anywhere.'

'I agree,' I said. Or almost, I told myself. 'But if we take that out, we're getting very close to home,' I said steadily.

'That's where we are too,' Roger said. I could see the muscles in Bill's cheeks working overtime. It wouldn't be long before frustration burst out again.

It wasn't. Two seconds or so. 'That garage, Jack. I was locked in.' He looked at me fiercely. 'But you know, I could have done that on purpose. Brandon found that out quickly enough, and I don't intend to find myself at the wrong end of a murder charge.'

'No fear of that,' I said without thinking.

'There is, and we know it,' Roger whipped back. 'There's some joker playing with dynamite round here. The sooner Joan's killer is found, the happier I'll be.'

'That message,' Bill said. 'Security never sent it. Brandon found that out. I could have wangled a text to myself. Easy enough. Brandon knows that too. We have to move, Jack.'

'Even if that means back to *Running Tides*?' I asked.

'Even that.'

By one thirty the last of us had been released and I drove back to Frogs Hill, much shaken. Roger had said filming at Syndale

Manor had been suspended perhaps altogether. Tomorrow, Saturday, they would return to Stour Studios and announce their decision about the film's future.

Louise was so tired that I persuaded her to go back to the hotel. That's what love is. She demurred. She wanted to be with me. That's love too. I kissed her and said the impersonal hotel would be better for what was left of the night, and that we had all the time in the world to be together. And that's really love.

Memories of Joan lying alone at Nemesis hung over me, naturally enough, as I turned off the Egerton Road into Frogs Hill Lane. Even the thought of home could not shake me out of the darkness of the day. There were no street lights of course as I drove along the narrow bumpy lane with the hedgerows high on either side. As I turned in at my gate the security lights came on, but tonight they seemed harsh, no warm glow. They merely seemed to underline my stark failure to find Angie's killer. It was no good telling myself that if the police could not track him down, how could I hope to do so? The police are hedged in with the need to find sufficient proof to convince the CPS before they can charge their suspect. I am not so constrained, at least in my thoughts, and I was all too well aware that Joan's ghost had now been added to Angie's in reproaching me.

Ahead of me as I drew up, the Pits loomed and in the stark light even they looked forbidding. Here be dragons indeed, one waiting round every corner. There was no sound, save the hooting of the occasional bird and the rustle of trees and tonight darkness was far from being a friend. I was relieved when I was inside the farmhouse again. No dragons lurked here, only the Glory Boot. I could have time to think a little and then sleep. Think how Joan Burton, friend of Margot Croft, could possibly have fitted into this crescendo of violence. How did it fit with Angie's murder? I could not believe that Nigel was so deep into car crime that it led to not one but two murders. Or was the fantasy of film throwing its mantle over the truth, blowing stardust in my eyes to disguise the real picture?

To my disbelief, the security lights went on again. A cat?

A fox? Nemesis? Then, for heaven's sake, there was a knock at the door. At gone two o'clock?

'Police?' I wondered as I dragged myself to open it. I realized at the last moment that this might not be such a good plan and put the chain on just in case. It wasn't Brandon's smiling face on the doorstep. It was, unbelievably, Pen's. Already she must have got hold of the new story, and being Pen, she was on to it.

'Story, Jack?' she asked hopefully.

'It's two o'clock in the morning, Pen.' I tried not to screech too loudly.

'Story, Jack?'

'No,' I bellowed ungraciously.

A foot was placed in the doorway. 'Cup of cocoa for a lone lady? Or have you got Louise tucked up in there?'

'No and no,' I snapped.

'Can I quote you on that?'

'No.'

'Do take that chain off the door. I feel unwelcome,' she complained.

I gazed at her wondering if she was a werewolf sent to haunt me. I struggled with reason. If she quoted me as refusing to talk to her, I would appear once more in print as someone with something to hide, and that wasn't going to do my reputation any good. If I did talk to her, I'd be murdered by Brandon and possibly Bill too. I chose truth.

'There's nothing I can tell you because I don't know myself. I'm knocked sideways and I can't think straight tonight. I liked—' I pulled up short. I nearly used Joan's name and that probably wasn't public yet.

Pen's eyes gleamed. 'Friend of yours, was he?'

So she hadn't got the full story yet. 'Fishing, Pen?'

'My job netting innocent minnows like you. Is my theory proven or is it not?'

Here we go again, I thought. 'No comment, sweetheart.'

'My guess is, laddie,' she replied thoughtfully, 'that it's got a whole lot closer to proof this evening.' Pen grinned. 'I'll give you a break, Jack. I'll leave. But I'll be back.'

'That I don't doubt, unfortunately.'

*   *   *

When I arrived at Stour Studios on Saturday morning, it was gone nine and I half expected to find that the film production had been abandoned, and indeed everything seemed suspiciously quiet. I checked in at reception where a very pale Jane was presiding. Filming, she told me to my surprise, was taking place in Studio Two: Miss Shaw and Miss Richey.

I found that hard to believe at first. Filming so soon? Then I realized that this could be Bill's way of dealing with the situation. Fine for him, but how did the cast feel about it?

When I reached Studio Two, I saw that 'filming was taking place' was somewhat of an overstatement. The crew was there, so were Louise and Eleanor, but they looked frazzled. Louise and Eleanor were sitting on the set of a drawing room, while Bill was giving the benefit of his blistering tongue to the crew. It appeared that perspective was wrong for a high-angle shot resulting in the mastershot for the scene being a complete failure. Louise noticed my arrival and came over to me.

'What's happening?' I asked. 'Is the film still going on?'

'Yes. Bill wasn't—'

Bill whirled round – he had sharp ears – and snapped that he wanted no 'garbage talk'. 'Yes, it's going on. *We're* going on. I don't give way to anything, not even this.'

I drew Louise out of earshot, sensing something might have happened that I didn't yet know about. I was right.

'Tom's been arrested,' she said.

My heart sank. 'For what?'

'Joan's murder, but maybe Angie's too. We don't know. That's why Bill's in such a state. Roger's going to make an announcement about the film at midday, but meanwhile Bill insists on filming as though it's going ahead. But Tom – oh, Jack, it's the last straw. How could he possibly have killed Joan? They were close friends.'

'Arresting him doesn't mean they'll be able to charge him,' I pointed out. I knew Brandon though. If he'd had his eye on Tom all the time and left it too long with the result that Joan had died too, he'd press on hard with every bit of evidence he could find.

'But Bill denies making any such arrangement with Joan

to go to Nemesis, and Tom's story about a radio call telling him not to come to the Manor with the storyboards turns out not to be from Bill but from one of the runners, but none of them admits to calling him. What does it all mean, Jack?'

I remembered Pen's theory that Bill had murdered Angie, and I remembered Bill's fury yesterday in Roger's office, when he himself realized that he might be being fitted up for Joan's murder. But Bill was a clever man – and knew both I and Brandon would see that the garage doors were self locking, and that in theory he might have killed Joan and then locked himself in. I warned myself that careful driving was called for here. Slippery surface ahead.

I slipped in to the canteen where the midday meeting was being held. Roger had decided on democracy by holding a vote for continuing or abandoning the film at least temporarily. Put that way, he won almost the whole company to his side, as perhaps he had calculated. It was a go-ahead. Sunday would be a free day but on Monday morning filming would recommence at the studios. One or two dissented and some of the crew and cast had other commitments, which would take some sorting out and the canteen and green room were both abuzz with talk while arrangements were discussed.

'How are you placed, Louise?' I asked her, fearing her answer.

'I'm staying,' she told me to my relief. She made a face. 'But I've had enough of that hotel. You were right about its being the right place to be last night, but now I need some distance.'

I held my breath. 'They say Frogs Hill has good air at this time of year.'

'That sounds just fine.'

A whole day to ourselves. Louise brought her luggage at lunchtime and settled into the farmhouse, because Roger had freed them from midday. That afternoon I had a date already fixed with Dave and Brandon, weekend or not, but on Sunday, glorious Sunday, I would be free and so would Louise.

'Let's go over the hills and far away,' Louise said.

'Seaside?'

'Countryside? Picnic?'

That was agreed.

Then fate stepped in. As it was Saturday, the Pits had officially closed at one o'clock before Louise and I had reached
Frogs Hill, but Zoe had stayed on to finish a job, noted Louise's
car arriving and came over to see us.

'I thought you and Louise might want to go the Marsham
Hall Fun Day tomorrow,' she said brightly.

It sounded ghastly. 'No thanks.'

'But it has that classic car show. I thought you knew it. It
was pretty good last year. I kept my ear to the ground, just as
you told me, and guess who tripped over it?'

'Rob?' I asked mildly.

A scathing look. 'Your chum Nigel will be there.'

FOURTEEN

The moment I walked in I could see Dave was in hedging mode. Shifty would be a less polite way of putting it. Usually he's happy to chat freely, but not today and not just because he dislikes having to work on Saturdays. Perhaps it was because I'd come to the dragons' den ostensibly to see what was happening on the classic car front, but in reality to find out why Tom had been arrested. Dave prefers his chats somewhere quiet – quiet in his view anyway – such as a pub where he fondly imagines he is invisible, but today that had not been possible.

'The film-set murders', as the media termed them, were high profile, with the eyes of the world upon them, and I knew Brandon must be feeling the pressure. Once upon a time, the answer was simple: 'Call in the Yard'. Nowadays the Serious Crime Directorate for Kent and Essex, which currently included him, had the spotlight of the world's press on it. Pen must be a positive pussy cat compared with what he must be facing.

Dave guessed quite well what I was here for, but couldn't give me the answers himself. 'Hopkins isn't yet charged. Looks possible though,' was all he could contribute.

'What's he got on him?' I asked. 'And is it Angie or Joan or both?'

'Pass.'

'I don't see it. Tom's no murderer.'

'Don't tell me he's not the sort.'

'He's not the sort.'

Dave sighed. 'That's why you're not in our shoes. I let Brandon know you were honouring us with your presence. He wants to see you. For all our sakes, give him good news if you can.'

Fat chance, I thought, as I filled Dave in on my latest Biddington theory. Police stations, like hospitals, march to a different tune from the outside world. Their rules rule, and no

arguing. By the time I reached Brandon's office, under the
protection of a PC in case I decided to rob the canteen till en
route, I was beginning to feel like a policeman myself. I was
glad I wasn't, even though I had no magic wand of good news
to wave at Brandon.

He nodded anyway, and informed me that it was good to
see me. I'd have liked a little more clarity on exactly why.
Until recently his sole ambition had been to throw me into a
cell and chuck the key away.

'You'll want to know about Hopkins. We'll have to charge
him soon.'

'Or release him.'

His eyes gleamed. 'Any reason why we should?'

Once I had bitten back my instinctive reply – 'Any reason
why you shouldn't?' – he indicated that the initial sparring
was over and we could get down to business.

'Dave Jennings tells me you're following a hunch about
Nigel Biddington being deep into car crime.'

'It's still a possibility.'

'Taking you anywhere?'

'Not far,' I admitted, 'but there's hope. Circumstantial at
present.'

Brandon did not look impressed and I couldn't blame him.
'Circumstantial is all we've got on Hopkins. He was around
at the time of both murders, he had a motive for Angie Wade's
murder and for Joan's too if she'd cottoned on to his role in
the earlier death. Bill Wade denies any plan to meet Joan
Burton at this temple place and Hopkins, like several people,
knew she was going there. The runners all deny calling him
to cancel the manor appointment and so does Bill Wade. What's
more, Hopkins admits he went up to the temple himself not
just the first time when filming was still going on, but again
after he got the call.'

That set me back a few notches. This was sounding bad.

'Bill Wade's story,' Brandon continued, 'is that he had a
dinner date with Sir John and was expecting to see Hopkins
before that. Then he was called to the garage by Security.
Denied by them. What we don't have on Hopkins – yet – is
forensic backup.'

'What's his explanation about going to the temple? Looks as if he really did have a call or why would he go up there?'

Brandon looked at me in a kindly fashion, and I couldn't blame him. 'Because he didn't have a call and he knew Joan would be on her own. That's our take. His is that he took this famous call around seven forty-five; it was a woman's voice and she was one of the runners with a message for him from Bill Wade. All quite normal, apparently. The message was that Wade was cancelling the meeting because he was meeting Joan Burton at the temple over some lighting problem. Hopkins claims that, not wanting to leave this storyboard question dangling, he went up to the temple half an hour or so later where he expected to find Bill. He wasn't there, and Joan was, highly annoyed at being kept waiting. Hopkins claims he found her alive and left her the same way. If so, she was dead not long afterwards.'

That call . . . I remembered the female gardeners whom Angie might have thought were calling her down to the garden. 'Could there have been two of them in it?' I suggested. 'The caller and the murderer?'

'Not likely in a murder case. Hopkins claimed he was in the canteen after he returned from the temple. No one confirms it so far.'

'Short on alibis then.'

'Precisely.'

'So where do I come in?' There had to be some reason Brandon actually wanted to see me.

'Nigel Biddington, if he's still in the frame for car crime.'

'It's wobbly. What worries me though—'

'Is that it's a big jump from car crime to double murder.'

'Precisely,' I commented. 'Glad you think so too.'

'You're too kind,' Brandon murmured. 'If there's nothing concrete over Biddington, however, it means I'll have to draw a line under your official collaboration. Anything more though, and you'll still be under an obligation to tell us.'

Not exactly surprising news, and nor was Dave's response when I asked him how his budget was looking.

'Bust,' he told me. 'Sorry about that.'

I believed him but so was I. The mortgage was due. I murmured about my last invoice which was as yet unpaid and he murmured about these things taking time to process. He did kindly add that he'd do his best. Apart from the Pits income (if any) all I had in the way of work was my obligation to Bill, which in the present circumstances can't have been high on his agenda.

The prospect of living with Louise, however temporarily, was both delight and torment. It had been a long time since I'd shared living space with anyone. Four years ago crocks and pans had flown across the room as Liz Potter had thrown me out of her house, and I was fearful of something similar happening again. That Saturday evening, however, daily life looked suspiciously easy, and I could grow used to Louise's help over dealing with dishwashers and conjuring up pastas. It was even easier as regards the romantic side of our relationship. Made in heaven it seemed, and living it was paradise. Too easy? Well, why knock that?

'It's good to be here,' Louise said happily. 'First of all, there's you. But you *here* is even better. I felt like I was living in a goldfish bowl at the studios and hotel,' she confessed. 'The eyes of the world are on us now, expecting us to be picked off one by one.'

'Not all journalists are like Pen.'

'If we were picked off one by one, no one would turn down a story like that,' she pointed out mildly, then managed a laugh as she saw my face. 'Don't worry. I'm not going to turn into a murdering serial killer or be a victim of one. It doesn't help that Julia Danby is the villain of *Dark Harvest* though. I could do with a spot of being whiter than white. Brian feels the same way as the duplicitous Lord Charing. We saw the rushes of our flashback sex scene this afternoon. Torrid stuff. They weren't good and we both knew it. So does Bill.'

'It'll be OK in the end,' I said, without much conviction I fear. 'You all feel bad, but you're pros. What comes out will be your best work.'

'I hope you're right,' she replied fervently. 'It's not just me. Tom's arrest really was the last straw.'

I couldn't tell her the true situation. 'He might be free by now.'

'Let's hope. It's hanging over us like a thunderstorm about

to break. It's as though misfortune were stalking us, giving us little jabs and big jabs alternately, and we can never shake it off. We won't until it's too late and we're all caught in the trap. Does that sound crazy?'

'No.'

'I was stalked once, someone who had a grudge against me because I got a part that they wanted.'

'That rings a bell. Some Victorian murderer. Can't place it.'

'It'll come back.'

'Like Pen.'

She laughed. 'I think we've seen her off for a while.'

'Do you?' I said politely. 'Ever optimistic, aren't you?'

'It's not funny, though,' she said soberly. 'We're none of us giving our best. The audience won't know that, but Roger does, and so does Bill. And yet they can't just postpone filming till we all feel better. It would cost the earth to get us all together again, even if it's practically possible. The end of next week is the absolute limit for me. It's not just the murders, it's this horrible feeling that some dark shadow hangs over us all. Whether that comes from the film or from somewhere else, I can't tell. It's like being in a cage.'

This sounded bad. 'Even at Frogs Hill?'

'No, thankfully.' She smiled at me.

'We've got tomorrow to ourselves.'

'At a car show?'

Louise had insisted that we take up Zoe's suggestion – she wanted to beard my fantasy about Nigel, as she called it, in a suitable den. Besides, she liked making up picnics, she told me.

'Classic car enthusiasts only have eyes for cars. They won't even notice you,' I assured her.

She giggled and the *real* evening began.

Fun Day at Marsham Hall is an annual event, and probably because of its name, I hadn't been here before. One look at it and I kicked myself for prejudice. Firstly, classic cars were going to loom large judging by the numbers and quality of those I could see in the parking area. Secondly, the hall itself was a marvel to behold. I'd looked it up on the Internet but nothing prepared me for the real thing.

It was built by an eccentric artist in the late nineteenth century who not only designed the house but the gardens as well. Fantasy was his line, so turrets, fairy-tale crenellations and towers abounded on the hall's exterior and the gardens looked an idyllic paradise of waterfalls, streams, and glades mixed with a child's fantasy world of witch houses, giant mushrooms, and ponds with delightful large frogs painted bright green. It sounds garishly awful, but it had been done with such taste that it wasn't.

The hall is now run by a charitable trust, and inside, apart from the private apartments in which the family still lives, is mostly devoted to displaying the eccentric collections of its successive eccentric owners. Events loom large in the trust's calendar, of which Fun Day is only one. Classic cars were awarded a large field adjacent to the gardens, which was gently sloped so that it could clearly be seen from the gardens if the admiring owners could detach themselves for long enough to join their families picnicking there. If the weather had the ill manners to rain during the day, we were told that visitors could make for the nearest pub or the restaurant in the house – or as third and best choice owners could sit proudly in their beloved cars.

Luckily for Louise, who did not reap the same pleasure as I did out of car-fancying, it was relatively sunny and would be possible for a welcome few hours to pretend that the world of Nemesis and murder was in some other galaxy.

Louise had decreed that we would take the picnic of our dreams, which thanks to an early opening supermarket was a dream that didn't turn into a nightmare. There had only been one awkward moment as we set off to drive here. Louise thought to ask me whether I would have bothered to come if it hadn't been for my fixation on Nigel.

'I've no idea if he'll be there or not,' I answered truthfully enough. 'Zoe could be wrong.'

She made no comment, but had snapped the lid of the picnic basket shut with considerable force. She and I had decided to drive to Marsham Hall in the Lagonda and Zoe told us vaguely that she would see us there.

'I'll leave you to your twenties replay,' she said.

'The Lagonda is a 1938.'

'Let's pretend,' Louise suggested. 'The twenties are more romantic, and I'm beginning to be heartily sick of the thirties.'

We had duly roared in about noon to admiring glances from aficionados. There was a great turn out. Talk was in full flood, with small groups standing admiringly by some cars, others ignored. I took a quick tour around and saw Zoe's Fiesta. I didn't expect to see Len. Mrs Len isn't a car person, but Zoe said he might turn up with his 'missis' later. I have rarely met 'the missis' or his children, who are now grown up with families of their own. That makes Len a grandfather, but to me his children are the classics he has serviced regularly for more than one generation.

As I looked around, I felt this was a world away from Stour Studios and despite my ulterior motive in wondering whether Nigel might be here in his possible role of spotter or organizer of a car theft gang, I was determined to enjoy it.

Picnicking was already under way in the gardens and indeed in the car park area where proud owners often prefer to sit in chairs to talk cars while they eat. My lingering here would hardly be fair on Louise, however, and having polished a tiny bit of dust off the Lagonda in the hope of winning Car of the Show award, I tore myself away from my second beauty in the interests of escorting the first.

We found a secluded spot by a small artificial stream with a particularly attractive frog, only to find that it wasn't secluded enough. Hidden by what we thought was a large bush, we found Zoe and Rob munching what looked like cold pizza. I hoped for Zoe's sake that I was wrong. They greeted me without enthusiasm.

'Hi,' Zoe said.

'Hi,' said Rob, just a second short of rudeness, as he decided whether to acknowledge our presence or not. 'Someone's looking for you, Jack.'

'Nigel?' Louise asked sweetly.

'Right. He's giving Clarissa a day out,' Rob told me. 'He knows the owner of this pile and thought she'd enjoy it. Cyril's a nice old fellow. Chum of my dad's,' he added.

'Of course,' I said. 'Who wants me?'

'Clarissa.'

'What for? About the Auburn again?'

'No idea.' That said, Rob returned to his pizza.

Louise and I retreated, found a Rob-free place to sit and threw ourselves into enjoying the day. She had dressed up in a floaty summer dress for the occasion, and though her outfit didn't run to a parasol I felt that the eyes of any Impressionist artist who wandered by would light up at the sight. Mine did.

This had all the signs of a great day for dads, mums, children – and sweethearts. There was a pleasant mingling of petrol smells, grass, and faint whiff of hamburgers in the air. Perhaps Nigel and Clarissa were taking their ease dining with Rob's Cyril in the hall, because I could see no sign of them in the car display area when I went back there. It would be tempting to enjoy the day for itself but even leaving Nigel out of the equation both Louise and I were conscious of the nightmare that hung over the studios. I had to keep a tight rein on what I could tell Louise about Joan's death, but in fact Louise told me rather more than Brandon had.

'It seems Joan had had a call to meet Bill at Nemesis, because she'd told several people about it. It seemed a reasonable arrangement if annoying for her that Bill should want to see her, because it would be for an exterior shot the next day and shadows in the dying sun would be important, especially as Joan would be in black. Bill denies making that call and so does his PA.'

'Who were the other people who knew about it?'

'I don't know.' Louise saw what I was after and didn't like it. 'I didn't, but Graham says that Joan wasn't making any secret of it. Anyone could have heard about it.'

'Including Nigel?' I forced myself to ask.

She flushed. 'Probably.' A pause. 'You really do have a vendetta against him, don't you?'

'Strong words, Louise. It's my job, remember? I work for the police.'

'Sorry.' But she didn't sound it, and there was an atmosphere between us at odds with the pleasure of the day. I went back to the subject of Tom.

'Do you think he invented that call?'

'No, but he might be scared that Bill murdered her,' Louise said defensively. 'After all, in theory Bill could have been hiding when Tom arrived at Nemesis, awaiting his chance. Loyalty comes first with Tom. He'd never voice any such suspicions.'

Why would Tom think that Bill might want to kill Joan, though? I was sure Pen would have her answer ready. Louise was tight-lipped, however, and we dropped the subject. We wandered around for a while and then I proposed to go back 'to work', although the array of cars here made that no hardship at all. She said she would prefer to find a place by the stream and wait for me with a good book. I had some breathing space for doing my job without having to feel guilty over darling Nigel.

Every age of cars from the twenties to the sixties was here, and such a mix of cars brings aficionados together in comradely fashion. Get a collection of classic Porsche owners together or MGs and there's a totally different atmosphere. In wider gatherings there's a general rejoicing that such wonders as classic cars exist for the common good.

At last I saw Nigel doing the rounds of the assembled beauties. It was still hard to think of his being bent on some criminal task on a summer's day such as this, with everyone wearing their best bibs and tuckers. Nevertheless I noticed he was inspecting a Sunbeam Tiger very closely and jotting down a few details.

'Hi,' I greeted him.

He didn't look in the least bit guilty. Again he looked pleased to see me, dammit. 'Is Louise here?' he asked.

'Somewhere around,' I said vaguely. 'I heard Clarissa wanted a word with me.'

He looked blank. 'Did she? You'll probably find her up on the terrace in her wheelchair. It's an electric one so she can drive up and down there giving herself what she calls a majestic overview of the proceedings. She likes it because people come up to talk to her without any effort on her part.'

I made my way over to the terrace, where I did indeed find her, complete with sunglasses, sun hat, and a book. Someone else was just leaving her, so I took the vacant chair at her side. Losing her memory or not, she remembered who I was, which was flattering.

'Ah, Mr Colby, how nice.'

I replied that it was equally nice to see her. 'I heard you wanted to speak to me.'

She looked puzzled. 'Did I? What about?'

'The 1935 Auburn?' I suggested.

'Do you have one? Lucky you.'

'No. I was looking for one when I came to see you and you were very helpful.'

'Oh yes,' she said triumphantly. 'I saw it one night. And dear Nigel tells me that you then found it in Gladden car park.'

'That wasn't hard after your tip.'

'I'm pleased to have been of help,' she said grandly. 'It's all very interesting,' she continued. 'That's why I wanted to see you. One of the car park guards who does odd jobs for me was telling me . . . I wanted to tell you . . .'

She looked puzzled.

'Tell me what?' I asked hopefully.

'That he likes crumpets. He came to tea one day.'

'Who? The guard?'

'No. Mr Shotsworth. Rob brought him. And of course, as you know, dear Nigel now owns part of the firm.'

FIFTEEN

The day brightened, as Louise and I looked forward to a peaceable afternoon. I left her chatting to Zoe while Rob and I went back to the car display where judging was in progress. I hadn't sought his company but Zoe thought it would be a good idea. Enough said. Anyway, I wanted to see whether my secret hopes of the Lagonda winning the Best in Show award were fulfilled. Len had crawled over it before I left Frogs Hill and I tried to give it the final spit and polish that the judges love. Whether it won or not, however, it was a good place to keep an eye on friend Nigel.

At last I might have the link I needed. Nigel had bought his way into Shotsworth Security and the probability was therefore that Mark Shotsworth had not been a stranger to him. As Nigel bounced up to me during the judging process, I was beginning to feel guilty for even suspecting him of any criminal activities, let alone murder. His rosy-cheeked beam hardly sat easily with a possible role in organized crime. But with the news of his co-ownership of Shotsworth Security, he was fitting that profile all too well. He might just need nailing down, although that was hard to contemplate on a day such as this when elderly friends were being wheeled out for a day's pleasure, golden lads and lasses sported in the sunshine and their elders chatted about the really important things of life, namely classic cars.

Oblivious to my suspicions, Nigel beamed at me. 'Hoping for the Best in Show, are you?'

'That'll be the day,' I said modestly. 'There are some good examples of *concours* cars here.'

He took up the theme with relish, and while he chatted on about Bentleys and Alvises, I wondered whether any of the cars he mentioned were destined to feature in some future list of Dave's missing classics.

'Clarissa said you'd bought into Shotsworth Security – is that right?' I asked when he ground to a halt.

'Bang on,' said Nigel enthusiastically. 'Great chap, Mark. Know him?'

'Not personally.' I was aware that my ribs were still aching from my encounter with his heavies.

'He's around somewhere.' Nigel looked vaguely around. 'Over there.' He pointed to a group of men huddling round an Austin Healey. 'The chap in grey cords.'

I'm not sure why I expected Mark Shotsworth to be a heavyweight macho guy, but I was wrong. He was tall, slightly built and looked as urbane as your average city gent.

'Want to meet him?' Nigel asked.

'Why not?' I was all for meeting 'great chaps'.

Nigel took me over to the group admiring the Austin Healey and detached Mr Grey Cords. 'Jack Colby, Marcus. Frogs Hill.'

'Of course.' Keen blue eyes with more than a hint of ice summed me up. 'Dave Jennings mentioned you,' he added.

He made me feel as though I was the villain while he himself was great chums with Dave. I put him down as the slippery sort that doesn't allow you a handle to find your way in. As no doubt he intended. We chatted briefly of Clarissa, of Harry Prince, and of Dave Jennings, and then he cut to the chase.

'You found that Auburn in Gladden.' He shook his head as in disbelief that such wickedness as stealing cars could still take place in this day and age. 'Bad deal that,' he continued. 'Pity we can't control who comes in and out of our car parks. On the stolen lists or not, there are so many clones and false IDs around nowadays, that there's no checking them all.'

'I'll have a word with Dave about improving the situation,' I assured him, taking pleasure in the way those icy blue eyes were flickering in annoyance. I could well imagine his urbanity giving way to macho ruthlessness.

'Good to meet you, Jack.' His tone suggested it wasn't as good as all that.

'And you.' I meant it. My brew was thickening nicely. With Nigel tied into Mark's operation, at least I had something to report to Dave, even if its place in Brandon's murder cases remained an open question. Satisfied, I returned to the Lagonda, where Louise and Zoe were now struggling to strap on the picnic basket. There was no sign of a Best in Show award. Some people have no taste.

And then there was Bill. Were my services still required on Angie's death? Not that I was going to give up, even if they weren't. Monday saw me back at Stour Studios and despite my best efforts I felt a metaphorical prison door clang behind me. There was little sign of life, although I knew filming must be proceeding in one of the studios – which meant Bill would be there and not amenable to discussions. At reception's direction, I went to the ops room in the studio building to double-check. I found no Bill, but to my relief Tom was back at his post, busily guarding the storyboards. No sign of digital influence anywhere. At least something was normal.

'They threw the book at me,' he told me gloomily, 'but released me without charge because they couldn't find enough evidence. And that's because,' he thumped the table viciously, 'I didn't kill either of them. You know what hurt me most of all, Jack? That anyone, even a flat-footed copper, could think I would harm a hair of Joan's head. After Bill, she was my dearest friend.'

'They might have thought you killed Angie and that Joan's death followed from that.'

He snorted. 'If everyone took a hammer to those they didn't like we wouldn't have a world food shortage. And as for killing Joan – do you think that's really likely?'

'No. That call you had, plus your second trip to the temple, were unfortunate though.'

'So what if I thought Bill was up there? Think I set out to kill them both, do you? Or that the idea of killing Joan just popped into my head when I found Bill wasn't there?'

He was red in the face with anger, not against me, but at the sheer lunacy of the idea, and I was in full agreement.

'You've been through a rough time, Tom.' I knew through bitter experience what a grilling by Brandon was like.

He relaxed a little. 'I tell you, Jack, they're not easily going to find out who did this, and so I might still be dragged back by the scruff of my neck.'

'Unlikely,' I said firmly. 'Look at it this way. Firstly, there's a cold-blooded murderer out there who killed two people; secondly there's the joker who poisons dogs and sends filthy anonymous notes, and thirdly the Auburn gets pinched. They must all link somehow but I can't see you being involved with all of them, so therefore it's none.'

'Thanks.' Tom's eyes strayed to the storyboards, perhaps as reassurance that a saner world was still to be found.

I abandoned Nigel at least temporarily as a suspect and went back to square one. 'Is there *anything* about Margot Croft or *Running Tides* that I need to know?'

I realized it was an impossible question when he looked at me helplessly. Give it one more spin, I thought. 'Who might still want revenge from those days, Tom, and for what? Margot's suicide?' I added.

Silence. Genuine bewilderment, I thought.

I tried to help out. 'Her family – her husband? He wasn't an actor but he could be here as an extra for *Dark Harvest*.'

A stirring of interest. 'Geoff Manning?'

The idea began to grow on me. I remembered what Joan had said about strong emotions festering.

'Did you meet him?'

'Sure. He was a nice chap.'

'How old would he be now?' I was busy calculating how much mileage there might be in this.

'He was older than Margot,' Tom said. 'Could have been mid-forties then – fifties now. But Bill knew him. He'd have recognized him.'

'There are an awful lot of extras and crew coming and going,' I pointed out. 'In costume and with different styles of hair and clothes, he might have escaped notice.' He could have retired or been forcibly retired, I thought feverishly. Maybe he lost his job.

At least it was a line to follow up. I'd look at the extras lists for a start, even though with evil intentions he could well be using a different name. The more I prodded at the theory the more possible it became. Why would Margot's husband want to kill Angie? Because, he might reason, Bill had been responsible for Margot's death, so he would kill Angie.

'Would there be a photo of Geoff around?' A long shot, but worth asking.

'Doubt it,' Tom grunted. 'Try the old celeb mags if you can get hold of them. Maisie might have some and she might have photos too.'

'Good idea.' I went straight over to the DOP's office and asked to see the pass lists. Frustratingly they showed nothing under Manning or Croft although there were one or two Geoffreys, which I noted down without much hope. Still, it was a beginning. Then I went to Roger's office to ask if Maisie was around. She wasn't, and when I explained what I was after, Roger didn't look convinced. Granted he must have other things on his mind – such as a film falling to pieces around him and a business that might soon be following suit.

'Check the pass lists,' he suggested.

'I've done so. No obvious lead. Do you think you would recognize him?'

'I guess not. I only met him a couple of times.'

'Would your wife have any photos of him?'

'I'll check that out.' Roger was looking more interested now.

'Did you keep in touch with Manning after the film?'

'Only to ask him to the premiere. Offer rejected as far as I recall, but I met him at the funeral.'

As yet anyway, my theory was holding water. Unfortunately I was outdone. When I reached the car park, there was the Queen of Theories herself.

'I've been thrown out again,' Pen told me cheerfully. 'Thought I'd wait here to net a couple of fish. You'll do.'

'Thanks. Why did you get ejected? Did you by any chance mention to Bill that he might have killed his wife?'

She looked hurt. 'Not yet. Joan Burton's death has thrown a spanner in the works. I've got to deal with that.'

So would her family and friends, I thought sadly. 'Are you planning to fit Bill up for Joan's murder too?'

'I like to do thorough research first,' she said primly. 'You know that. I'm doing some scuffling around on Joan.'

'And what have you dug up?'

'Not a lot. Divorced. No children. Husband beat her up.'

'No secret love affair with Bill? Or one with Roger perhaps?'

'I hadn't thought of that angle,' she said seriously. 'You're right. That's possible. Roger and Bill at daggers drawn over her.'

I groaned, hoping I hadn't played into her hands. She looked highly pleased with herself.

'How's Louise?' she asked.

'Staggering on without your kind attentions.'

'She's all right, is Louise.'

'I think so too.'

She looked at me pityingly. 'Careful, Jack. They're a world to themselves, these film and theatre folk. Step outside their magic circle and they can't cope with the big wide world.'

'Which of us can?'

She considered this light comment carefully. '*I* can.'

'Tell me your secret.'

'No secret about it. You know what Billy Shakespeare said? All the world's a blinking stage. Just build your own and invite suitable guests for the play of the moment.'

'Am I invited?'

She grinned. 'Any time, Jack.'

It took two days before I saw the photos. In the meantime I had tried my theory out on Louise and she had agreed it might hold water, given some backup. I was champing at the bit to get it moving, but the Internet and other sources had not yet produced anything on Geoffrey Manning's life after Margot.

'I've asked Graham and Chris if they can recall this Geoff Manning,' Louise told me, 'but Graham said they hardly knew him. He rarely came to the set and didn't socialize with them anyway. Chris asked around but no one heard from him after the funeral. They all moved on, naturally enough.'

Moved on. Geoff Manning may not have been able to do that, I thought. I had another burst of hope when Maisie brought the photos but they weren't good. She had also kept a scrapbook of the filming of *Running Tides* but Geoff had not figured in more than a couple of the photos included. The face was blurred and rang no bells with me or Louise. Nor unfortunately with the casting department. 'Might be one of ours,' I was told. 'Can't say for certain. It's an old photo.'

Which left Bill.

He bearded me in the canteen. 'I hear you've been busy,' he said accusingly. 'Geoff Manning, Roger tells me.'

'A possible line. Would you recognize him now if he was one of the extras here?'

'I would.'

That was something, I supposed.

'If,' he continued, 'I *saw* him. But you know how many of my extras I actually *see*? One in a hundred. I look at the shape of the group, the height, the girth, the clothes, the movement, but the faces? Rarely. They're there for a purpose, that's all. *Background*. Louise, now –' he passed a hand over his face – 'I see her as a character. Same with Ellie and Justin. Even Brian Tegg. But the other extras – even those playing silent characters, the Prince of Wales, von Ribbentrop, Mrs Simpson – I don't *see* them. Sorry, Jack, but that's the way it is.'

'You still want me to carry on?' I asked. 'The situation has altered since Joan's death.' I had to bear in mind that Bill himself must have been investigated by Brandon.

'Let me tell you something. I want this ugly business over,' Bill told me. 'The chances are one in a hundred you'll turn up anything, but because of that one, I won't take the risk. If you contribute anything at all, it will be worth every cent.'

'Even if it leads nowhere – as this Geoff Manning theory might?'

He thought for a moment. 'You know why I go to twenty takes sometimes? Because sometimes that's what it needs to get there. Nothing you can do about it. Just get there, Jack.'

Geoff Manning. The elusive husband who might or might not be amongst the *Dark Harvest* company. His target – the film, then the personal revenge. He was preying on my mind, almost as if he were mentally stalking me. Intangible, but out there.

Louise was worried about me and insisted after we had eaten that evening that we went for a walk along the River Stour. It was good, it was quiet, the dog roses were in blossom, a few ducks quacked annoyance as they were disturbed.

'Tell me, Jack,' Louise said at last. 'You can't go on brooding like this.'

'There's a cough in the engine,' I said, burrowing down to the root of my discontent.

'Tell me.'

'Joan. Her death doesn't fit. By my reckoning Angie was the end of the trail for our joker. I can only think Joan wasn't part of the killer's original plan, but was killed for something she knew. Or someone she knew. Geoff Manning, perhaps. She was certainly worried about something and yet if it was obvious, she wouldn't have hesitated to tell Bill or the police or even me.'

I hardly dared go further, but I had to face it. I had been assuming the killer's original plan had been a gradual build-up of the dirty tricks, then the theft of the car, climaxing in the death of Angie. So how did Joan present a threat? Identifying him as a killer? Possible but suppose identifying him would interrupt his *completion* of the plan?

Pen was way off the mark. I was convinced I was on the right trail now. The killer had steadily deprived Bill of what he cherished most, but it didn't end with Angie's death as revenge for his losing Margot.

Now Geoff Manning wanted something just as precious. Bill's own life. Bill had been the ultimate target all along.

SIXTEEN

I forced myself to sleep on this scary deduction. After all, if it was so blindingly obvious why hadn't it occurred to me earlier – and even more significantly why hadn't Bill considered that his death might be the final goal? There could be a chance that I had been suffering from an end-of-the-day fog and imagining bogeys that weren't there, in which case morning could present a more balanced view.

It did not do so. I was still convinced I was right, with all the terrifying implications. Louise announced her intention of rejoining the cast at the hotel for the Thursday night before filming ended on the Friday. Those two days would see the remaining scenes shot, including a big one for her.

'Is it a difficult one?' I asked as she didn't seem to be looking forward to it.

'No,' she admitted. 'It's just because it's the last chance to get things right before the final wrap.'

'And after that you'll disappear with a merry wave of a hand.'

She avoided looking at me. 'There's the wrap party to come that night.'

I knew about wrap parties but hadn't realized one would be coming up for *Dark Harvest* – especially in the circumstances. 'That means everything's finished? For the film,' I added, in case she thought I meant between us.

'No. It just marks the end of shooting. Then it's over to the editing team to do the hard work of fitting the scenes and shots into some semblance of what Bill is trying to achieve. The *mood* in other words. The cast returns to the cruel reality of the outside world.'

I refrained from bleating, 'And what about us?

'Bill's hosting the party at his home,' she continued. 'Roger's laying on buses to take us over there and bring us back.'

The last part sounded good, the first didn't. If my instinct was right, it would play into the joker's hands – and increasingly I was giving a name to him: Geoff Manning. 'Does it have to be at Bill's home?'

'Bill has spoken, and it shall be. My guess is that he's deliberately sticking his neck out. The show must go on at all costs, and be seen to do so. Normally at a wrap party everyone lets their hair down.'

'Dancing on tables?' I asked dubiously.

'And drunk under them.' She made a face. 'I hate them, but I have to go. It sounds worse than it is, though. Usually once I'm there, it somehow works. This time, though, it wouldn't be right to have that sort of do. Bill and Maisie have planned a communal dinner and then they're showing the rough cuts of *Dark Harvest* in his cinema in their correct order, so that we can see that *something* at least has been achieved.'

'Has it? Are you happy with it?'

'I never am, but that goes with the territory. But I have faith in Bill – he could edit a stone statue into giving a performance of emotional depth.'

I wondered whether to point out the risks, but Louise wasn't stupid. She must see them. Even so . . . 'Has Bill considered that the announcement of a plan like this could be a red rag to a bull?'

'Yes,' she said. 'He has. I think that's what he wants. Jack, I'm scared.'

I woke up to an empty bed again on Thursday, because Louise had had a dawn start, and by the amount I already missed her I realized she was fast becoming part of my life. I wasn't sure of the wisdom of this as I've never seen myself hitched to any kind of star, but then Louise was different. Not a 'celeb', but a woman with a job that she did well and a dream that was all her own. I supposed I was more or less in the same position, but without the 'star' tag. The question was: whose dream would come first if they met head-on?

I had a clear agenda for the day. I had to talk to Bill and fast. If he was the target and the cast and much of the crew would be dispersing after the wrap party, the killer would have precious little time to lose – and so therefore would I. Bill

however was going to be pinned down to a film set, and wasn't
going to welcome distractions such as chatting to me. Tough.
He would have no choice.

I drove over to Stour Studios once more, marvelling that
so much could be going on in such a relatively small industrial
area, surrounded by a rural scene to tempt Constable. I
reminded myself that currently I was part of it, and asked Jane
to get a message to Bill that I needed to see him urgently. I
watched the runner depart on her mission, from which she
returned unexpectedly quickly.

'Bill says wait in his office.'

The word had been spoken. I went over to the farmhouse
and tried to be patient once I got there, but looking down on
the garden where Angie had died made it hard. Pen's daft
theory jumped around in my mind. Bill kill Angie? No way.
I'd been with him when we found her and that shock and grief
had been genuine. I remembered reading how one should play
being drunk on stage or film: don't stagger around all over
the place, but do one's utmost to stand still. That's how I knew
Bill wasn't putting on a show for me. He had gone inside
himself, not wailed his grief to the heavens.

In a way Pen and I were both right, however. There was a
story here somewhere, and Bill was my first priority. It was
thirty minutes before he arrived and I wondered again how a
man so relatively slight and not particularly tall could convey
so much energy and strength. He wasn't hurrying, and yet he
gave the impression once again that Montgomery had suddenly
joined me. I almost saluted.

'What have you got?' he barked. 'Make it important.'

'It is.' I explained my reasoning and like all good generals
he listened, without reacting.

When I had finished, he said calmly, 'I take that on board,
but it doesn't wash.'

'It does if Geoffrey Manning is behind it.'

A long pause, while he weighed this up. 'I doubt that. You're
working on the premise that *Running Tides* or Margot has
something to do with what's been happening here. I tell you
it's coincidence that Angie and Joan worked on that film. Angie
barely exchanged two words with Joan let alone Margot. Both

film and tragedy took place over ten years ago. Stick to your cars, Jack. That's what you're good at.'

I felt like a schoolboy slinking out of the headmaster's study but at least my 'caning' hadn't been too severe. He'd thought about my theory and rejected it. I believed he was wrong to do so, but I could do no more where he was concerned. I'd have to make my own way round the problem.

He called out to me as I left: 'Come to the wrap party tomorrow night, Jack. You'll see I'm right.'

I was all too afraid that I would see something rather different. I went over to the canteen where, finding myself alone apart from the staff busy chatting in the kitchen, I put through a call to DI Brandon.

At least he too listened to what I had to say. He didn't reject my theory either. Indeed he sounded almost relieved as he pointed out that Sissinghurst wasn't in his policing area. I persevered with a plea that it would be a good plan to have police in attendance. He said he would pass on my advice – and make some enquiries about Geoffrey Manning.

Had there been sarcasm in Brandon's voice? For once I didn't think so. Two murders on his patch in the same company had achieved what one could not.

Encouraged, I then rang Dave. 'Nigel Biddington,' I began. 'Any news?'

I'd reported to Dave on Monday about Fun Day at Marsham. The fact that Nigel brought an old lady with him as cover didn't rule out a role as spotter for some scam. I had added that he'd spent a lot of time observing cars. Dave had pointed out that it was a car show. That I had granted, but maintained that Nigel was ideally placed with his links to both insurance and cars. Dave had given his usual grunt and said he'd bear it in mind. Today he seemed more interested, however.

'Still got him down for murder?' he asked.

'Way down the possible list. I'll keep an eye on him at the wrap though.'

'Eh?'

I explained what that meant plus my theory about Geoff

Manning, and Dave listened more intently than I thought he would. 'What are you planning to do about him?'

'Stop him, I hope.'

Dave didn't laugh. 'Whether it's Biddington or Manning, there's a man with a gun and nasty habits out there, Jack. Get some kit to wear. I'll sign the order for it. If it *is* Biddington, remember he's killed two people already. If it's this Geoff Manning, who's harboured a grudge all these years, he's a maniac, which means if you stand in his way, he'll blast a path right through you.'

'Anything more?' I was taken aback by the seriousness with which Dave was suddenly taking this. If *he* believed it was a real threat . . .

'Nothing more that Brandon and I can do. That's the problem. Get that gear, Jack. You're on the payroll again.'

I hardly saw Louise during the rest of that day. I took Dave up on his advice to get myself bulletproof protection, which took so long on the Thursday that I returned to the studios to find that filming was over and Louise had left for the hotel.

It was a different picture when I arrived on Friday. Everyone looked under pressure – not unusual of course, but today there was a sense of time running out. Louise made a brief foray into the canteen and warned me they were running late, but her scene was called for two p.m. It turned out it had been shot much earlier in the production but Bill had decided he wasn't happy with it, and needed another go. The 'go' took all the afternoon and at six p.m. he was still not happy with it. Yet another take.

I'd had no calls from Brandon or Dave so I was forced to leave matters in their hands, cursing cuts and protocol and everything else that stopped them from being able to put a twenty-four-hour guard on Bill and indeed on everyone going to this blasted wrap party. Including me. For Bill, organizing a Custer's Last Stand was all very well, but it was the men who might go down with him that he should think about.

I drove myself over to Sissinghurst early to give me a chance to look round the gardens and house before the guests arrived. I was somewhat peeved that Louise told me she'd elected to join the bus group with her mates once the shooting was over and she had changed into party gear. But I could see her point. If ever solidarity was called for, it would be this evening. If Geoff Manning was present, however, his mind would be focused only on killing Bill Wade, not on the togetherness of the company. How could Bill not see it added up? A series of hits against the film, the loss of his precious car, followed by the far worse loss of his precious wife and his own life in danger.

Now that the joker had taken on solid form, it helped focus me on what Manning might be planning. There was always the chance that I would be wrong, but I couldn't afford to take any risk. Was it just Bill he was after, or was it the film and everyone connected to it? I pondered the frightening possibility that Manning might intend to burn down the whole house, or more likely the marquee where everyone would be eating, or the cinema. If the film was his target, Bill would have all the rushes there tonight, but I comforted myself that in these days of digitalization there would be copies somewhere even though he shot on film. If Manning's target was the film, moreover, he'd had plenty of opportunities to sabotage it without waiting for tonight. If he was going for the cast and crew, on the other hand, then the marquee or the cinema in the house would be his best chance.

But if he was after Bill . . . anywhere, any time, any place. Manning had only to wait for the opportunity. No, that didn't figure. He would want to cut Bill down in his moment of glory. Bombs? I thought uneasily. Manning had had plenty of time to plan for such a scheme. Mass murder by food poisoning? No, not certain enough. Bus or car brakes tampered with? Nor would that be certain to achieve his objective.

I took the Alfa to Sissinghurst. No risking nasty tricks in the Lagonda or my noble Gordon-Keeble. There were to my surprise and relief two uniformed police at Bill's gates. Good work on Brandon's behalf. Although with that thought came its counterbalance: he must really think something was afoot. My passes were carefully scrutinized.

Mayden Manor was buried deep in the countryside behind Sissinghurst on the Cranbook side. It was in the Weald, a gentler area of Kent than the Downs, with farmhouse and mills and red tiled houses tucked away almost invisibly among the trees. I could not see the house itself from the gates, but as I turned into the forecourt I saw a striking medieval Wealden house, with red brick additions from Tudor and maybe later dates. A hotchpotch of architecture that worked, as so often with Kentish buildings. I could see why it had appealed to Bill.

In the evening sun it seemed impossible that I was really thinking in terms of its being blown up or set on fire, or of anything more violent than the popping of champagne corks. As I drove up to the forecourt, I saw to my surprise that the Auburn was parked right in front of the main entrance to the house. The creamy paint glowed in the sunshine, seeming to dare anyone to defile its beauty. Was it there just temporarily? I doubted it. To me it had the hallmarks of a Bill Wade gesture of defiance. Tempting the bull, however, was by no means always a good plan. Bulls were noticeable; our joker was not.

I parked the car, checked in with Maisie who was super-intending the caterers and then went straight into the grounds. The police and two security guards would have checked them of course, and the house too, but these gardens seemed to me the most vulnerable place if there was going to be trouble. In the setting sunlight they looked at peace, however. On the main lawn there was a huge marquee and a subsidiary service area. Tables were already set up inside, and I could see staff dashing around making last-minute arrangements for the seventy or eighty guests that I'd been told were expected. There were also half a dozen uniformed security guards around it.

I walked round the perimeter of the garden, more to satisfy myself than with much hope of finding anything suspicious. It took some time, as it was more a small estate than a mere garden. A brick wall, eight foot or so high, surrounded it; there was woodland on the western and southern sides, plus a stretch of trees inside the wall which ran parallel to it for part of the way. It wouldn't be thick enough to hide a killer for long, although the shrubbery on the eastern side could easily do so.

I was assuming that the potential killer would be trying to get in from outside the walls, but it was probable, alas, that he would be amongst those seventy or eighty guests. Not good. Any one of them could 'smile and smile and be a villain' as

Shakespeare realized. I wondered what the Bard would have made of the Bill Wade plot so far.

Maisie had said I was welcome to tour the house, and I took her up on it. As in Syndale Manor a semi-basement room had been converted to a home cinema, where the unedited *Dark Harvest* would obviously be shown. The living area of the house and bedrooms added up to a pleasantly relaxed atmosphere, which was surprising in view of its owner's taut energy. Angie must have had more going for her than my brief brushes with her suggested. Attics? Again, as the killer was in all probability known to everyone here, there would be no reason for him to hide. And yet I checked what I could, telling myself it was a precaution, although in fact it merely meant I could persuade myself I was doing something to help in a situation where – if I faced it starkly – we were all effectively impotent. As Manning was no doubt gloating over at this very moment.

At eight o'clock the two buses arrived and duly disgorged their passengers, and it was then I felt the first real chill of apprehension. What had been a mental exercise in trying to second guess the killer's intentions had become an all too real situation. I saw an added touch of defiance in that Bill had, presumably with Nigel's collaboration, arranged for the other three classics to join the Auburn. The front of Mayden Manor was glorified by the Bentley, the Fiat and the Horch, although amid them the Auburn reigned supreme.

Louise looked fabulous in a short silvery evening dress. I was so used to seeing her in thirties gear or in casual clothes that to see her in her full glory was breathtaking. Eleanor on the other hand, in a skimpy brown dress with too many ruffles, looked like a particularly cross hen.

As we all moved to the lawns, the women's dresses and party food and champagne livened up what could have been an awkward evening. Talk seemed to centre on the future and not on the traumas of the past few weeks. I watched Bill carefully as he circulated. He seemed preoccupied, but as the evening progressed he looked more relaxed, even – to my horror – standing up to make a speech at the end of the excellent meal. Not a good idea. I expected a shot to ring out at any moment with such a clear target.

Nothing happened. I didn't know whether to be relieved or whether this merely raised the tension level. I took them alternately, relaxed when coffee and liqueurs were circulating, then felt my muscles tensing as we left for the cinema.

'The film won't make much sense to you at this stage,' Louise warned me. 'It's nowhere near finished.'

I was almost lulled into relaxation myself, by the time the lights dimmed for the film show. That quickly came to an abrupt end. I'd been expecting the film to begin with the 1935 Jubilee Ball. What we actually saw with the opening shot was First World War fighter planes flying over fields of poppies.

There was a general gasp, someone cried out, but most of us sat in frozen bewilderment. Bill lost his cool. 'What the hell is this?' he yelled at the unfortunate operator.

That at least was clear, as we had only recently seen this shot. It was the opening of *Running Tides*.

'Some mistake,' Louise muttered to me, as Bill and the operator struggled in the projection room to get the right film running. I had a renewed fear that the *Dark Harvest* rushes had indeed been destroyed, but apparently not because its first scene duly appeared, with the arrivals of the cars for the Syndale Manor ball.

'I hope you're right about its being a mistake,' I replied.

She stiffened. 'The joker again?'

'Yes.'

It was clear to me that Geoffrey Manning had thrown down the gauntlet. It was his open declaration of war. The question was what would come next.

I was in a state of jitters as the film progressed, but nothing more happened. Not until after midnight when the party broke up, and the buses were ready to leave. And then, just as I was beginning to think it was all over, Nigel came rushing into the house and made straight for me.

'Trouble, Jack. The *cars*.'

I was out there in the forecourt like a flash. Bill's gesture of defiance had been noted. The Auburn's creamy paint now had a gaudy decoration. The word 'whore' had been painted in bright purple across the bonnet.

Amazingly, Bill took this in his stride, merely demanding

of police and security guards what they thought they were paid for. It was his very quietness that made me nervous. I was well aware that this was just the warm-up. Manning was not going to be catching the bus back home.

'Shall I stay, Jack?' Louise asked.

'No, pet. I'd be worrying about you as well as Bill.'

She took that. 'But you . . .'

'The police are here,' I said lightly. 'Plus the guards.' The extra security guards round the marquee had now left, but there were still two remaining, plus the two police and every security light and alarm yet known to man.

Louise didn't believe me, but I managed to persuade her to go. Everyone went, save for Bill, myself and our security. Plus, I feared, Geoff Manning.

'You go too, Jack,' Bill told me.

'As if,' I said briefly, and for once he didn't argue with me.

I checked with the police that the same number of guests had left as had arrived, and tried to believe their assurance that this was the case. Manning was clever enough to have sorted that one out, however. I walked out on to the terrace where I could see the marquee, now empty of all but the bare tables waiting to be picked up the next day. Maybe that was when Manning would come, I thought, and already I could feel the adrenalin dying down inside me. I roused myself. That would be what Manning was counting on.

'No sign of anything yet, Jack,' Bill said neutrally as we walked back into his living room.

'You call that *Running Tides* switch nothing? Or that attack on your Auburn?'

'Guess not, but it's good. It means that's his last shot. No murder in mind.'

'It's not over yet.'

A pause. 'You still thinking Geoff Manning is going to come?'

'Yes.'

He sighed. 'Whoever does come, it won't be him. I checked him out. He died three years ago.'

SEVENTEEN

We sat in our comfortable armchairs in silence, Bill and I. I wished I could have believed that the storm clouds had passed. There was a police car in the forecourt, containing one constable. Another one stood at the gate. Two security guards had replaced the earlier ones for the night patrol, and the house had been minutely searched to their satisfaction. Bill had told me enough to convince me that Geoffrey Manning was indeed no longer in the picture – whatever the picture might be. No switch of identities or false funerals in this case. The information had shaken me, but not to the point where I could shut up shop and go happily to bed. Either my fears had been one gigantic fantasy or I had taken a wrong turn in my thinking. I hoped it was the former, but every gut feeling told me it was the latter.

At one thirty Bill told me that he was going to get some sleep; I could do what I wanted. There was a bed ready for me upstairs, third door on the right, or I could stay here with the whisky bottle, or I could lay me down and sleep on the floor outside his door in the good old-fashioned way if I preferred. I opted for staying put – without the whisky bottle. Why stay? Obstinacy perhaps, or a feeling that if and when our killer arrived I needed to be on the spot, not lying vulnerably in bed.

After Bill left there was no temptation for me to sleep. I went over the evening again and again in my mind. Not everyone had attended the party, as the last day's shooting had not included a full crew and extras. I thought of the two incidents of the evening: the intrusion of *Running Tides* into the film and the paint on the Auburn. There had been – and must still be – some joker in our pack. So where was he now?

It was a scary feeling that he was around *somewhere*. In all my oil company days I'd had experience of being in the midst of the desert and yet knowing that danger was lurking near.

Even though the security lights blazed out fiercely at the slightest move and we were safely indoors, I felt prickles at the back of my neck, as if I were a particularly stupid mouse who had been lured into a trap that would shortly slam shut. I saw a security guard passing, but it gave me little confidence. Shotsworth Security? I wondered. Was Nigel in on this deal too? He'd been present this evening, but I had seen him drive out in the Bentley. He'd wanted to take Louise with him, but she chose to go on the bus with the others. Perhaps she preferred that to Nigel. Had he bargained on that, and had not in fact left at all? All sorts of scenarios buzzed through my mind.

Except the one that exploded outside.

No security lights flashed on.

Only *noise*.

Noise so deafening that it shot me out of the armchair, rushing to the windows to look out into the darkness of the night. Nothing to be seen. Only heard, as a woman's voice magnified a thousand times shrieked out endlessly in desperation:

'Bill, Bill! Come to me. Come.'

Intermingled with it were snatches of music, music I remembered. We'd heard it earlier this evening. It wouldn't stop. It assaulted the eardrums, it tore at the nerves, blocking out reason. It brought Bill bursting back into the room with white face and staring vacantly. He wasn't focusing on me, and as he clutched at me and missed I thought he would collapse. He didn't, but stood there, swaying in a trance.

'It's Margot,' he whispered.

No need to ask more. There was only one Margot. And all along she had been the missing character in this crazy script.

'Margot,' he repeated, as the racket continued, lights blazing out. If the guards and police were shouting, I wouldn't have heard them.

I tried to shake Bill out of his stupor, shouting over the din. 'What is it?'

I could feel him trembling, not with fear, but with disbelief. *'Running Tides,'* he said. 'The last scene.'

I remembered now. Ramble, Margot's code name in the film, was in prison, calling on the man she loved, the British fighter pilot Bill Brackley.

'Stop it, Jack,' he whispered as I rushed for the door. '*Stop* her.'

Without working out what the hell I was going to do, I ran over the terrace and down to the gardens, as the security lights blazed out. The noise was coming from the woods on the far side of the boundary wall. Or was it this side, where the line of trees ran in front of it?

I reached them at the same time as one of the two policemen. 'Over there,' I panted. I could hear it nearby. At the same time he was yelling at me and pointing in a different direction. The security lights didn't reach through these trees but we rushed for the wall – anything to stop that *noise*. I wasn't looking down as I ran over the uneven ground, and I tripped on something. I nearly threw up.

It was a body. The policeman was waving frantically for his mate, who was just catching up with us. I fell to my knees to see what had happened. It was a security guard – probably the one I had seen from the house. He was alive, thank heavens, groaning and even conscious, although my hands were sticky with blood.

'Where is he?' I asked sharply. 'Ahead of us? Over the wall? Behind us?'

I thought he couldn't speak but his lips managed to form one word: 'Woman.'

Woman? Dear God, what was this? Thoughts raced through my mind. Could it be a woman who had killed Angie and Joan? A woman had rung Tom. A woman had driven the Auburn. No time to think back. Think forward. Do, not think. The police were giving first aid and calling for back-up, the other security guard had arrived. I rushed to get over that wall to the source of the noise. One of the PCs was over first, but then my brain clicked into gear before I followed him.

Where the hell was Bill? If one security guard was on the ground, the other with him, and two police here, Bill must be on his own. Whatever that racket was, the joker knew Bill wouldn't be going in search of it. Its aim was to lure me and anyone else that might be around out of the house. Whoever this woman was, she wanted Bill all to herself.

To kill him.

'Back,' I yelled to the PC still with me, leaving the wounded security guard with his mate. I was already racing towards the house, my breath coming in gasps. I realized the PC had hesitated, so I had to shout back, 'Bill Wade's alone there.' More time lost while I did so.

I didn't wait to see whether he was following me. I just hoped to heaven that he was. I could take on any woman I reckoned, but one with a gun was a different matter. I needed the advantage of surprise. I had to hope that Bill was still in the living room and thanks to the angle at which I was approaching the terrace, with the marquee shielding me, I might be out of their sight line if the woman was already with him. I might be able to think of something. But suppose I didn't? I pushed that thought away. Of course I would. At times like this, reason isn't always to the fore.

As we reached the house, reason obliged, and I clutched at it. There was a way into the house at the side of the building, *if* it was open. The killer would be expecting any relief operation to be through the French windows, not through a door from the house. I looked round to see where my cavalry was. At first I thought I was it, but thankfully it showed up. The young PC had caught me up as I pushed my way into the house. 'What on earth is this door doing unlocked?' I muttered fleetingly. Had Bill's killer come this way? Could be. And where were they? Was Bill still in the living room? Had he been frogmarched somewhere else? Was he already dead? I cut through all this. Find him first. Try the living room.

Then I heard the sound of voices. They were there. Voices raised. I could hear Bill's. I could hear a woman's husky voice too. Was it the same that had been calling out *'Bill, Bill, come to me'*? Was it Margot's?

I tried to cling to sanity. How could this be Margot Croft herself? I remembered at last the Victorian murderer who had flashed through my mind earlier. He'd killed the actor/manager William Terriss at his stage door. He just waited patiently for his quarry to come along and stabbed him to death. *In revenge.* This woman was the same. She had a plan and calmly executed it bit by bit. Somewhere there had been a pattern, which I had not picked up.

This woman really did not care if we arrived provided that

Bill was dead. Was she planning to kill herself too? Another suicide? I was advancing all the while step by step. The woman's back was to me as I pushed the door open a little way. I could see Bill. He was facing her, as though he'd always known her. I couldn't read his face. Montgomery meets Rommel face to face. No time for crazy thoughts now. She was chatting almost conversationally to Bill.

'Never me, never me, always you, Bill.'

She must have known that people would soon come so there must be something she wanted to tell him, part of the plan. Now *I* needed a plan. Who was this woman, her back to me and clad in a long bedraggled skirt? That voice . . .

'She killed herself because of you, Bill. You took her from me and everything else too.'

The gun was trained on Bill. If she intended to kill herself and saw me, I stood a chance. But if she saw me and Bill was her sole target, she would shoot him first before I could grab her. It would be blindingly stupid for me even to try it. And then I remembered the bulletproof gear I wore.

'Are you armed?' I whispered to my cavalry.

'No.'

Silly of me to have asked. Budget cuts. 'I'll go then. You follow.'

My hand felt sweaty on the knob as I pushed the door fully open. No going back now. Dear God, was I mad? Too late to change my mind. The cavalry was behind me, at least.

As she heard me and turned just fractionally Bill leapt forward, bless him. I heard a shot as I threw myself forward and bore her to the ground. The gun went off again, but wherever the shot went it wasn't into any of us. As I gripped flailing arms, Bill tore the gun away. The cavalry and I had her in our grasp and pulled her over on to her back.

I froze. Chalk-white face plastered like a painted clown's with heavy lipstick, massive blue eyeshadow, a long brown wig, skirt, jacket, but no full breasts. No woman. This was a man. And one who had been with us all the time. No gentle face now. Why had I never noticed that his eyes were so completely mad?

It was Chris Frant.

*　　*　　*

Stand on a tower in the middle of a maze and look out over the pattern of the hedges below and you have an overview of all the little innocents trying to find the right way round it. Be one of those innocents yourself, and you'd be just as adrift as I felt. In theory I could have put all those indications of a warped personality together. Mazes have plans behind them. Work out what it is and you're there. Or should be. Plenty of innocents are thwarted at the last hedge before the centre.

Bill and I sat in his study as the night hours ticked on. We'd been checked over by the first-aiders, given our preliminary statements, ignored everyone's recommendations for shock relief and assured the police we'd be here the next morning when the SOCOs returned. Not a murder scene, thank heavens, but attempted murder provided that the security guard pulled through. The police were a new gang to me, being in a different area to Charing, and it was a relief to find I was actually 'known' to their computer because of my work for Dave Jennings. It saved the hassle of explaining how I came to be wearing bulletproof gear.

Neither Bill nor I could face sleep. Something had to be said between us before we could do so, and it had to start with Bill.

'That racket,' Bill said eventually. '*Running Tides*, of course. He must have taken it from the film and made his own recording of that speech. Easy enough for him to get hold of it from the studios given enough time.'

'And that he had. Over ten years.' The police had already found an intricate sound system rigged up in the trees outside the wall, with small powerful speakers and an amplifier. They were high up, where the patrolling guards would not have noticed them. They would have been searching at ground level. Bill told me that Chris had driven over early that day to set the system up, then gone back to the studios, joined the bus to attend and leave the party – and once back at the hotel driven back again to stage his coup.

'He wanted to tell me the whole damn story before he shot me,' Bill said with a kind of wonder. 'He was convinced Margot would have loved him if it hadn't been for me. He was an extra; I doubt if she'd even have noticed him.'

'I remember his telling me he auditioned for the lead in *Running Tides* without success.'

'Yeah. He brought that grudge up too. I had no idea. Wouldn't have stood a chance.'

Like Terriss's killer, I thought, who believed Terriss had ruined his stage career. 'He blamed you for that?'

'Yeah. And for the fact that his wife walked out on him last year. My fault too, apparently. He tried for Robert Steed in *Dark Harvest* too. Another black mark against me. If he did, the news didn't reach me. He'd have been ruled out right away.'

'Because of his acting?'

'No. There's just something about star quality that stands out, and he hasn't got it.'

I thought of all the non star players in this world, and of how the Bill Wades brush them aside. Unfair to blame the Bill Wades though. They have to reach for the best. Others find their own level, their own achievements, but once in a while there's one who doesn't. And Chris was one of them.

'Margot Croft was the starting point though?'

'Margot. Yeah. You know, when he was there, in the room, he really thought he was Margot. That caricature of a face. He was wearing identical clothes to those she wore in *Running Tides*. Who'd have thought it? He looked so normal. And I thought I was a good judge of character.'

'Is he clinically deranged, do you think?'

'Not to him. Pure logic, the whole damn charade. He told me calmly how he planned to take everything from me because I'd driven Margot to suicide, and before I died I'd know exactly how he felt.'

I'd been working on the right lines then, but the thought gave me no comfort.

'He said he disliked Louise because she had taken Margot's place as lead actor. Next he decided to blow my wife away just as I'd taken Margot from him. And then it would be my turn. But Joan . . . I couldn't understand that, and told him so. He looked at me as though I was the crazy one. She'd guessed, he said. So naturally he had to kill her or she would spoil his plan for killing me. He strangled her, then returned with Graham to have a witness to finding the body. He was quite matter of fact about it. He was sorry, but it had to be done.'

'Would he have killed himself after you?' I felt cold at heart.

'Who knows the answer to that? I doubt if he did.' He paused. 'It's gone five, Jack. Feel like a kip? I guess I'll just stay here. You?'

'Me too.'

'We'll catch up sometime, Jack. A few days maybe. I've some thinking to do.'

My mobile was ringing. Louise was frantic with worry. The first news bulletin had been that there had been a shooting at a house in the Weald of Kent, the second that it was the home of film director Bill Wade. I assured her that Bill and I were safe, but that everything else would have to wait until the police had done with us.

I could hear a sob of relief in her voice. 'I'll be at Frogs Hill, waiting,' she said.

That sounded good. The police had come back at dawn which was precisely thirty minutes after Bill and I had decided to call it a day and nod off. They had left us alone for a while because they were at work in the woods, and didn't move into the house until an hour later. The security guard had come out of surgery, was in intensive care and expected to make a full recovery. Good news there, then. Something to cling on to, while Bill and I still floundered in a morass of whys and might-have-beens. We left the police to their job, and some time later that morning we gave them formal statements in the incident van. The van looked out of place drawn up by the Auburn, still defiantly parked outside the front entrance, its purple paint addition still in evidence. Bill didn't give it a second glance. The first was enough. 'Time for that later,' he said briefly.

I thought I should ring Dave before I left Mayden Manor. He was at his desk, Saturday or not. 'Heard the news, Jack. Bit of a scrap, eh? Glad you're OK. So's Brandon.'

My stock had indeed risen! 'Give me Mark Shotsworth's crowd any day,' I tried to joke. 'At least I know what sex I'm dealing with.' That white mask of make-up had haunted what

little sleep I had had, and it wasn't going to go away for quite
a while.

'At least it wasn't Nigel Biddington.'

'How's that going?' I'd almost forgotten that he'd been one
of my suspects for murder.

'Big time. We're doing a stake-out. Let you know what
happens.'

Stake-out of what, I wondered, but hadn't the energy to ask
him. 'Thanks for your help, Dave.'

'Over what?'

'The bulletproof gear.'

'I'd forgotten about that. Useful, was it?'

'Turned me into a cross between Superman and Bonnie
Prince Charlie. I felt safer going in.'

'That's what budgets are for. Speak to you later on the
Biddington front, Jack. You're going to love it.'

I didn't give a second thought to Dave's gleeful quip. I
wasn't in the mood. Nevertheless coming back to the security
of Frogs Hill was bliss. The sound of a newly tuned engine
in the Pits, and the sight of Zoe's clapped-out Fiesta were
comforting. I parked the Alfa, but saw no sign of Louise's.
My spirits dropped even further. Had she given up on me?
The farmhouse felt empty and lonely as I walked in.

But I was wrong. Louise was there. She told me her car
was being given a loving once-over by Len and Zoe. All was
suddenly right with the world again. I should have told her
all about what had happened. I should have told her how much
I loved her. I should have shown her how much.

I did none of these three things.

Instead, I fell asleep.

I seemed to be on automatic pilot for the next few days. On
my own. Louise had a job in London and I had a general
feeling of waiting in the wings for something to happen on
stage. There were a lot of comings and goings with the police
both at Charing and Sissinghurst in whose areas Angie and
Joan's murders had taken place. I was questioned so closely
I half expected to be arrested myself for attacking Chris, but
this didn't happen. The guard was already off the critical list.

Chris had been formally charged but whether his mental condition would enable him to stand trial or not was doubtful. I'd
even had to pay a visit to the Studios, which seemed full of
ghosts without Louise and the cast of *Dark Harvest*. Editing
was in progress, and all was quiet as I walked around.

There was of course also Pen Roxton. I opened Wednesday's
Graphic to find that this time I was the hero of her fantasy.
I read the article with some trepidation, expecting to find
heavy hints that Bill was the real guilty party rather than
the poor misguided actor. Fortunately Pen hadn't thought of
that one – yet.

I rang her to congratulate her – not quite the right word
perhaps but it would do – on the story, and she seemed pleased
to hear from me.

'Great,' she said. 'Now show your gratitude. I've dug out
all I can about Chris Frant and his sad quest for stardom and
all that, plus his crush on Margot Croft.'

'He's been charged, Pen,' I said patiently. 'You can't use
it.' Bang, the trap shut.

'So now you can tell me the *real* story, darling.'

'You've got it,' I said through clenched teeth. Big mistake
to ring Pen about *anything*.

'Come on now. You're hiding something. I can smell it a
mile off.'

'*I-am-not-hiding-anything.*'

'Someone is,' she said brightly and rang off. Two minutes
later she rang again. 'Girlfriend going strong, Jack?'

'Yes, no thanks to you.'

'She there with you?'

'In London. Got a job.'

'Casting, actually.'

'Casting for what?' I asked blankly.

'Haven't you heard? Major series coming up on TV, Moore's
Esther Waters. Being shot somewhere up north. She's tipped
as hot favourite for Esther.'

Louise hadn't told me.

EIGHTEEN

A nd then Bill rang. I hadn't seen him since the Saturday it all happened, four days ago. 'Feel like coming over, Jack? We can meet at a pub if you can't face Mayden Manor again, or eat here if you can.'

I was about to choose the pub, but then had second thoughts. If I visited the manor again, it might help put the whole experience into perspective, instead of its being a memory from which I shied away. If it wasn't still a crime scene, and if Bill was happy to stay there, why should I object?

Without the marquee, the gardens looked altogether different. Mayden Manor was a peaceful country house albeit with massive security – but all such houses needed that nowadays. This was a fairly remote dwelling but I reflected that even so the sound of that noise in the night must have had some neighbours complaining, not to mention quite a few sheep shocked into running for their lives.

We settled on lunch in the garden. With a beer in front of us, a salmon salad at its side and raspberries to follow, this seemed to be what summer was all about. No maniacs running around here.

'So,' I began at last, after we'd covered all the small talk. 'Why did you ask me over?'

'Let's kick off with this. You saved my life, Jack. I reckon I owe you.'

'Pay me with the Auburn,' I joked.

He laughed. 'It's cleaned up OK, and I can just about afford the respray it needs. I don't feel the same about it, Jack. It's an unlucky car.' He paused. 'I'll settle up for your time spent on my behalf, Jack, but I owe you more than that. An explanation. I want to tell you about Margot Croft.'

I was instantly alert. At last. 'Margot and Chris Frant?'

'No. The real Margot Croft, her life, her death – and me. OK by you?'

I nodded, and he began.

'I knew the lady long before *Running Tides*. I'd seen her in her early movies, even directed her once in a bit part. There was something about her – you ever see that Griffith movie *Broken Blossoms*? The original not the remake. Margot reminded me of Lilian Gish. She didn't need words to act, she used herself. She was dedicated, like Gish. She wasn't just a good actress, she was, well, a mood, a dream, in herself, something you couldn't quite grasp, beyond direction, but it left you trying to pin it down. She was delicate, yet had this strength that could carry her past that quality into something mighty glorious. Opposites: fragile; strong; inspiring love; inspiring hate; unselfish; selfish; giving love; taking it. All those. Except she never hated anyone in her life.

'When I first directed her,' he went on, 'I knew little about her offstage. I knew she was married, even met Geoff quite a few times, but I was solely interested in her performance. I'd had a bad first marriage, and wasn't looking for anything permanent, or even mildly serious by the time I was looking to cast *Running Tides*. I'd wanted to direct it ever since the script landed on my desk. It was based on this short novel, based on a true story and written by the head of intelligence involved. You've probably heard it was based on a short novel published in the early twenties in a magazine – not Pulitzer Prize material, but it had potential and I could see what I might be able to do with it to turn it into something special. I remembered Margot Croft and that was it. I knew I had to have her play Ramble.

'I don't know which was the first obsession, the film or Margot. Did I have this great idea about the movie and fitted Margot into it, or was it the other way about? I reckon it was Margot first and the dream of the movie grew out of her. Whichever, we were in bed together within a few days. After that days and nights seemed to become one, feeding each other. Sleeping with her, loving her, seemed part of the vision for the movie. I don't like that word, but what could replace it? Only dream maybe, but if it's realizable it's no dream. You see what you want and try to create it. Margot was part of that, maybe the whole of the inspiration. She threw

herself heart, soul and body into *Running Tides*. She could
see exactly what effect I was after and created it for my sake.
She loved me all right, and I loved her. That went on for four
months or so, while we were shooting here and in France. At
what point does passion become obsession? For the movie
and for each other. Where's the dividing line? I didn't know
then and I don't know now.

'The problem is that some day filming ends. What happens
then to the passion and obsession? Continue with it? How do
you channel it? If you can't, there's disaster staring you in the
face. If it's obsession it's more serious. Margot and I had
reached that point. We realized that at the wrap party. The
movie would be a success, and we'd go off into the sunset
together.

'So what went wrong? You'll have heard everyone's version
but mine, and mine's the truth. Margot's part in the movie was
over, while I was still obsessed night and day with getting what
I saw as my dream expressed exactly as I wanted it throughout
the editing stage. Margot was restless, she had another filming
job to do, and I was still caught up with *Running Tides*. She
wanted us to be together right away, but I wasn't ready. The
movie wasn't finished for me. You could put it crudely and say
that I was just falling out of love with her now the shooting
was over. But that would not be the case. I was still in love
with her, but I had to get the movie finished. The more she
badgered me the worse it grew. She wanted me with her every
minute and if I wasn't, she'd come to track me down, crying
that I no longer loved her. It got to the point where I realized
I was more *sorry* for her than in love with her.

'Then she told me she was pregnant with my child, and I
believed her. I went to see Geoff to discuss it and he told me
she was lying. She couldn't have kids. They'd tried. I refused
to believe him, but Margot admitted it when I tackled her.
Then I did cool. I couldn't take that. When I delayed, made
excuses, then the real problems began. She'd ruin my career,
she'd kill herself, she'd do this, she would do that.

'I talked to Geoff again. He hated my guts, incidentally,
which was hardly surprising. He admitted I wasn't the first in
Margot's extra marital life and that suicide threats had been

made before, without her acting on them. So I didn't take her ranting as seriously as I should have and I told her it was over. Geoff said he loved her and that he would look after her. They lived in London and I was down here in Kent by that time, so when the threats ceased I thought everything was calming down.

'Then I had a phone call from her in the middle of one night to say she was going to kill herself. She had driven down to the spot where we had shot a scene in *Running Tides* on the cliffs near Folkestone. I still didn't take it seriously, but I had to go. I drove down there in the Auburn, half thinking she wouldn't be there when I arrived. But she was. Sitting in her car, waiting for me. I wondered if she'd taken pills but she said no. Not yet. She wanted me back and the threats began all over again. She'd ruin the movie and me. All nonsense but I began to see what life with Margot would have been like.

'I'm not proud of myself, Jack, but I realized I was beginning to hate her. "I knew you'd come, Bill," she said complacently. "Just like in the film. *Bill, Bill, come to me,* and here you are." You can imagine how that sound hit me the other night, Jack. Chris couldn't have known about our meeting there, and yet he hit the weak spot.

'Margot told me quite calmly that she had bought a gun, just like mine. She thought we might have a suicide pact. She'd shoot me and then herself. Great! She whipped the gun out and I tried to get it away from her but it was no use. She was shrieking with laughter and getting wilder and wilder, waving it around. I tried reason, I tried telling her how much she was needed, about how much she had to offer as an actress and finally, lying, I told her how much I loved her. She didn't believe me, and I knew if I tried to run, she would kill me. This time it was for real. I knew that. She put the gun to her head –' Bill swallowed – 'then to mine. I thought she was going to pull the trigger, she was talking so wildly. So I put my hands over hers on the gun and wrenched it back the other way. It went off. Who pulled the trigger? No idea.'

I was cold with horror. 'So in effect—'

'I killed her.'

*   *   *

His hands had been over hers, not on the gun, and there was
no other proof of course. Even if Bill decided to turn himself
in, there would be nothing to back up his story. Had it been
accident or self defence, or had he intended to kill her? He
didn't know himself, and I believed him. I thought of what
he had said to me as I left.

'No one liked Angie, Jack, but she was the best thing that
ever happened to me. Except for Roger and Maisie, everyone
thought that Margot was the goodie and Angie the baddie. But
for me the opposite was true. Margot was sweet and lovable
but as implacable as stone; she cast a spell but spells can be
bad as well as good.'

'So what now?' I had asked him.

He knew what I meant by this. 'I do movies, Jack, like you
do cars. Angie and Joan died because of me. I owe them something. I do movies best.'

Dave rang me about Nigel, not that I cared now. I still felt
drained. 'You can put in your invoice now, Jack,' Dave said.
'You've earned your dosh.'

'You've nailed Nigel?' I felt almost sorry.

'Nope. Biddington was just an innocent decoy. We've nailed
the organizer.'

'Anyone I know?'

'Yes. Her name's Clarissa.'

When I'd picked myself up off the floor and Dave had
stopped chuckling, he told me that being in a wheelchair and
pretending to be forgetful had been the ideal cover for her.
When she was questioned, she had been proud of herself, and
in view of her age the case might have to disappear for lack
of supporting evidence. She was a tough lady, and no one
wanted to be on her wrong side – especially in view of the
heavies that she employed, many of which worked for
Shotsworth Security. Mark Shotsworth himself was as clean
as a whistle and so was Nigel Biddington, nor was there
anything amiss with the cars for *Dark Harvest*.

Clarissa must have been raking in a fortune, I thought. Dave
read me part of her statement: 'Everyone is so kind. They
come up to chat with me and tell me about their cars as I

know so much, thanks to my father. I can be so helpful to them, telling them how good Nigel is as a broker. Dear Nigel and Rob are so good to me. They know how much I love cars and I can usually get one or the other of them to drive me where I need to go. Of course there are taxis, but that would be an extravagance.'

'Why did she put me on the right track over the Auburn?' I asked, bewildered. As a car detective it seemed to me I was a washout. 'Even though she was wrong about the woman driver.' I did a double take. Or was she? Had Chris in his madness dressed up as Margot to take the car? It was all too possible.

'She sticks to the woman driver, and as for telling you about it, she was highly annoyed that the Auburn had been stolen so publicly and that the thief had had the audacity to put it in *her* car park, as she put it, although she had not authorized the theft. Pure chance I gather. Chris heard from Ken about the car park and thought it would suit his purpose nicely.'

And then I had come along and been led by the nose to find it. I didn't think I'd dwell on that aspect to Dave.

No need. He thought it up for himself. 'Don't worry. I won't take it off your invoice.'

'You're all heart.'

'If it's any consolation, she rates you highly as a sleuth, hence her decision to risk giving you only the slightest hint where the Auburn could be found.'

I felt better. 'Are you charging her?'

'Yes, though I doubt it will come to court. She was quite aggrieved about it. Told me the government kept on urging older people not to retire but to continue working as long as they could.'

Which just left one more outstanding issue. Louise.

She came back to me at the weekend with eyes shining and with good reason – for her, at least. We loved with great passion that night, although even then I suspected it might be for the last time. The next day we went for a walk through woodland that in May had been thick with bluebells, and now as July opened had a canopy of green leaves so thick

there was little light for undergrowth. You need undergrowth
for a strong relationship, and that's what Louise and I would
never have while those trees reached higher and higher
towards the stars.

'I've got the part, Jack,' she told me. 'It'll be in the press
soon. It's going to take me away for at least six months.'

I knew what that meant. I congratulated her on getting the
part. Sincerely, but . . . 'You'll be leaving me then.'

'Me or my heart?'

'They're both the same, my love.'

'The answer is that I don't know. Perhaps . . .'

'I'll be here.'

'There'll be someone else sooner or later.'

'Probably, but not you.'

'Will it hurt?'

'Yes.'

'For me too.'

I wanted to say, 'Then don't leave me,' or 'We'll work
something out.' But I couldn't. That's the trouble with wandering
stars. They wander. That's what they do. If you haul them down
to you, they're not the star you wanted.

'Come back some day, Louise.'

'I will.' A pause. 'Come with me, Jack.'

I thought about it, I thought of what I had here, I thought
of Louise and I knew I had to cut her free. And myself too.

'Some day,' I said. 'A few things to sort out here.'

After she'd gone, I looked around at what I'd chosen. In
the Pits I could hear Zoe and Len singing. Well, not exactly.
Zoe was singing and Len was grunting some unrecognizable
ditty. In a few moments I would go to join them. First, I went
round to look at my Lagonda and my Gordon-Keeble, both
awaiting my pleasure. Then I went into the Glory Boot. Dad
did not seem to be around, but after a while he condescended
to drop by for a minute or two. What was it he used to say?

'There'll always be classics, Jack. Remember that, son. You
can rely on cars.'

THE CAR'S THE STAR

James Myers

Bill Wade's 1935 Auburn 851 SC Boattail Speedster
The Auburn's classic year could well be 1935, with the addition of a supercharged straight-eight for the 851 series and the strikingly beautiful boattailed Speedster body refined by Gordon Buehrig from an earlier design by Count Alexis de Sakhnoffsky. You could therefore say that this design was born out of aristocratic inspiration. But it had performance to match its looks. The Cummins supercharged Lycoming straight-eight produced 150-brake horsepower and each car was guaranteed to have been test-driven at more than 100 miles per hour. Unfortunately, Auburn lost money on each and every one of these heartbreakingly gorgeous cars and so the model continued for only two more years. If you'd like to see one today, visit the National Motor Museum at Beaulieu in Hampshire, UK, or in the US the Auburn Cord Duesenberg Museum in Auburn, Indiana.

Jack Colby's daily driver: Alfa Romeo 156 Sportwagon
The 156 Sportwagon is a 'lifestyle estate', which means that it's trendy, respectable to have on the drive, although it lacks the interior space of a traditional load-lugger. For those who value individuality, its subtle and pure styling gives it the edge over rivals such as the BMW 3-Series. It gives a lot of driving pleasure even with the smaller engines.

Jack Colby's 1965 Gordon-Keeble
One hundred of these fabulous supercars were built between 1963 and 1966 with over ninety units surviving around the globe, mostly in the UK. Designed by John Gordon and Jim Keeble using current racing car principles, with the bodyshell designed by twenty-one-year-old Giorgetto Giugiaro at

Bertone, the cars were an instant success but the company was ruined by supply-side industrial action with ultimately only 99 units completed even after the company was relaunched in May 1965, as Keeble Cars Ltd. Final closure came in February 1966 when the factory at Sholing closed and Jim Keeble moved to Keewest. The hundredth car was completed in 1971 with leftover components. The Gordon-Keeble's emblem is a yellow and green tortoise.

Jack Colby's 1938 Lagonda V-12 Drophead

The Lagonda company won its attractive name from a creek near the home of the American-born founder Wilbur Gunn in Springfield, Ohio. The name given to it by the American Indians was Ough Ohonda. The V-12 drophead was a car to compete with the very best in the world, with a sporting twelve-cylinder engine which would power the two 1939 Le Mans cars. Its designer was the famous W.O. Bentley. Sadly many fine prewar saloons have been cut down to look like Le Mans replicas. The V12 cars are very similar externally to the earlier six-cylinder versions; both types were available with open or closed bodywork in a number of different styles. The V-12 Drophead also featured in Jack's earlier case, *Classic in the Barn*.

The 1935 Horch

The Horch was a prestigious German marque of the 1920s and 30s, one of the four brands that were incorporated into the Auto Union Company together with Audi, DKW and Wanderer. The famous 'four rings' Audi badge was a symbol of these four car marques, DKW being the most modest and affordable, while Horch was the most powerful and sporty, not to mention the most expensive. The 853 model was introduced in 1935. It featured a five-litre straight-eight engine. Horch cars were extremely well built and engineered, featuring straight-eight engines (a few were available with V-12 engines) and four-wheel independent suspension.

The 1935 Bentley Silent Sports

In the 1920s, Bentleys enjoyed numerous racing and

record-breaking successes, most notably five victories at Le
Mans. But the cost of all this was massive losses and the
company was bailed out by millionaire adventurer and Bentley
racing driver Woolf Barnato, one of the famous 'Bentley Boys'.
The Bentley 'Silent Sports Car' series was introduced in 1933.
This new model was very different from the previously huge
and muscular Bentleys.

The 1935 Fiat Tipo 508S 'Balilla'
In the early 1930s, Fiat introduced an important new small
car – the 508 Balilla. A sporty overhead-valve engine, four-
speed synchro gearbox and hydraulic brakes made for a lively
driving experience. As one might expect from an Italian design,
it featured a sleek body, with a long bonnet, cutaway doors,
wire wheels and a finned tail, which gave the car an elegant
and sporting air.

*For more discussion of classic cars, see Jack Colby's website
and blog at jackcolby.co.uk.*